TRADED FOR A TRIFLE

ABETY GWANDI

DESIGN House, Limbe

Published by DESIGN House
P.O. Box 321, Limbe

ISBN 10: 9956 26 063 0
ISBN 13: 978 9956 26 063 8

Cover design by Spiffing Covers

DEDICATION

For ex-servicemen of the
Royal West African Frontier Force
Who gave their all for the British Empire
May their memory never be blotted out

CONTENTS

PART ONE

TO WAR AND BACK TO WAR

CHAPTER ONE

From bench to trench

1941

He had reasons to be happy as he strode towards home. School had finished at mid-day because it was a Friday and the following day was Big Market Day. On such Fridays, no one returned to class after the long break. Pupils went instead to their parents' farms to bring in produce. His headmaster wisely accepted the half-day holiday assumed by the pupils; it was a choice between letting them go early and teaching benches all day.

Ayonchugu was happy because he was only a short distance from his home and from Ngelem. She always chose to be arranging their sparsely furnished room about the time he would be arriving home, and whenever he dropped his box and started giving her a rather close hand, she would shove away his hands and remind him that his food was getting cold. He was looking forward to that today, and not to the mournful spectacle that was in front of him when he stepped over the threshold and came into his yard. Ndi and two of his uncles – Teneng and Kwende – were sitting in front of his house, looking pensive, heads bowed, and not drinking.

'I greet you, my fathers,' Ayonchugu said, studying the men's grim aspects. 'Is anyone dead?' he asked.

'No,' Teneng replied. He stood up and the other men followed suit. 'Something is at stake, though. Keep your school things inside and join us in your big room.'

Ayonchugu went into his room, placed his wooden box on a bamboo shelf and grudgingly went to meet the men. He found Ngelem sitting with them and his mood brightened up when he saw her welcoming him with a soft smile. The basket that usually contained his food was set on a low table. She fetched a calabash of water from one corner of the room and took it to the men; they all shook their heads. She brought it to Ayonchugu, stooped and poured it out for him to wash his hands. He untied two bundles of banana leaves containing his meal, spread them out on the table and started eating. The men chatted in low tones until he was half-way through his lunch.

'Ngelem came over to Big Compound to report to me that the fon's messenger was here today and left you that,' said Ndi, pointing outside. Ayonchugu's eyes followed his big brother's fingertips and fell on a spear he had not noticed before. He stopped eating and stared at the spear as though it was an evil omen.

'Me! What would anyone want me in the palace for?' Ayonchugu asked, his voice growing louder as he pronounced each word. 'We will make ourselves known to the palace when we are ready. We barely got married. You can see Ngelem's state. I don't think it's a good idea to go dragging her up to the palace to drink from the fon's cup now. I know couples who were married for five years before they could hold a conversation with the fon. I'd made it clear that we would progress to that stage only when I finished school and found a job.'

'This has nothing to do with *kwiemuluh*,' Teneng said patiently. 'No one can force you to do that. This is more urgent.'

'Rumour has it that the fon is in need of young men to send to Tishong at the request of the Native Authority,' said Ndi.

'Well, I regret to say I won't respect this particular summons. I need to go to school.' Ayonchugu was relieved to see Kwende nodding in agreement. He resumed eating his food.

'Son,' said Kwende, 'if I were in your shoes, I would say the same thing. The real problem we have now is this spear. Tell us what we should do with it.'

'Just let it stay there!' Ayonchugu said defiantly.

'Ayo,' Ndi said calmly, 'this spear has never stayed the night in anyone's compound. The fon can be defied only by his equal – another fon. If you keep this spear, *Kwifon* will come and plant his spear in your compound tomorrow morning. Your fine thereafter would be big enough to be paid right down to the third generation of your descendants, or you must go on

2

self-exile.'

Ayonchugu sat staring at Ngelem, whose sudden sniffs and tearful eyes were now tearing his heart into shreds. They all knew he could not escape what was coming next.

'I'll finish the food later,' he said, pushing the rest of his meal to one side.

Ayonchugu was one of many young men who that evening went to the palace to return the fon's spear. He was accompanied by Teneng and Kwende. Their fears were confirmed when they saw that the fon was with the District Officer and a Chief Sergeant who was attended by some soldiers.

The young men and their parents were shoved into a darkened hall in the palace where a team of the Colonial Film Unit was busy setting up equipment. Ordinarily, the films would be of the humorous genre from Hollywood and the arrival of cinematographic equipment would ignite excitement and anticipation among the villagers. That evening, the atmosphere was subdued and the purposefulness of the officials was truer to the peremptoriness of the functionaries.

When the reels were ready to run, the Chief Sergeant told them he was going to show pictures of things that were happening in some African countries – things which if they did not take urgent action to guard against, would soon be happening in this very village.

The Chief Sergeant lectured them in Pidgin English about the fascists and how they had invaded Libya and, thereafter, the independent nation of Abyssinia. They had driven away the emperor of the country, who luckily, had found refuge among the British, and was now, thanks to His Majesty's government, in a struggle to throw out the invaders and get back his throne. He said that for Africa to be safe from Fascists and Nazis forever, every African who loved his continent ought to show it then. He was there that day to ask the brave people of Libah, old and young, men and women, to join in the fight against cruel invaders, whose goal was to maim the populace, wreak havoc everywhere and undo the development the British had brought about.

Ayonchugu watched the pictures of the atrocities Italian troops had committed in North Africa going back thirty years, from the time they set out as belated colonisers to conquer the adamant sands of Libya, to when they occupied Abyssinia. The pictures were harrowing; the barbarism surpassed any that had ever been known in Ayonchugu's world. Haile Sellasie was shown in the glory of his coronation and imperial power, and then as a refugee appealing for help in meetings in Europe. The film concluded with footage of a flawless British army battling in semi-arid mountains in Abyssinia.

The Chief Sergeant ended his presentation with promise of payment for the services of the young men. He sat down beside the fon, who stood up, plucked his spear from the ground, and gesticulated energetically with it as he spoke.

'Libah people, do you hear the fon?' he asked in a powerful voice.

'Mbeh!' the people answered.

'Libah today reassures our august guests that this village is committed to the cause of the liberation of Africa which Britain has championed. Strangers are putting our house right for us. Is that the way it should be?'

'Ngang!' the people answered.

'When you leave your door open, the devil walks in. You can't afford to look away while strangers chase thieves from your cocoyam farm. Or can you?'

'Ngang! Ngang!' the voices of the people echoed.

'My own very son,' he continued, 'has already signed up. Natural warriors that the sons and even the daughters of this land are, everyone is to follow my son's example. Warfare is second-nature to us. It ensured the survival of our clan for centuries. Did our fathers not fight their way through hostile territory from the North to our present location? Yes, we have the battle instinct. But we are not a people to get into a war without being sure that the prize is worth the blood. You have heard that you will be paid. The gods of the land, Kwifon, the British government and we guarantee the safety of all young men who sign up. We guarantee the success of their mission. We have spoken! Can anyone doubt the word of the Lion?'

'Ngang! Ngang!' answered the men in a prolonged chorus,

stamping their feet, while the women ululated, with their hands over their mouths.

The fon sat on the throne, placed his legs on his elephant's tusk foot-rest, and nodded to parents as they came up in a file and did the ritual of allegiance to him, while the young men were having their names written down as potential combatants.

The following day was less decorous. The initial selection of competent fighters was done with strict military promptness, which left the unschooled enthusiasts feeling out of their skin. It began with a short physical check. The Chief Sergeant and a doctor were seated at a makeshift table with fountain pens and writing pads ready. They were attended to by four burly charcoal-black soldiers who had prominent tribal slashes running down their cheeks and spoke Haussa. On a prod from a private who was ushering them, each volunteer walked up at a fast pace to the table forty metres away to be assessed.

Ayonchugu joined a queue of about a hundred and fifty potential recruits, ranging from fourteen to forty years old, and waited for his turn to be assessed. He was a sturdy fellow with curled bushy hair. He was above average height and walked with legs somewhat apart, for his limbs, either by nature or because of a childhood illness, were slightly curved. His arms were shaped like his legs, and because of their distinctive muscularity, gave him an intimidating look. Ayonchugu's skin was dark-brown, and the tone was accentuated by the processed palm oil with which he had rubbed his body after bathing that morning. He was chewing on a bitter stick reputed for its hygienic as well as therapeutic properties.

When it was his turn he walked up smartly and stood in front of the Chief Sergeant and the doctor, his curvy arms hanging loosely by his sides.

'Let me have his name,' the Chief Sergeant said.

'My name is Ayonchugu, Sir,' he said before the translator could speak.

'You speak English?' asked one of the privates.

'Yes.'

'You no answer Commander. You answer me, right?'

'Yes.'

'Ya name!'

'Ayonchugu.'

'Ya age!'

'Nineteen.'

'Righ' turn!'

Ayonchugu executed the command.

'Lef' turn!'

Ayonchugu executed the order and faced the table again.

'Head up!'

Ayonchugu looked up. The private held his head and jerked it abruptly backwards.

'Open ya mop!' he shouted.

Ayonchugu opened his mouth and the private took a brief look inside.

'All good, sah!' he said to the Chief Sergeant, who nodded and wrote down on his pad.

'Enter de pan!' the private ordered.

Ayonchugu took off his canvass shoes and stepped into a basin containing a chemical which killed jiggers. He had just made it through his initial physical assessment. The medical check-up was done shortly after behind closed doors, and its success thereof put him on the way to being Private Ayonchugu, volunteer in His Majesty's Royal West African Frontier Force, The Nigeria Regiment. That same day, the recruits had their hair shaved and scrubbed until it shone. Petroleum jelly was applied to the scalp, which glittered like looking glass in the tropical sun.

One week later, Ayonchugu returned home to bid family and community farewell. His people gathered in Big Compound, with the aim of speaking with one mouth and giving him their blessings. He came in his uniform, causing quite a stir among the children who crowded around him, asking him to execute military salutes. When everyone settled down finally for the meeting he took his place among the young men of the family and studied the gathering of humble villagers, and thought about how their daily preoccupations were as distant from the issues at the back of the war as was the distance he was going to travel to engage the enemy. His eyes did the round of the house and settled on Ngelem, seated among the women in a corner of the room. Her hands were reposing on her belly and she looked withdrawn. Tried as hard as he could, their eyes never met.

Teneng dipped his hand into a soot-stained fibre bag hanging on the wall and brought out the family cup – a gnarled buffalo horn which had belonged to his great-grandfather. He filled the cup with palm wine, and holding it in front of him, invited Ayonchugu to come to the middle of the room. He then addressed the assembly.

'Our son has suspended schooling because he is now a soldier in the Army of King George. He is on his way to fight the king's enemies, and therefore our enemies. If our family is divided, we shall be a source of woes for our son in the face of a destiny that is filled with danger. By our words of supplication and by this wine that I'm pouring, I call on our ancestors, who were all great warriors, to show him the way on this journey. He shall not lose a toenail in battle. When his foot hits against a rock, the rock only shall break! Indeed, he shall tread only on clay! When the bullet comes from the right he shall be on the left. When it comes from the left, where shall he be?'

'On the right!' the people responded in a chorus.

'Whoever looks at him with the intent to harm, shall it not be the evil-intentioned person's head that shall pay the price?'

'His head shall pay!' they answered.

'This is for you who come with an evil intent. You shall not cross the doorstep. Have yours out there and leave now!' He stood by the door and poured some wine outside. 'This is for you who come with good intentions.' He dropped some wine on the floor inside the room.

'And now, our son, I invite you to drink from this ancestral cup. It is a source of the energy radiating from the dead and the living of this family being channelled unto you. Drink!' said Teneng, holding the cup to Ayonchugu's lips. He swallowed two gulps of wine from the cup. 'Empty the cup!' Teneng said. Ayonchugu did. 'We will now join our ancestors in saying farewell to our son.' Teneng refilled the cup, took a sip, and then passed it to all present to drink from it.

'I have a headache that has been keeping me awake for the past three nights,' one of Ayonchugu's cousins complained. 'It gets worse when I drink. I should normally be in bed now trying to catch some sleep. But I couldn't afford to miss today's occasion.'

'I think you should go and have a rest since the main thing has been done,' his wife suggested from one corner of the room. The man promptly left, holding his head as if it was about to explode within.

'The venomous snake begets its kind,' said Teneng. 'This moment is too precious to dwell on old family feuds, however.'

Senior members of Ayonchugu's family spoke, wishing him well and offering assurances that his wife would be well taken care of. The people ate and drank some more, and thereafter, each person came up to Ayonchugu and had a chat with him before retiring to their homes.

On their way home, Ngelem held her head high up as Ayonchugu strode beside her.

'You were tight-lipped at the family meeting,' Ayonchugu remarked.

'There was nothing to say.'

'I thought maybe you did not want to be there.'

'Why would you think such a thing of me?' Ngelem asked. 'You are a hero! My hero! Just look at the spectacular way you went through the selection process! Where would I have hidden my head if you had been rejected like Nange's husband? He has become a laughing-stock.'

'The poor man's health was not good. It wasn't his fault.'

'Tell the women that. A song has already been composed about him. Do you want to hear it?'

'Yes, my darling,' Ayonchugu replied. 'But not now.'

'I've composed a song for you too. I'm not sharing it with the women. It's for your ears only.'

'Indeed? I thought you did not want me to go to war?'

'You have to go. You will make a great soldier for the Empire.'

'You are so unpredictable.'

Shortly after they went to bed that night Ngelem nudged Ayonchugu and asked, 'Do you want to hear your song now?'

'Yes, wife,' Ayonchugu replied, and rolled over and faced her.

'It's called "Tell me Chirpy Little Bird".'

'And who is chirpy, little, and sings like a bird but you?'

'Look at my belly again before calling me little. I'm talking to the little bird that sings from the palm trees behind our house and wakes you up every morning to go to school. The song goes like this:

> *Chirpy little bird,*
> *Tell me what to feel*
> *I'm young and barely married*
> *My husband's on his way*
> *To fight enemies*
> *That he never made*
> *I'd rather he did not go*
> *I'd rather he did not fight*
>
> *Chirpy little bird,*
> *Tell me what to feel*
> *My husband's taking on Italy*
> *Where's it? North or South?*
> *I know not, he knows not*
> *Where's Germany? Left or Right?*
> *I know not, he knows not*
>
> *Chirpy little bird,*
> *Tell me what to feel*
> *If my gallant husband were killed!*
> *Oh, unthinkable thought!*
> *Close my door, lest evil walk in!*
> *Now alone to bear my tears*
> *My comfort? Kicks and turns*
> *Here within.*

'Why are you not saying anything?' Ngelem asked after a long interlude. 'Don't you like the song?'

'I like it. You sing so well. You could call it "Lamentation of a Departing Soldier's Wife".

Ngelem touched Ayonchugu's face in the darkness. His cheeks were wet.

In the morning Ayonchugu went to school to tell his teacher that he was going to war. Mr Ngu was already aware that he was leaving and gave him a lecture.

'Congratulations on your recruitment,' he said. 'When you return, do well to complete your education. Your destiny is not in the army. But this war, I believe, will be shorter than the first one. I look forward to the day you come back home, have your GSSC and go to the teachers training college.'

Although the ability to do long treks on bare feet was a standard recruitment requirement, boot training was a main activity in their training. They had feet as wide as their palms, with each toe tuned to an angle of its choice. Years of wearing shoes occasionally, as on Sundays, meant the feet of the new recruits had to be recast to fit into conventional boots. Experienced as the trainers were, they gave recruits with problematic feet boots one or two sizes bigger.

The first day he trained with them, Ayonchugu's felt like he was carrying a log underfoot. He tugged his cumbersome boots along bravely, pining and sweating under the punishment they inflicted on his feet. He looked out for Fingoba, a fellow who had bragged that he would return from the war with the skull of an Italian, and saw him limping about and falling ever so often. Saji, the oldest of the recruits, was an old hand at the business and was coping well, having donned, he claimed, even heavier boots in the German days. Their trainers let them have a field day on the first day. They could take off their boots sometimes to let their feet breathe. From day two, just when their toes were showing the blisters from the previous day's torments, they were ordered to keep them on indefinitely. Limping was banned, as was whimpering. The young recruits sweated it out, locking the pain within all day, and collapsing onto their straw mats at night, their painful raw feet reminding them that they were still alive.

They did the journey to Tishong on bare-foot, and were told by their trainers that this was a foretaste of the kind of trekking they would do in the military. Life in the army, they said, was more of marching than fighting, and coming face-to-face with enemy troops was often relieving because it saved one a long pernicious march either pursuing or retreating from them. When the new contingent arrived at Tishong, good news awaited them. Boots that were specially designed for them had arrived.

Tishong was once a seat of the German colonial administration. To the natives it was a place to avoid coming to, except as an employee. It was grandiose and absolutely intimidating. Here were located the courthouse and the inevitable prison, the inspectorates of the different government departments, and the residences of the British administrators. The most eye-catching sight was the former German garrison built around the turn of the century. There was an administrative section and a military camp. The administrative structure was built of stone blocks and roofed with stone slates. It was a massive rectangular structure, built to last. A gate led into a large courtyard from which stone-paved footpaths led to the different offices. In the bigger of these offices, raised two storeys high and overlooking the budding township of Abakwa that lay two about thousand feet below, was the District Officer's office.

Across the road, about half a mile from the administrative section, were tens of semi-circular robust structures, each eight feet high, fashioned out of solid corrugated steel. The German colonial army once headquartered here.

The surrounding countryside once luxuriated with mountain vegetation of stunted trees and tall grass. During the dry season, wild fires burnt everything down, leaving behind the sooty trunks of craggy trees from which fresh foliage sprang as soon as the first rains sprinkled the earth. The plateau were reforested with stands of eucalyptus and made a no-go territory for local hunters and loggers. The reforestation project was already paying dividends, for every now and then a careless soldier lost a boot to an inquisitive monkey. A snaking thoroughfare that went peeping through the bushes told that beyond the walls of the forest lived the villagers who had been obliged to donate land for the building of the government houses. A stream of water gushed from the rocks beyond, cut through the forest, caressed the back of the barracks before flying over the edge of the mountains to splash in the valley below, into Abakwa.

Troops were harvested from all the villages around the region and brought to Tishong. They were all young and tough. Some were enthusiastic fighters and believed they knew exactly what it was they were fighting for. Others had fighting in their blood, and were hot on wielding a gun and blasting it off at whatever target they were shown. There was the raw bulk that did not know the difference between a fountain pen and a pencil, and were going where the wind blew them. One thing even the most rustic was sure about was that the Empire needed their services and they were there to serve King George with their lives.

Every morning, they each hurled a bag weighing fifty-five pounds onto their backs and set out on a ten-mile run. When they returned, they were split into small groups for Basic English classes. They regrouped two hours later brandishing wooden objects in the shape of guns, and confronted mock enemies in the forested land around the garrison and its network of World War I trenches. They were drilled in military discipline, hand-to-hand combat, and sent through gruelling physical and mental exercises to boost their stamina.

Two months later, they discarded their dummy guns, and were transported to Victoria, where the promise of a refreshing sea turned into abhorrence when they learned its water was not drinkable. On board a carrier to Lagos, men panicked when the stormy high seas tossed them about, and they thought their vessel had missed its course and brought them to the ends of the earth. They were all miserably seasick by the time they arrived in Lagos and came off the ship hoping they had reached the war zone. More troops boarded the vessel and within a week they were back in the tepid waters, sailing for the Gambia where other fresh recruits were waiting to board.

CHAPTER TWO

Home again!

May 1946

The returning soldier was being transported to his village in the back of a Land Rover jeep. The vehicle ploughed headily and noisily along a dusty highway that wound its way precariously along the edge of one hill and the inevitable next one like a meandering scar on the face of the mountains. It would charge down into the depths of one precipitous ravine and after a long spell, it would re-emerge on the slope of the adjoining hill, spewing out black exhaust gases on its ascent.

Ayonchugu squinted into the dust and smoke, trying to see the landscape. The rainy season was overdue. Wild fires lit by worried nomadic herdsmen were burning on the hills. Crackling burning grass rose listlessly, danced about in the wind, broke up into many fragments and fell slowly, carpeting the ground in black and grey ash. The white and black of his one good eye moved from one familiar landmark to the other, the recognition of each sending gentle shivers of excitement into his inner being as he anticipated every glee of a heroic home-coming.

His coarse hair and eyebrows had caught a rusty film of dust, which made him look like an albino. Five years of a rugged and disciplined life had left him tough-skinned, and this was nowhere more visible than in his angular facial features which emitted a silent stoicism.

His khaki shorts which extended just below his knees had taken on a brown hue and were criss-crossed by numerous darker lines where they had rubbed against his hands and other objects around him. The massive soles of his extra-large black boat-like boots were caked in the dried mud of the treacherous roads that sneaked and snaked all through hundreds of miles of dense, cluttered forests between the coast and these airy hills of the hinterlands.

The end of the war had given him high expectations. He had cash in his pocket, and some more at the Post Office, and believed the future held further remuneration. The relevant papers were carefully wrapped up and stowed away in a polythene bag, which he treasured for its weighty content. The bag contained his official documents, articles and clippings he had found intriguing from newspapers abroad; it contained addresses of friends-in-arms whom he had met from a multitude of Commonwealth Nations, and some memorable pictures of himself and soldiers from his unit taken the day they learned they were victorious over the Japs. There was a picture of a British woman and souvenirs from places he had visited. He had all these items stashed away in the depths of his military kit, which inevitably contained needful things he had carried along in his time in the army.

Ayonchugu was now doing the last leg of a journey inland. Following their discharge four days earlier at the Victoria Demobilisation Centre, he and forty-five other survivors whose hearts lay homewards had boarded an old coffee lorry that the Resettlement Officer had hired. They had spent half of the journey pushing and tugging the lorry on the tattered roads which linked the hinterlands to the coastal towns. Their route had afforded them a brief peek into French Cameroun, by which the only viable road through Nkongsamba led to Abakwa. The battered lorry had groaned and rumbled all the way, puffing out black suffocating fumes. To their relief that morning, it had crawled safely into the expanding town, most of its parts still clinging headily on the chassis. They had been dropped off at the Dispersal Centre adjacent to the District Office.

They had stopped singing *Home again again!* which they had spent the afternoon of the previous day and all night delightfully chanting in spite of the violent yanking and jerking of the ancient lorry. The District Clerk, doubling for the Resettlement Officer, had arrived, greeted them briefly and had them finger-print various documents before getting his cashier to pay their fare to their final destinations. The official had told them he would contact them as soon as information relating to their well-being came in from the High Command. He had then summarily dismissed them.

Ayonchugu had stood by for a while with six other

comrades – Fuochu, Afungchwi, Mbah, Niba, Teneslaw and Kangno – taken aback by the off-handed and summary reception he thought they were being subjected to. Then it had fully dawned on him that despite his uniform he had indeed been a civilian ever since demob at the Victoria Demobilisation Centre, where they had been hurriedly educated about their new status. They had been warned not to expect any special treatment, or assume any prerogatives other than those they enjoyed before being enlisted in the army. This had been another shocking anti-climax for Ayonchugu and his mates. Their performance in Burma had been well appreciated by their commanders, who had written letters recommending them for special privileges. Before leaving the Victoria Demobilisation Centre, he was searched by the Military Police and a locally acquired pistol retrieved from him. He protested, brandishing a letter recommending he be allowed to buy a Raleigh bicycle and keep a gun. The MP directed him to the general office, whereupon airing his grievance, he was shown a letter which colonial officials had written to the HQ in Burma requesting they stop their commanders from sending such recommendations.

'Can I see the reply to that letter?' he asked the clerk.

'There is no reply. Black Tarantula or not, the orders are simple: No recommendations. No guns. No Raleigh bicycles. Go home, soldier!'

In Abakwa that morning, while the ex-soldiers were still consulting among themselves whether to tarry around town for some fun with free women or go directly home, they overheard the District Clerk's driver telling another staff member that their boss was going to Pond. That meant his jeep was going to drive through their villages. Ayonchugu, oblivious of the niceties of protocol, walked up to the administrator and saluted.

'Excuse me, Sir,' he said. 'Corporal Ayonchugu. Chindits Brigade, Burma. If you are going through Libah gif me a lif Sir.'

The District Clerk looked him over and, at a loss for words, said, 'Okay, chum. Hop on.' Ayonchugu and his six comrades all clambered on. The District Clerk's guards made some uncertain moves to stop the unlikely invasion, but their boss signaled them to stay put.

Thirty minutes later they were being driven out of Abakwa. Among the passengers was the District Clerk's cook. He was sitting next to Ayonchugu and was gazing at his medals. Ayonchugu gave him a friendly nod.

'Chei! Four medals!' the cook exclaimed eventually. Ayonchugu nodded and smiled.

'I haf one of dis,' the cook said.

'Indeed? Which one?'

'Dis one,' said the cook, taking hold of one of Ayonchugu's medals and painstakingly reading out the inscription on it. 'D-e-f-e-nce Medal.'

'Where did you earn it?' Ayonchugu asked.

'From Ekoko. He was ma broda. He wen' to No' Africa in '41. He never retorn. His comrade bro' it to me in '43. Ma broda was very strong.'

'I believe he was,' Ayonchugu agreed, nodding.

'He attack enemy soja's truck. He killed eighteen enemy. He alone!'

'That's bravery, my friend.'

'He go to check de truck. A bomb jus' bomb boom! He is killed.'

'Sorry! That was probably a grenade. Personnel carriers don't normally carry bombs,' Ayonchugu explained.

'I haf Ekoko he picture in ma haas. I know he is died. But when sojas are retorning, I tink he go jus' retorn too.'

'Oh! oh! Ashia,' Ayonchugu said.

'I tried go war too,' said the cook. 'Ma master – da was de former Distri' Clerk – said, "Sango, I need you to stay and cook at GRA Canteen in Victoria. Okay?" I say "Yes, sah." So I stay. De new DC cam and say I can go to war. I lef ma job at GRA Canteen and goes to join army. No recruitment. De war end. I be jobless. I go see de DC agin. He coming transfer here. He offer me to recruit as he persona cook if I cam wit he to Abakwa.'

'That was nice of him.'

'He na good man. You never-never dream to climb Distri' Officer he Land Rover. Only Natif he carry na he cook and he houseboy. Sometime village fon, if na urgen' bisnis. I be hear he tell ma DC to not be friend-friend wit educate Natifs.'

'Did he? Why?'

'He say da educate Natifs are plenty trouble and da sojas especial, are total corrup'. He say da be *rigratable*. Da na de exak wha he say.'

'But we are just normal people who have been doing their job. How could he say that about us?' Ayonchugu asked.

'I listen to de whole convasation. De Distri' Officer cam visit. I serving dinner. You know, dey talk all time like I no dey dere. Dey do da agin-agin. De DO say in he nose: "Di survival of di colonies, and so di British Impaya, dipendit on di perceift invincicility of di amistrator. Da's why British manage to rule whole small continent of India wit jus few thasand sojas." He say da Sah Lucas' promonotion about Nangeria sojas go come happin for sojas from Kamarons when sojas retorn. I tink da he word don come happin today.'

'All I did was ask for a lift. Who is Sir Lucas?'

'You no savy de big govina da was in Nangeria?' Sango asked.

'Aha! Sir Lugard!' Ayonchugu said.

Ayonchugu's comrades hopped off the jeep on the outskirts of Libah and took various directions to their hamlets. He was the last to be dropped off, and this happened at the Libah village square. The District Clerk came out of the car, said a few words to him, to which he answered 'Yes, Sir!' looking at him straight in the face. A sprinkling of curious onlookers mushroomed from nowhere and watched the District Clerk give him a handshake and a pally pat on the shoulder before entering his jeep and taking off, leaving behind a swirl of rusty dust. Ayonchugu stood back in a stiff military salute pose. He could see Sango waving back at him until the vehicle disappeared around a bend. He bent down and picked up his luggage.

While the villagers were staring at him as if they had been immobilized by an ominous wave of collective shock, two teenage boys whom Ayonchugu recognised as relatives of his but could not exactly recall how, came over to greet him. They took his bags, slung them over their shoulders and set off in the direction of his brother's house.

'I say, little brothers, you're going the wrong way,' Ayonchugu said. 'My house is towards Bamboo Valley.'

'We thought you would want to go to Big Compound first,' replied one of the boys.

'Of course! I can't miss not going there today. But a married man should be able to tell his kinsmen how his family is doing when he visits his father's compound.'

The boys looked at each other in dubious complicity, unsure as to what more to say. 'I err...guess your wife is err...living in Big Compound,' stammered one of the boys.

Ayonchugu was a bit surprised but not bothered. It was normal for one's brother to look after one's wife. It was even expected, especially when she had a child. Had he died, his brother would naturally have married his widow, without the fuss of a formal ceremony or a bride-price. Ndi was his only brother living in his father's house, and although the original family house had been reconstructed, the place was still considered to be the seat of the family. His wife and his child could not be in better hands.

As they got closer to their destination, Ayonchugu's thoughts focused increasingly on his family. His father had lost a leg in the Great War, but this had not deterred him from bringing up a family, at a time when it was abnormal to have one wife. Ayonchugu was the last of five children – four boys and a girl. The oldest was in Jos working for a tin mining company and had not been seen for a long time. Every once in a while a wayfarer delivered a parcel to Ayonchugu's mother from his brother, bringing rare joy to her cheerless existence.

The second child was the lone female. She was married in a nearby village. She used to come home quite often to visit her parents, but never stayed beyond three days, lest her husband start threatening that his bride-price be returned. Third in the family was Ndi. He had always been the one to stay in the village when everyone was out pursuing adventure. Ayonchugu tended to be close to him, and looked up to him.

The fourth child, Tongembe, had lived in Nkongsamba from a young age, having gone there as an apprentice carpenter. After her husband's death, their mother could not withstand the void, and eventually followed her son with the intention of staying just a few weeks before bringing him back. She ended up being trapped in French Cameroun. It was in the years after the Great War, after Kamerun was partitioned into two wobbly entities and handed out as spoils of war.

The last of the lot was Ayonchugu. When his mother was leaving for Nkongsamba, she sent him to live with his newly married sister. People who did not know the family well took him for his sister's first.

Big Compound was located about two miles off the road. Ayonchugu took in the familiar sights and smells of his village and felt an intensely increasing sense of anticipation as he got closer to his destination. He noted with his one good eye the changes that had taken place in his absence. More land had come under cultivation of coffee. As the three wove their way along well-trodden paths, the smell of blooming coffee lifted his spirits even higher, and the buzz of bees, as they went about their chores of pollination, was like music to his famished spirit. He saw two new houses built of stone and roofed with corrugated metal sheets. He could have asked the boys about the buildings, but they seemed intent on not talking to him. There will be ample time for them to update him on all developments, he said to himself, and took in deep breaths, as they had been taught to do in the army, to calm a mounting excitement.

They crossed a brook by stepping on stones that were not so visible but whose positions were well known, walked up a craggy winding path which brought them to a hedge at the back fence of the compound. The boys took a short-cut leading into the compound by squeezing through an opening in the hedge. Ayonchugu walked the length of the fence, came to the front entrance and stepped over the threshold.

He saw the main house at the far end, across a spacious yard. He could hear the voices of women chatting. As he walked further into the compound, the women's section, located adjacent to the main house, came into view. Ndi's wives – Megemuo Senior and Megemuo - were crouched in front of their kitchen, using their hands to fill a basket with beans which had been spread on mats outside to dry. They both looked up and saw him, and their eyes widened in alarm. The younger wife ran into Ndi's big room screaming, 'Oh my mother! My mother!' Megemuo Senior placed her hands over her mouth as Ayonchugu marched towards her, smiling, a look of euphoria on his face. She gave a guarded ululation, ran towards him and held him.

'It is indeed you!' she exclaimed. 'Our ancestors be praised! Ayo! Is it really you?'

'It is indeed I! Megemuo Senior, how are you?'

She did a jig of excitement, put her hands on his head and brought them down on each side of his body until she reached his feet in a symbolic cleansing motion, all the while murmuring words of welcome and prayers of thanks.

She led him to Ndi's sitting room. Ayonchugu's luggage was just by the door; the boys had sneaked off without talking to anyone. Ndi sat slumped at an angle in a wooden seat at one corner of the sparsely furnished room, mouth agape, a calabash of stale palm wine and empty bottles of beer strewn all around him. Megemuo was trying desperately to wake him up from an afternoon slumber. 'Get up and welcome your brother! He's back! Get up!' As she spoke, she placed her hands on his shoulders and shook him.

'From the land of the dead?' he growled, moving his head from side to side.

'Don't say things like that,' said the senior wife. 'Ayonchugu is here and you have got a lot to tell him.'

'Stop taunting me, devil of a woman! I've got nothing to tell anybody. Keep out of my sight, both of you!' Ndi spat out.

'I will get him some food,' said the senior wife to her companion. 'Go and inform Teneng and Kwende that Ayo has returned. They will know what to do.' The women left the room.

'Brother!' Ayonchugu called, moving closer to Ndi.

The drunken man managed to sit up. He peered through bloodshot eyes at his brother; then he started weeping.

Although Ayonchugu had seen lots of tears in the war, some of which were his, it tore his heart to see his brother break down so unabashedly. Ayonchugu had always known him to be a heavy drinker, but never to be a drunk. As a weeping drunk, he was all the more pathetic. This was no mood for women to see a man in. He turned around and pulled the door shut. The poorly ventilated room took an even more sombre look, and Ayonchugu moved over to a small wooden window, pulled back the latch and pushed it open.

'When did you start getting drunk? I smell something unhealthy happening around here.'

'Did you say unhealthy?' Ndi's voice was an unsteady drawl. 'It is Death itself. I will tell you what this is all about in good time. But for now, let my tears flow for the House of Ndafuh. For you – you that have been treated as dead...for Ngelem who now warms another man's bed...for Bimeh – an innocent baby whose mouth was ripped off the nipple. Oh ngeuh!'

Ayonchugu felt a painful jolt from within and crumbled into the nearest seat, shielding his face with his hands as he relived for a few traumatic seconds a scene he thought he had left behind him.

'You think I'm a drunk?'

'I don't have to think. I can see you are a drunk. Brother, why have you let this happen to you?'

'Do I drink? Yes. When you've been shackled down by your own impotence the calabash is a reliable sedative. If I do not drink, I'd do something that could land me in the rotten prison.'

'What happened to Ngelem and my child?'

Ndi leaned against the sun-dried brick wall and, rolling his sweaty head from side to side, began narrating a story which sounded most surreal to Ayonchugu's ears.

'Ajong, the fon's eldest son, has been the devil's incarnation in this family. Sometime after you left for the war, Ajong came out of hiding and started paying visits to Ngelem. No one thought anything serious was happening. Was he not our kinsman? And she was heavy with your child. But before long rumour had it that something that could burn down a house was going on. When the baby came it lived just long enough to be given a name. 'Bimeh' we called her. We were thinking more about you, who had left behind wife and family to go and fight. Nobody ever resembled her piteous name more. She was a delicate little thing, shrivelling as each day went by. It would seem that on Ajong's instigation, Ngelem deprived her of milk and comfort. She was branded four-eyed, and given the treatment that is the unfortunate lot of such children. Yet she was a strong one in her way, and hung on, hoping someone would notice the injustice and rescue her. No one did. I was blinded by rage against the mother to see the victim in the baby. One month to the day of her birth she breathed her last. Oh ngeuh-oo!'

'I do not remember a history of four-eyed babies in our family. Who ascertained that she was four-eyed? Was Munumi consulted?' Ayonchugu's voice was loud and incredulous.

'I got Munumi to come, but he only showed up at the very last minute. We knew nothing about the deprivations until a few days before the baby passed on. It was all in Ajong's master scheme, as I would later conclude.'

'And what about the women who came for the *ndamu*? They allowed something like that to happen?' Ayonchugu asked, his voice rising even further.

'When rumours about Ngelem and Ajong were proven true the women abandoned her. Only her mother showed up for the birth of the baby and stayed for two market days. Out of shame, and because she was being brandished an accomplice to them she left. Ajong was free to do his worst.'

'So are you about to confirm my worst fears that Ngelem is not in this house but elsewhere?'

'Have you gone deaf? She is not *elsewhere*. She is at Ajong's house – a happy mother of two – a boy and a girl.'

Ayonchugu sprang into action like a whirlwind. In seconds he had a pistol in his hand and ran towards the door. He had not anticipated opposition from Ndi, who jumped on him from behind, locked his arms around him and put his whole weight on him. The two went sprawling on the bare floor, with Ndi still holding on to him tightly.

'Ayonchugu! Little brother! Don't do something stupid. Listen to me! Listen!'

'I will kill him! Let me go, please!' Ayonchugu pleaded.

'No. You shall do no such thing. Have you heard?

Whatever has happened shall be fixed.'

Ayonchugu lay on the floor and waited for Ndi to release him. 'I thought I had shed all the tears a man can at the war front. Evil has touched my fence today! How could such a thing happen with men in this village? Where were you? Where were our uncles? Where were the elders?'

As he talked he loosened his grip on the pistol and Ndi took it from him. He sat on the dusty floor and held his face in his hands. Tears dribbled down onto his medals, and dripped on the earth floor, which instantly absorbed them, without attenuating the rage he felt within.

'Calm down and I will tell you the whole story. It takes a cool-headed man to do the right thing in circumstances like these. Call me a drunk, but I know what you can and what you cannot do now.' Ndi, staggering slightly, went into an inner room and hid away the gun. When he returned Ayonchugu was more collected, although he was still sitting on the floor.

'My brother,' Ayonchugu said eventually, 'I'm calm now. Let me hear what you have to say.'

'You are supposed to be strong enough to take any news after what we heard you boys went through in Boma.'

'Boma was war. This has struck me right home.'

'Then you must be a man and listen. I'm supposed to be the one with the heart of a bird here, not you. Take a seat.'

'I'm listening,' Ayonchugu said.

'News came that you had died. Fingoba was your undoing. My brother, in this village you are dead and fully buried,' pronounced the brother, pointing downwards and letting his head drop listlessly over his chest.

'No doubt that I am. If you could allow this to happen then I'm certainly dead. But you will all have to bury me again, and I won't go alone!' Ayonchugu looked wild, but he painstakingly collected himself, got up from the floor and slumped into a low wooden chair in one corner of the room. He covered his face with his hands, stretched out his legs in front of him and crossed one leg over the other like a woman in mourning. He cut an unbecoming picture.

'You remember our father's land at Ntako,' Ndi said.

Ayonchugu nodded. 'I do. The forested one.'

'It is no longer forested land,' said Ndi. 'It is a massive plantation of coffee belonging to Ajong. He and his father own a quarter of all the coffee farms in this village, and are still not satisfied. They have been land-grabbing ever since the demand for coffee soared. They are the only two farmers in this village recognised by the Marketing Board. Everybody else is supposed to be their employee. They buy our coffee for the price of groundnuts and resell to the Board at the official price.'

'Tell me what happened to our land,' Ayonchugu said.

'Ajong cleared it and started planting on it. Our uncles confronted him. He told them off. There was a scuffle. Ajong actually chased them off with a gun. They went to see the fon the following day. The fon told them they really had no case. He claimed the former fon, his father, had only leased the land to our grandmother for farming purposes. The person to decide to whom the land belonged after her death was the fon, he said. And although he had not sent his son to occupy the land, our uncles had no mandate from our late father, as far as he knew, to defend any property of his. That could only be done by our father's designated successor. How many times had he asked them to name a successor and have him recognised by the palace? Our uncles said they were waiting for you to return from the war before naming the successor. The fon said that whatever the case was, they had no right to get into a fight with a prince over property, and one to which he had a just claim.'

The door opened and Megemuo Senior stepped in carrying food in a basket and water in a calabash. She looked as though she wanted to say something, but when she sensed the mood in the room she quickly placed the items by the hearth and nimbly bowed her way out.

'It was clear the fon had taken sides in the matter. Ajong became terribly arrogant. He built a house on the land, on the very foundation our father had started building before his death. Then news of your death circulated like wild fire in the village. We had our doubts because we had no confirmation from any official. We went to see the District Officer, and his clerks told us they had no such information. They promised to contact the High Command and find out. We decided to do nothing and wait. Have we not been told before that a son of this village had died from forced labour, or from that horrible forest-land disease called malaria in the coastal plantations, and then one day he had turned up looking like a ghost from beyond?

'Yes, it has happened before,' Ayonchugu agreed.

'A messenger came from the palace to see us. I sent for our uncle Teneng. The messenger said the palace wanted us to say when we intended to perform the traditional rites on our late brother. We replied that until we were certain you were dead, we could not do anything but wait and hope to see you one day. He said news of the death of many braver men had been confirmed. What made us think you were still alive? One day Fingoba showed up.'

'Fingoba? Is he alive?' Ayonchugu asked, sitting up.

'Alive and thriving,' said Ndi. 'He confirmed your death in Binghashi.'

'My what? In Benghazi!' Ayonchugu sprang up.

'Sit down and listen,' Ndi said. Ayonchugu did a few paces around the room before returning to his seat. 'Fingoba said you were shot in an attack by Italian fighter planes in Byssania where there's nothing but sand. He said you refused to obey orders, and instead of lying flat on your belly when a raid was on, you stood up and ran. He said he lay flat on the sand and brought down an Italian plane as it flew over him. He survived the attack, sustaining a bullet wound to his right leg. He is *Finjongfinchugu*, a titled war hero. He is also Ajong's errand man.'

Ayonchugu gaped at his brother as he recounted the tale which was as improbable as one told by a bird. He knew more than anyone else, the truth about what happened to Fingoba after they left for the training camp. At least he knew what happened until the day he disappeared.

Fingoba and Ayonchugu had joined the army at the same time, while Ajong, who was physically very strong as well but known among his peers as a bully, had simply disappeared at the time the drafting was going on, adding 'coward' to his qualifications. Ayonchugu suspected he had been hiding in Kwifon's den.

CHAPTER THREE

Kwifon's den

News of Ayonchugu's return spread with the winds, and that same evening, his family members poured into Ndi's house bearing baskets of food. In normal circumstances they would have been celebrating with dancing, singing and even gun firing. This meeting was tinged by a sense of gloom and urgency. Ayonchugu was supposed to be dead. The family had been most reluctant to do the burial rites, but had finally given in.

The folks sat down and spoke in low tones, sharing palm wine and kola nuts. The men consulted among themselves in little groups, and a plan of action was devised.

Teneng cleared his throat a few times before speaking. 'The elders of the family have conferred. Ayonchugu will stay with his brother until his compound is cleansed. A man can't see his own grave. A man can't enter a compound wherein his spirit has been laid to rest with the ancestors. It will provoke a malediction.' Everyone nodded. 'The dilemma as we know it,' continued Teneng in a sombre tone, 'is that cleansing can be effective only if we get the accord of those who insisted that the rites be done in the first place. We must act urgently. We will begin by taking news of Ayonchugu's return to our fon.'

Kwende and Teneng were designated to report the return of Ayonchugu to the palace and get the requirements for the cleansing rites. It was not unheard of in Libah that someone returned from the dead. However, it had not happened in a very long time that someone for whom final funeral rites had been performed returned. No one could remember with certainty the standard items the palace demanded to perform cleansing rites in a case like Ayonchugu's. The information was available with the archivists of the palace who could subject it to negotiation.

The following evening the two envoys reported to an assembly of the senior members of the family.

'We have good news for you all,' said Teneng. 'The fon and the councillors have made no special requests. They say the palace has been very happy to see a son of the land return home safely. The palace intends to bestow a title on Ayonchugu as soon as he is fully settled in. As a gesture of good faith, the fon gave us this cam wood to present to him,' he concluded, pulling out a little bundle from his fibre bag.

Ayonchugu was the only one not feeling flattered by this unexpected largesse.

The next destination for the two kinsmen was Kwifon's den. The two men were aware that Kwifon made decisions independently of the fon and his councillors, and that of the two authorities, Kwifon was more unpredictable. Kwifon had no face but that of his messengers. He was thought by some to be a group of men sitting in council. Others thought kwifon was a family of powerful masquerades or spirits, and still others thought it was a group of mystical old crooks backed by very talented musicians. Certain things were clear: Kwifon was mysterious and unfathomable for the non-initiated; his power was paralysing, and no one had succeeded to see him and go free. It was popularly believed that when the non-initiated saw Kwifon, the transgressor simply *turned red* and shrivelled up.

Kwende and Teneng arrived at the mouth of the den early in the morning and prepared to wait there for any of the messengers to show up. They placed a large calabash of raffia-palm wine at the entrance and stood from across the road and looked expectantly at the narrow track leading into the den. They coughed and cleared their throats until an elderly man wearing only a cap and an *ntum* – a length of cloth expertly girded around his waist and loins – emerged from the narrow path and stood just behind the raffia fibre curtain that was the gateway to the shrine.

'Two coughing so loudly so early in the morning. It creates panic here in this abode of peace and next thing you know, Kwifon is complaining that one of his children got scared and ran into hot embers, scourging his feet in the confusion. What have you got to say to that?'

Kwende was the more tactful speaker of the two men. 'We would truly regret such a misfortune,' he said. 'We never opted to fall prey to the tempests this morning, but when one has spent two sleepless nights following many years of worrying about the whereabouts of one's child, Kwifon can understand why our health is poorly.'

'The one with the last word is Kwifon. But I'll give you the benefit of the doubt. When the dog defecates in the house it should not have as an excuse that the door was shut. What was it with your child?'

'He was gone for five years to fight the war of the Europeans and news came to us that he was killed,' Kwende said. 'As the gods of the land would grant it, he showed up two days ago, bringing along his entire luggage.'

'Whoever dwells abroad for a long time should return home with his entire luggage,' said the old man. 'Kwifon will hear the good news. A son of the land that is a successful warrior anywhere is a hero here, even if we still have to see the colour of his luggage.'

Teneng stated their immediate concern. 'The only problem is that when news of his death came, burial rites were performed. It now turns out those rites were done on a living person. A heavy log lies on our shoulders and only Kwifon's hand can lift it.'

The messenger shook his head slowly from side to side, and after a thoughtful spell said, 'It is not for the messenger to say what the master will do. I will take your concern to Kwifon.'

So saying, the old man lifted the calabash of raffia-palm wine the two men had brought and bore it along with him. The men watched him in silence as he disappeared gravely behind the bushes, and then turned and acknowledged each other's performance.

'Not a bad start, is it?' Teneng said.

'By the look of things so far, yes. But don't forget that with these people you never know what is coming next,' Kwende cautioned.

'At least Nformi has a better reputation than the others,' observed Teneng.

'You are right there,' Kwende said. 'Nchumuluh would have started by telling us the calabash of wine we brought was not enough to awaken Kwifon's senses after a rather busy night fighting the forces of evil.'

'Shush. Here he comes already. He sure wasted no time cooking up what to say.'

'Mind what you say yourself....'

Nformi looked at the two men rather solemnly, cleared his throat melodramatically and said, 'Kwifon says when he sees a good thing he calls it good. Kwifon's eyes are the very grasses you see all over, and those eyes were glad to see the son of the land return from battle. If he were not a great warrior, he would not have survived the massacre that we hear went with that war. Kwifon is happy too that he would be duly honoured by the palace. With regard to your quest, Kwifon has got this to say: The hand that goes to the anus returns with fart. He who buried should exhume.'

'Only Kwifon can give us the power to do that,' said Kwende.

'You took it upon yourselves to bury,' Nformi said. 'You were very aware that when an adult dies in this village Kwifon must come to the burial.'

This was delicate ground and Teneng should have let his companion carry on, but he started explaining on a wrong note. 'We had no corpse and....'

'So why are you people calling for Kwifon?' Nformi cut in.

Kwende took back matters in his hands. 'We wish to cleanse our brother's compound and the grave behind his house in which was buried the banana sucker which represented him. He would be able once again to return, and live in his home. By tradition, burial rites cannot be repeated on the same person. Neither can they be done on a living person.'

'You are not informing me,' said Nformi. 'However, this is a rather uncommon request. When the dog defecates in the house it should not take excuse that it was leashed inside. I will take your request to Kwifon.'

The pair watched the old man as he turned around and did the solemn walk he had done for many years through the mysterious path that led to the abode of the secret society. He did not take too long to return, looking a bit more severe.

'Kwifon says he values all his children, both those deserving a beating and those that are obedient. Issues must be sorted out in an orderly manner. You will have to provide the standard twenty goats, twenty cocks, forty baskets of achu, and forty calabashes of palm wine – of course you know what size to bring, and thirty heaps of bitter-leaf. That will be for the burial you performed in Kwifon's absence. When you have done that, return to the mouth of Kwifon's den to discuss the cleansing.'

'We accept our short-sightedness in the matter,' Kwende said. 'We have learned by our mistake. But when you beat a wayward child, you should do so while pulling him into the homestead. These things will take time to put together. Our bags are light and government taxes for the past years have left us scrounging around for our very survival. We wish to ask Kwifon to combine the two rites into one.'

'I can't decide for the powers that be; I will take your proposal to Kwifon,' answered Nformi. He turned around and gently snaked his way back into the den. He soon came back with a message from Kwifon to the effect that he had accepted in principle to combine the two rites, on the condition that they doubled the number of items requested. Kwende and Teneng found this unacceptable and couched their answers in proverbs. They knew only too well that Kwifon's bag never got full. If you were stupid enough to show him that you could satisfy his appetite, then he would keep asking until you confessed your utter helplessness. It was like using your bare hands to channel water to irrigate your farm. No one dared challenge Kwifon to an encounter about riches; that person would end up bankrupt.

The messenger kept going back and forth, in the infinite patience that was the trademark of those who had to engage with powers too demure to be rushed, until after his sixth visit to the den, Kwifon gave his final demand. Kwifon would be provided fifteen goats, twenty cocks, thirty baskets of achu, twenty-one large calabashes of wine and fifteen heaps of bitter-leaf.

'Kwifon has chosen to be benevolent after due consideration of the fact that your son is not an initiated member of kwifon, and therefore owes no substantial food debt here.' Nformi paused, studied his interlocutors, and seeing no battle left in them continued, 'I've also made it known to Kwifon that you two gentlemen have spoken rather well and Kwifon does not remember having any grudge against either of you. You are advised to act quickly lest the spirits become annoyed,' Nformi concluded, with his back already turned on the men.

That evening the two men reported back to the family. Everyone listened in dismay as the pair explained what had happened. They were all shattered at the enormous cost of the rites. They each offered to contribute an item or two to help Ayonchugu out. By the time the meeting ended, he had been promised five goats, thirteen cocks and all the palm wine by the men. The women, under the leadership of Megemuo Senior, promised to provide all the achu and bitter-leaf.

Throughout the meeting Ayonchugu barely managed to contain his disenchantment. He sat head bowed, and no one talked to him directly or looked at him in the eye.

That night he lay on a creaky bamboo bed in his brother's house and thought over what he had gone through in the war. It was indeed a wonder he was still alive. Of the hundred and sixty-eight young men who went to war in his group from the five surrounding villages, less than half survived. It was not that the dead were not brave, but rather that they had faced the enemy on the most vulnerable occasions with the most basic weapons. They were never trained to handle sophisticated tanks or fly planes. They had had only their rifles with bayonets and grenades, and the occasional cannon and anti-aircraft mounds with which to face the Italians and the Japanese. He had been exceedingly brave, and inexplicably lucky, losing only an eye. His greatest problem was in his mind. It needed a rest, but whether asleep or awake, it dwelt on the war. He could not stop thinking that they had been ordered to attack treacherous Japanese positions before elite troops could be allowed to venture into the same terrain; that he had once been ignorant enough to allow himself to be defiled by one of his top commanders who had strange urges; how he had seen far too much blood, and tasted gobbets of flying human flesh following bomb blasts, which sometimes left nothing behind to be buried.

He thought about Idrissu, a boy from the Gold Coast with whom he had become good friends. They were fighting side by side in Burma when he was wounded grievously. He was later driven off to a hospital. Like many others, he was never seen again. All the grievously wounded soldiers were simply never heard of again. Did they all die? Ayonchugu wondered. Was it not intriguing that mostly the able-bodied soldiers returned home? It was known that European veterans of the first war were still being taken care of in hospitals or care homes across Europe. Where did the thousands of seriously injured Africans end up?

His worst memory was of the slaughter of personnel belonging to a contingent of South African forces who had engaged Italians in distraction tactics for some days. The South Africans were about to be overpowered when their commanding officer made frantic efforts to join his command post in order to obtain a dispensation allowing him to arm unarmed men under his command. Every gun was indispensable for putting up a successful resistance or beating a retreat. The response was categorical: "No! No carrier will be allowed to use a gun! Not even against the enemy!"

The South Africans were overpowered and hundreds of soldiers taken prisoner. The carriers did not fare so well. They were all herded to a mine field and ordered to run about. The mines exploded, maiming half of them. Some of the men figured out that if they ran in single file, they could make it, with those at the front detonating mines, giving a chance to those at the back to survive. The Italian soldiers realised what was happening, and used heavy artillery to wipe out the remaining men from a distance.

A day later, Ayonchugu's company and fighters from the East African Rifles engaged the Italians and pushed them back. They retreated in a hurry, leaving behind the South Africans. In a change of spirit, the South Africans retrieved the corpses of their decimated comrades, which had all the while lain in the sands awaiting the arrival of vultures, and buried them with full military honours, at the risk of a court martial.

Ayonchugu's sole solace had been the hope of returning home and picking up his life where he had left it. He had been looking forward to seeing the child his wife must have given birth to. It would be a joy to pick him up and cuddle him and forget the horrors of the war. He had hoped to have another baby. Ajong, now, more than before the war, was the cause of his frustration.

Ayonchugu had always known Ajong to be a bully. He was physically built for the role, and worst of all, he was power drunk from an early age. His desire for power increased when he became wise enough to understand that as the fon's eldest son he was disqualified to be the ruler of the village. Anyone who called him by his name without the princely title *Muontoh* was sure to get into his bad books, or, as Ayonchugu's people would say, add a twig to his pile. Whenever he drank with his peers, Ajong was known to start a fight over petty things like who got a lob of kola nut first.

Ayonchugu still remembered how at one social gathering, Ajong bullied a man into giving him the gizzard of a chicken when he clearly was not entitled to it. On other occasions Ayonchugu had downplayed Ajong's bigotry with a derisive smile and a shake of the head. This time he did not stay silent.

'When you take your mouth to ask for something that is obviously not your due, what would you use to eat it?'

'Did you just ask me a question or is my imagination playing tricks on me?' Ajong asked in turn.

'I did,' Ayonchugu said calmly. 'People have lost their lives over things of taboo because they had a deep stomach. Princehood does not entitle you to eat gizzard when your elders are present.'

'Well, I have the gizzard here in my hand and I want to see you stop me from eating it,' Ajong retorted, firing up and edging towards Ayonchugu.

'I won't stop you. But you dare not eat it either. Ignorance is forgivable, but bigotry and greed are not.' Ayonchugu by this time was standing up and looking unflinchingly into the challenging eyes of Ajong who was now edging closer.

Others called out: 'Stay calm! Stay calm!' Two smart men held Ayonchugu firmly and pulled him away from the confrontation. Everyone knew he was correct and that he had made a bold point, but it was important to save face for Ajong's benefit. Ajong did not eat the gizzard then, but he was too proud to give it to whom it was due. The following month, during the same meeting three additional chickens were roasted courtesy of Ajong. He must have listened to sound advice for once or used his initiative to make such reparations. He sat tamely quiet until someone handed him his share of the chicken.

Their other major clash had been over Ngelem. Bobe Chia, her father, worked as a cook for Europeans for many years. She had grown up in a more enlightened community far from the village, and no man had claimed her for a future bride. When her parents retired to the village, there was a scramble to marry her. Ajong arranged things with Bobe Chia who, wishing to carve a place for himself among the palace nobles, had welcomed him eagerly. Ajong cornered her one evening as she was returning from bathing in the stream and attempted to get too intimate with her. Ngelem fought him off. Ayonchugu did the opposite, wooing and winning Ngelem's affection, to her father's disappointment. Between the two young men, family blood turned into bad blood, resulting in a fight from which neither emerged a clear winner. A truce was finally brokered, but they both knew neither of them could have a peaceful sleep in the vicinity of the other.

Ayonchugu stirred uneasily in his bed as his mind dwelt on the day's happenings. Everyone in the family was strained to the limits putting together the items for the cleansing rites. He had some money which he had intended to use to acquire land and develop plantations of coffee and other cash crops. If he were to meet the demands of Kwifon and satisfy other parties involved in the rites, he would be left with nothing.

In the wee hours of the morning, just when he was finally falling asleep, he heard shouts of distress coming from somewhere in the village. He rolled out of his bed, quickly put on some clothes, took a torch and stepped outside. From a distance, he could see tongues of fire lighting the night sky. He went and knocked on Ndi's door.

'I think there's a house on fire over in Bamboo Valley.'

'Indeed? Then we must go over and help.'

The two men dashed out into the darkness and took the direction to Ayonchugu's house. They dared not say what was in their minds lest it turn out to be true.

When they arrived at the house Ayonchugu stayed by the road, while Ndi joined a despairing team of villagers who were trying to put out the fire. They witnessed in dismay the last wooden pole go down. What was left of Ayonchugu's house was a heap of smouldering and exploding embers.

Thatched roof houses were susceptible to fires especially during the dry season when women made *mankare*. A spark from burning grass could land on thatch and set it ablaze. Investigations in the morning showed that there was no farm nearby. No one had made a fire inside the house that day either. Ayonchugu was convinced that this was arson. It was the closest an enemy could get to taking his life.

Two days later, Ayonchugu assembled his family and addressed them. 'My dear kinsmen,' he said, 'I must ask you to stop making preparations for the cleansing rites. I know this comes as a surprise. Just let me speak. Since my return from war, you have shown me that I have people I can call mine. Right now, I do not wish you to endure all the trouble you are going through for my sake. This village has become too uncomfortable for me. Someone has declared war on me, and I know he won't stop until he gets me. I would be staking my life if I stayed. If you see the back of my head, know that my face is already facing the way out.'

'Our brother,' said Teneng, 'if we say that you are comfortable here, we would be lying. But what I know from experience is that running away from a problem does not solve it. Your enemy is our enemy. We are ready to support you.'

'During the war, intuition saved many a life,' replied Ayonchugu. 'Mine tells me to move on, and I have to do so in spite of your counselling, which is in good faith. Leave I must.'

Other family members spoke, trying to dissuade Ayonchugu from leaving, but his mind was made up. 'I'm going in the direction in which the sun rises,' He said. 'I'll send word to you when I'm well settled.'

He gave money to each man and woman. The women

wept and laughed at the same time. The men were pensive, and afterwards, tried again to talk him out of his plans.

After midnight, eleven days to the day he returned from war, Ayonchugu brought out his bulging military kitbag and strapped it on his back. Armed with a locally crafted pistol, he lit his way with a torch and walked briskly out of the village.

CHAPTER FOUR

Welcome to Ngonibi

Ayonchugu felt cold in spite of the thick clothes he was wearing. He had travelled a long way. His journey had taken him onto increasingly higher altitude. His breathing was a bit laboured, and this fact annoyed him. He came to a cliff, and saw a peaceful enclave lying before him down in the valley. Thick patches of morning mist, immobile like white decorations on a green picture, obscured his view of parts of the dwelling below. He had reached his destination.

Just about the time that palm wine tappers set out on their rounds, Ayonchugu walked into Ngonibi. The men he met as well as a few women who had had an early start greeted him and asked where he was going and whether they could be of help. He could barely infer what they were saying. He did his best to reply, gesticulating as much as speaking.

An elderly man who understood some Libah language interviewed him briefly and offered to take him to his house. The two men walked silently for about a quarter of a mile off the main track and arrived at a compound with several chalets. Ayonchugu was shown into a room where a fire was burning slowly on logs of wood. He dropped his luggage at one angle of the room and settled down in front of the fire.

His host was called Ndamgu. He was an elderly balding man, and what was left of his hair was already grey at the temples. But he looked solid and carried himself with an aura of authority. Ndamgu woke up his wife, Manyi, and introduced her to the wayfarer, and then went out to continue doing his morning chores. She quickly prepared him breakfast, consisting of leftovers of the previous evening's meal. He ate heartily and thanked her. He then clambered onto a bamboo bed by the hearth and immediately fell asleep.

Later that evening, two men came at the invitation of Ndamgu to have a discussion with Ayonchugu. Tanteh was the quarter-head in Ndamgu's neighbourhood. He normally would not have been the one to come to Ndamgu's, but he had a lot of respect for the elderly man, and had offered to come and meet the stranger. Tachum was a blacksmith who was well thought of by everyone. The men were excited to hear that Ayonchugu was from Libah, and they talked to him in an imperfect form of his language.

'How is Libah now?' Tachum asked. 'My father and I used to travel to your village. The market for kola nuts was good there.'

'I was away from home for a long time,' Ayonchugu replied. 'I don't know what business is like there now.'

'Trade was quite good in your village in the old days,' Ndamgu said. 'My family sold hides and rare feathers to Libah middlemen who in turn travelled to Calabar to sell them. My gun, which used to be my father's, was made by Libah smiths of old. A German official who was going about collecting old things asked me to sell it to him. I refused. He offered me a bag of money. I told him my inheritance was not for sale.'

'He possibly could not have been asking you to sell him the *atifang*?' inquired Tachum.

'That gun has a lot of history behind it. It was given to my father by the fon of Libah himself when he helped Libah citizens in their fight with the Bikwun clan who were enemies of your people then.'

'I have heard the story of an Ngonibi man who helped Libah people,' Ayonchugu said. 'Only, I have never fully understood what happened.'

'He overheard their war plans and revealed them to Libah people,' said Ndamgu. 'Your people at first took him for a spy and imprisoned him. They were going to behead him. When things happened as he had told them they would, he was rewarded with honours and an *atifang*. It was that simple. Libah was prepared when the Bikwuns attacked.'

'He did a lot more than Ndamgu has described,' said Tanteh. 'We know that Ndamgu is not a man to boast. Libah warriors had the *atifang* which shot without missing, but the Bikwuns had charms that made them invincible. His father managed to steal the medicine which the Bikwuns were using, and applied it on Libah warriors. Now, they not only had the *atifang*, but were also invincible. That is how the Bikwuns were stopped in their wars of conquest by Libah.'

'Ndamgu was the best warrior in his youth,' Tachum said. 'He is still our undisputed army commander in inter-village wars. Is it not a wonder that after fighting a dozen wars, he has no disability at all?'

'These scars were not caused by enemy weapons, but by accidental slips and falls,' said Ndamgu, showing healed gashes on his legs, arms and face.

'So my host inherited both the *atifang* and the Bikwun charms?' asked Ayonchugu.

'Are we speaking German?' Tanteh asked.

'We understand you've just returned from war,' Tachum said. 'It's a pity you did not see him before going to fight, as did many young men from all over this region.'

'Maybe my eye would have been saved,' Ayonchugu said. 'But that is the least of my problems.'

Ayonchugu told them his story. When he finished, they expressed their sympathy.

'We understand your feelings,' said Tachum. 'You have been all over the world and have seen better places. Why have you decided to come to our village of all places?'

'I want to forget all I went through in the war. I wish to live in as peaceful a place as possible and absorb myself in work. *Arbeit macht frei.* I hope this formula works for me here,' Ayonchugu said with a bitter smile.

'You were too young to know what we went through,' said Ndamgu. 'You were not even born when we did *Njogmassi*.'

His interlocutors understood his meaning of the word only within the context of their own experience of what they had endured at the hands of their former protector nation, and it was not a precept with which they readily agreed.

'No, I was not,' Ayonchugu agreed. 'But I've been through a lot. By the end of the war, I had come to know men and women of all creeds and colours, and had seen the world, and the human heart at its most evil and at its best and bravest. We lads all grew up the tough way, some into rational men, while others, unable to face up to the shocking barbarity of war, became shadows of ourselves.'

'That, son, is what war does,' said Tanteh. 'War is a teacher with two faces – one evil, the other good.'

Ayonchugu nodded and continued speaking. 'I have known men for whom war was fun. I have known men who would gladly return to play at it and stack their kill as if they were stacking pebbles in a game of *minjang*. War has shown me that brothers can come from different wombs. At the front, it was all about survival and bravery. With a lot of good fortune, I made it through. Now, all I want is peace.'

'Welcome to Ngonibi,' said Tanteh. 'This is the best possible place for you to find the kind of life you long for.'

'We must warn you,' said Ndamgu, 'that neighbouring villages are hard-pressed for fertile land and have encroached on ours many times. We've had to fight back.'

'Right inside this village, you must tread with care; sleep with one eye open, or you could pay the price with your head,' Tachum warned.

The men talked and drank palm wine until late into the night, and then left, each brandishing a fire torch to light his way home.

Ndamgu's hospitality was boundless, as was Manyi's. Their two younger children were twins and immediately took to Ayonchugu who had many stories about his travels to entertain them with. By constantly interacting with Ndamgu's family members, especially the children, he quickly learned to speak Binibi.

Ndamgu took Ayonchugu to introduce to the palace.

'The fon was very happy to learn that a son of one of our allies was here,' said the monarch. 'We hope you would stay. Land is available. Help will be provided.'

Two weeks later Ayonchugu and Ndamgu went back to see him to request land of his own. They brought along a large calabash of palm wine and a goat. The fon sent out five members of his council to map out land for Ayonchugu at the peripheries of the village. It was a coveted site, three compounds away from Ndamgu's estate. This was indeed a great honour for him, as the land owners around the fringes of the village were all tough warriors and were there to serve as a buffer against invaders. Here the land was a lot more arable. Ayonchugu was shown three different allotments, demarcated by natural landmarks. He chose a piece of land that was bordered by a stream and a large gully which had no water running through it during the dry season. On the humid side of the land, there was a lush forest which gradually petered out into mountain grassland as one moved upwards, towards the centre of the land. There were no trees at all on the dry side of the land, which was instead rich in fodder that could also serve as material for thatching. He found his choice just perfect for the plans he had in mind. Since a man must have neighbours, the adjoining plots were allocated to two brave young men who already had families of their own, but had still been enjoying the hospitality of their parental homesteads.

It took one month for a team of competent builders working under Ndamgu's and Ayonchugu's directives to build a four-bedroom house, which was a novelty in Ngonibi. Normally, a compound had a number of detached single-room houses, depending on the size of the family.

Ayonchugu quickly set out developing his land. It was not an easy task for a man without a family, but he never lacked help. Ndamgu's thirteen-year-old twins – a boy called Ibonge and a girl called Nibonge – were never beyond earshot. Subsequently, their father sent Ibonge to live with Ayonchugu. Nibonge was always around and willing to give a hand with domestic chores. Within a year his land showed promise of becoming very productive farmland. All around his house he planted coffee, interspersed with suckers of plantain and banana. Knowing that too much water made for diluted palm wine, he planted a raffia-palm plantation on the dry side of the land. He had brought eucalyptus seeds wrapped up in a polythene bag. He nursed them and within five months, he had over five hundred seedlings. He cleared natural vegetation along the humid side of the land and planted the seedlings. Few people in the village had seen a eucalyptus tree before and wondered why he was interested in this particular plant. His estate was lush and green by the end of his second year in Ngonibi.

Ayonchugu prospered faster than many of his age mates in the village and was the envy of many a young man and the perfect prize for a maiden. Everybody expected him to marry one of many pretty virgins, but he never showed any interest in women. Often, a courageous mother would send one of her daughters bearing a basket of delicious food to him, or send her to give him a hand with cooking or some farm work. He accepted their hospitality graciously, but never bothered to look at any of the girls below the neck. Some people joked that he was waiting for Nibonge to grow up. He liked her very much indeed, but it was the same as liking one's little sister; the thought of marrying her one day never crossed his mind.

Few people knew about the deep pain he carried in his heart. Yet there never was a single night he did not silently mourn the loss of Ngelem and the death of his baby. Dreams about them jumbled up with nightmarish images from the war and marred his sleep. He went to bed very late and woke up with the birds. He spent the day toiling on the farm, letting the bitter memories of war and family drip off in the sweat from his brows.

CHAPTER FIVE

Neighbours at war

As time went by, Ayonchugu became well established in Ngonibi and the mishaps of the past receded slowly to the back of his mind. The mental wounds were still there, throbbing, but no longer bleeding. No man could live his war experience and return to being oneself soon, unless one was made of the stuff the Nazis were made of. Yet, he knew that even Nazis were not totally without their own soft spot somewhere. He had recently read a post-war newspaper article about the former commander of a concentration camp, who when asked what he regretted most about the war, said he regretted not spending enough time with his family who lived within a mile of the camp.

One morning on a *njuelah*, the sacred day of the week, Ayonchugu joined a committee of elders whose duty it was to map out contingency plans for the security of the village. His opinion was taken seriously. As he helped put them together, he hoped that these plans would never have to be executed.

Later that same afternoon Ndamgu educated him amply about the history of the conflict between the people of Ngonibi and their immediate neighbour to the east, the Nambems. It was a non-working day, but the two men could not afford to be idle. They occupied themselves by selecting bad coffee beans from Ndamgu's harvest which was spread out on a mat to dry in the courtyard. Ndamgu had a lot to say, and Ayonchugu mostly listened.

'Just about the time the Germans came here, a group of dissenting villagers broke off from their clansmen and went in search of a new homeland. They were led by a prince called Jungwi. They travelled over two hundred miles, but were turned away from many villages because of their arrogance. They finally found temporary abode in Ngonibi. They were of a totally different extraction.'

'I can tell from their language,' Ayonchugu said. 'It sounds alien to all others in this region.'

'It does,' Ndamgu concurred. 'Their practices are also very different. Nambem women spaced their children by two years.'

'Like European women,' Ayonchugu remarked.

'Yes. With the difference that our neighbours went on to multiply like ducks. They refused to worship our deities. They were spiteful. They refused to recognise the sovereignty of our fon.'

'What insolence!' Ayonchugu said.

'Insolence indeed! But that's not all. They behaved as if they had an indisputable natural claim to everything that belonged to us. Inevitably, skirmishes occurred between their youths and ours. During one such incident, a young Ngonibi native died. This angered our young men and they spontaneously set out in rage to avenge the murder of the youth. News of the impending confrontation reached Kwifon who quickly gathered the Nambem people and planted his spear in their midst. The youths retreated, swearing they would be back one day to deal with the ingrates. Kwifon, meanwhile, herded the Nambems to our eastern borders and resettled them there temporarily.

'The prince of Nambem got his people to assemble some goats, a bull, a cow and thirty chickens, which he sent over to the Ngonibi palace. The lead emissary bore along the nkeng to show that they came in peace. When our people saw the peace-plant their rage was tempered and they allowed the gifts to be delivered to the palace. The emissaries apologised for the death of the youth and gave their word to the fon that such a thing would never happen again.'

'Was their apology accepted?' Ayonchugu asked.

'Many councillors were against accepting the apology until two men had been killed to avenge the death of the youth. But our fon at the time was a peace-loving patriarch. He reminded the unforgiving councillors that when one beats a wayward child one should at the same time be pulling him into the homestead. He kept the cow and Kwifon took the bull. A goat was given to the family whose son was killed, and the rest of the goats were given to the councillors and quarter-heads.'

'And the chickens?' Ayonchugu asked.

'They were mostly used to entertain the guests,' said Ndamgu.

'I see. How did Nambem finally become a village?'

'Each of the villages that made up the Mingembale tribe accepted to concede some land at the point where the five villages intersected. The land thus carved out was big enough to accommodate the new-comers. The Germans later mapped out the area. Jungwi was crowned fon.'

'I see,' said Ayonchugu. 'There was peace at last.'

'For many years the villages lived in a truce which, though not perfect, was harmonious enough to allow each village to develop. Nambem grew in population. Girls married at thirteen and had babies every one to two years until they could no longer have them. Nambems wanted to maintain the purity of their bloodline. They broke taboos. Second-cousins married one another, and two brothers could get married to third-cousins.'

'That was incestuous,' Ayonchugu said.

'To them it was very normal. Our people spited them for that, naturally. For a while all was fine with the Nambems, apart from that population growth meant they had more mouths to feed. Very gradually they started farming on their neighbours' land. And because they knew on what side of the bed Ngonibi people lay their heads when they went to sleep, they expanded mostly on our side of the border. Trouble started when they pitched up the first houses on Ngonibi land. It suddenly dawned on our people that we were losing territory. Diplomacy produced no results; Fon Jungwi claimed the houses were only farm huts.

'On a Nambem market day, a group of Ngonibi youths went down to the occupied land in a surprise attack, rounded up all the children and locked them up in one house, and within a short time razed thirty new houses and flattened all the farms. They returned bearing goats, chickens and pigs.'

'The farmhouses were actually permanent homes,' Ayonchugu said.

'Yes,' Ndamgu concurred. 'The Nambems responded by calling our people cowards. "Ngonibi people are our wives," they said. "They took it out on the kids when we were not around. We did in one of their own in their land and they could do nothing about it. We shall deal with them again. We shall go up to their palace and return with their fon or their Kwifon. They will never again lift a hand against a descendant of Shamiakuba!"

'They executed a counter-attack. There was bloodshed, which ended only when the colonial administration intervened six days later. A truce was brokered and the best warriors on both sides were subsequently drafted into the German colonial army and sent to fight in the first big war.

'Over the next few years, the villages rebuilt their relationship. On market days traders moved freely from one village to another doing business. The Nambems had no raffia-palms, and so they bought raffia fibre bags, baskets and reinforced decorated calabashes from Ngonibi traders. They loved our wine! The Nambems brought *musanga* jewellery and weapons acquired from Pond smiths, who for centuries, have been masters of the art of mining and smelting of iron ore. The Bifus came with palm oil, traps and animal skins. The Bitehs came with pottery. On such days it was difficult to tell that these same people had not so long before been at war with one another. Men from Ngonibi haggled harmoniously with men from Nambem whom they had taken a shot at a year before. In the palm wine huts, while keeping a smart eye on their cups, former warring enemies told callous jokes about women over a calabash of strong wine. As you know, it was, and still is taboo to talk about war with one's former enemy in times of peace, unless such an exchange is coded in proverbs and riddles.'

'Only cowards go for each other's throats when away from the battle front,' Ayonchugu noted.

'That's true,' said Ndamgu.

Barely three weeks after Ndamgu enlightened Ayonchugu on the history of conflict between Ngonibi and Nambem, peace was compromised, and Ayonchugu found himself taking up arms.

Mamun ran three businesses in one on market days. She had a bar in her home where she sold palm wine and imported beer. There too, she served illicit brews to a select few from an inner chamber. In yet another innermost chamber, she ran the third of her businesses, of which she and her daughter were the wares. They would alternatively go into the chamber to serve a client who himself had sneaked in through a side-door.

Among their discrete regulars was Nkenalu. He was one of the king-makers and a hereditary councillor to the fon of Nambem. He had seven wives, the youngest of whom could well pass for the grand-daughter of the first. Nkenalu would walk all the way from his village with a load of wares, and after selling them, would slip into Mamun's, and there, surrender every shilling to either the matron or her lubricious daughter. When he did not have money, he bled his wives dry of the day's earnings from the sale of their vegetables and spices, sent them home, and used the funds to feed his secret addiction.

He soon ran up a debt at Mamun's. The total amount owed varied at the whims of the women. One day he left the market and was trying to sneak away when the two women accosted him in public. It was an embarrassment for him when a little crowd gathered to watch how the drama would play out. No matter how hard he tried to negotiate, the two women held on to his *ntum*, demanding he pay every shilling he owed them.

Some Nambem men and women happened on the scene of the incident and intervened physically to free him. The Ngonibi lookers-on stepped in to support their sisters. The result was a general scuffle which ended in sprained limbs, gashed faces, and torn clothes on both sides. A trickle of blood was running down Nkenalu's nose.

News of the market brawl travelled like wild fire in the harmattan and reached Nambem even before the belligerents limped into the village that night, calling all sorts of curses to befall the people of Ngonibi. And it would have all ended there were it not for Nkenalu's protracted nose bleeding. No herb could stall the flow. By early morning, the haemophiliac had bled to death. A village medicine-man, without even seeing the corpse, concluded that he had been poisoned in Ngonibi market. The reaction was spontaneous: His death must be avenged!

The people of Ngonibi woke up that morning to cries of

woe from the outskirts of the village. Many homes were up in flames. A young man and his wife had been abducted.

Talking-drums soon erupted, churning out a coded message calling all able-bodied men to rally in front of Kwifon's den to prepare to take the war to the aggressors.

Ayonchugu thought the cause for war was not well grounded, but he could not stay back while others went to fight. Was he not once told that soldiers did not seek justification for wars but had to fight and win them at the behest of politicians? He went along with his pistol which had six rounds of ammunition. It was a battle of dane guns, spears, and bows and arrows. It raged on for two days before everybody came to their senses and hostilities ceased. Nambem lost seven men; Ngonibi never recovered the abducted couple.

CHAPTER SIX

Medicine-men to the rescue

Ayonchugu returned from the inter-village fray with a gash on his left tibia from an arrow. The wound did not look fatal, but fatality was not in the look; it was in the poison that the tip of the arrow was laced with. Even that was not fatal if one knew exactly the kind of poison that was used in *cooking* or *spoiling* the arrow and acted fast enough. He had reacted swiftly after he got shot at by taking a combination of antidotes that had been handed out to every fighter. A village medicine-man did some laceration around his thigh and applied medication there to prevent any poison from flowing up into the rest of the body.

As the wound healed, his leg got heavier. He finally was immobilised and started using crutches to move around. The infected leg swelled, turned hard and hot. The pain was unbearable and Ayonchugu had to muster the courage not to cry. The nearest health centre was a long way off and was not reputed for successfully dealing with local poisons. Munumi, the renowned medicine-man from Ala'a Okuk was called in. He prepared a thick poultice and smeared it all over the leg.

'In two days the problem will be gone,' he reassured Ayonchugu.

Two days later, the mouth of the wound reopened and pus spilled forth in quantities that Ayonchugu did not remember seeing before, not even in the hospital in the Imphal, where all the patients had lost at least a limb and were decorated with severe jungle sores. For many days, it was as if the whole leg had transformed into a mush and was wasting away in an unhealthy milky flow.

'You are a lucky man,' said Munumi. 'I think it was simply not your day because you are the first person I know to have survived this particular poison.'

'How can I thank you for coming? You have refused to take any money. Please, choose any animal from my herd of goats.'

'You don't have to worry too much about that. I do what I have to do, just as my father taught me. I'm happy you are getting well. For this treatment, my pay is a chicken. I also need transport fare back home.'

The man hardly gave himself credit for his cures, attributing them to the will of the gods that breathed potency into his herbs. A good healer needed no publicity. He was the most sought-after medicine-man in the region.

Ayonchugu's leg healed, but it looked thinner and felt heavier than the right one. He could no longer walk long distances without the use of a cane. He bought a bicycle. He could no longer work long hours on his estate and had to accept more and more help from others. Help was always available, but he knew he was not going to depend on the benevolence of others for the upkeep of his farms. He thought about employing people to work for him as Europeans did in their homes and on their large coastal plantations. That was not the practice in Ngonibi. Here, people owned and worked on their own farms, and only a man without any self-pride would work for pay on another person's farm. That kind of person usually was a foreigner who had not been brought up in the mores of the Ngonibi people.

One wet evening, Ayonchugu was sitting in his house looking through the open door at the rain drizzling monotonously on the fields, his thoughts for sole company, when he spied someone emerge from the bushes and approach his residence. As the person came closer, he recognised him as Nyarong. The visitor came to the house, leant his machete against the outer door frame, greeted and walked in.

'I hope you came on a good footing. Please sit by the fire.' Ayonchugu pointed towards a number of carved stools of different sizes, and Nyarong chose one and settled his bulk on it.

'It has been raining hailstones,' said Nyarong.

'Indeed. I have not done much work today. If it continues like this, crops will be destroyed.'

'I have had a hard time finding some of my herbs.'

Nyarong was best known for treating epilepsy. Sufferers came from tens of miles away to receive his treatment. Some patients got cured fairly soon and returned to their homes while others, because the forces binding them to the illness were thought to be too strong, stayed longer, sometimes for more than a year.

'So how will you manage?' Ayonchugu asked.

'I have some reserves, but they will run out in two days. People are so wicked these days. Do you know that a majority of my patients are non-natural sufferers?'

Ayonchugu had an earthenware pot of steaming palm wine on the fire. He poured in more fresh wine from a *badi*, rummaged in the bamboo shelf behind him and brought out a soot-stained deer horn. He turned the cup so that its mouth faced down and tapped it several times with his forefinger, and then held it up and inspected its interior with his good eye. Having thus ascertained that the horn was free of bugs, he handed it to his guest, who in turn held it out for him to fill with hot wine. Nyarong tasted the white liquid and smacked his mouth in satisfaction.

'How do you tell the difference between a natural illness and one caused by men when the symptoms are the same?'

'You underestimate what we know. To you the symptoms may look the same, but to me there are stark differences.' Nyarong paused for a little while, and then let Ayonchugu in on one of his secrets. 'Quite often the sufferer's family already knows who or what caused the illness.'

'And you only confirm it for them?' Ayonchugu asked.

Nyarong shook his head. 'I confirm nothing. *Njoh* does it.'

'But njoh is only kola nut peelings which you throw on the floor. There is no logic as to the direction any is going to take. How can it give you any reliable information?'

'I'm surprised at you, son. You can't question at your age what our ancestors relied on. After all your travels, I guess you should be wiser. Njoh never lies.'

'But you can lie and the people will be none the wiser.'

'The success of our healing has been based on the honesty handed down from our ancestors. Many a medicine-man who started asking for more than what his forbears asked for quickly became a quack. Take Nkabalum for example. He inherited the treatment for *ngunibom* from his father and turned it into a commodity. He is very rich as a consequence, but which clever person still goes to him for treatment? Go to his place and you'll see people dying in pain with distended stomachs. He has nothing to pass on to his children except greed. Meanwhile, people have to travel all day now to Ala'a Okuk to get treatment that works.'

'It's so sad, isn't it?'

'More than sad,' said Nyarong. 'He claims to treat everything now. When did you hear of such a thing? Even Munumi does not treat everything. He refers to me people suffering from epilepsy and other things he can't handle.'

'Does he? One would think the man can handle just about any illness.'

'I did not feel affronted by Munumi's coming in for your leg because I knew he is good in poisons, even if I can handle just any ailment. Honesty pays off for the sake of the patient in this business.'

'It sure does,' Ayonchugu said.

'How's the leg now?' Nyarong asked.

'It's not fine. It aches in the night and I hardly can fall asleep. And then I suffer shattering headaches the following morning. My farms are suffering.'

'I will send Mengen tomorrow evening with something to calm your headaches, and another for the pain.'

'I hope she won't have to do any scarring.'

'Are you allergic to the touch of a pretty woman?' Nyarong asked and burst out laughing.

'No! I....'

'You what? She is quite good at the job. And whatever the case, this house of yours needs warming up.'

'I certainly don't need a woman to do that. I've been down that way once, and don't wish to be scalded twice.'

'Are you a man?' Nyarong asked. 'Perhaps. To be a complete man you need a woman.'

'Do I? I'm doing fine without one now.'

'That is just for now. You need children. You will have to marry. It has always been like that and will always be that way,' said the medicine-man, punctuating his words with gestures.

'Perhaps I was meant to be the exception,' Ayonchugu

replied.

'You see, for now people can tolerate your being without a woman. But in a few years you will not be able to fit into respectable society without being married. Your neighbours won't trust you. But all of that is secondary. You have one of the biggest plots in this village and you need hands to farm it.'

'And my wife will provide the labour?' asked Ayonchugu.

'She, your other wives, your children,' Nyarong said.

'Mm. I hear you,' said Ayonchugu with a touch of sarcasm in his voice. 'We were talking about my leg. As you can see, this leg is smaller now than this one. I fought in a war where the weapons produced fire and thunder and only lost an eye. I could have completely lost my leg in a war of bows and arrows!'

'War is war, irrespective of the weapons used. The purpose ultimately, is to annihilate the enemy. You are lucky to have survived two wars. I would add that it was not your time to die.'

'No, it was not. I saw entire armies wiped out in the sands of Abyssinia and in the jungles of Boma in a rage of big gun bangs, buried and flying bombs. On one occasion, over three hundred of us left for battle on a boat. We came under Japanese fire. Only forty of us managed to swim back alive to shore. I still can't tell how I managed to swim so well.'

'The good news is that your side won ultimately.'

'I lost good friends. My village lost young men. I returned home to meet my family in a shambles. Would it have made any difference to the folks in this village whether the English or the Germans won?' Ayonchugu asked, even as he felt a tingling sense of betrayal for the army he had so valiantly fought for.

'I hear you were paid a lot of money?'

'Mm? Where did you hear that?'

'The news was all over the place,' Nyarong replied. 'You boys had cash to spend when you came back. Every woman wanted to marry an ex-soldier.'

'Women wanted us for the pride of it. My pay was not enough to cover the cost of my funeral, let alone the death celebration. So what money are you talking about?'

'You surprise me indeed. How much did you say your pay

was?'

'First thing, I was paid four times less than others with the same rank for the same job. I'm not extravagant. I'm comfortable. I have to thank the people of this village for their generosity.' Nyarong looked at Ayonchugu in disbelief, shook his head slowly from side to side, and continued doing so as he spoke. 'Do you know that the prince who avoided joining the army is the one whose bed my wife is warming this very moment?'

'Mm...young man, I can only say one thing: She did not deserve you for a husband. Stop mourning the past and forge on with your life. There's no misfortune that does not beget some good.'

'What good comes from being shot at?' Ayonchugu asked.

'You went and saw the world for what it is,' Nyarong replied. 'You interacted with people from every nation. That was a good education. Now open your eyes. Start doing something with that knowledge. A lazy hunter thinks his traps have been bewitched.'

'You speak words of wisdom. Yet, it would take me more than wisdom to get healed of what I have lived through.'

'You have shown that you are a man,' Nyarong said. 'Live the life of men.' He leaned towards the door and peered outside. The rains had ceased and only a mild wind was now shaking off drops of water from the leaves of stunted savannah trees. 'I will be on my way, lest the rain start falling again. Tomorrow morning Mengen comes to administer your treatment. If you open your eyes, you will see.'

The medicine-man emptied his horn, picked up his machete which he had propped by the door, collected his herbs and set forth. Ayonchugu watched him as he wound his way through the lush savannah elephant grasses like a huge wild animal and disappeared in the direction of his home.

Although Ayonchugu thought Nyarong spoke a lot of wise words, he had his misgivings about medicine-men. You entrusted your life to them and they gave you what it pleased them to give. You could visit them and thankfully collect your own death in the form of a poisoned potion. Yet people had a blind trust in them; people had no choice; the understood ethic of their trade required medicine-men to give you what was good for you. But the choice was theirs, and they could give you death in lieu of health.

How did this differ from fighting in the big war? He had gone with the bravest of his compatriots in all patriotism to fight, with the assurance that their sacrifices would be rewarded. Recently, the village was treated to a public projection of a film about the Chindits Special Penetrating Forces of which major battalions of The Nigeria Regiment had been an integral part. He had watched the black and white images in excitement, but had returned home bewildered when no one from his battalion featured in it. Was his life indeed worth only as much as the banana sucker that lay rotting in his grave behind what was once his house in Libah?

CHAPTER SEVEN

The medicine-man's daughter

Sure enough, Mengen showed up the following morning, just after sunrise. Ayonchugu heard her singing even before he saw her. She approached the door, stopped singing and asked cheerily, 'Who's in the house, eh?'

'I'm in. Come right in,' Ayonchugu replied, trying as much as he could to emulate her spirited mood.

'You are home?' she greeted as she came in.

'Yes, I am. You'r welcome.'

'I've come with some herbs for you. I'll need to crush these ones. Where's the grinding stone?' she asked, looking around the sparsely furnished room.

Ayonchugu pointed to the stone behind the door. She set to work promptly. Ayonchugu went about doing his morning chores, and stole looks at her as she crushed the herbs, crouched over the grinding stone. He took in the healthy laps and her rounded arms as well as her ample hips. Her well-endowed bosom heaved to and fro as she moved her hands expertly in rhythmic movements.

'Where's palm oil?' she asked when she was done with the grinding.

'There, behind you in the tin container on the shelf.'

'I'll add a little palm oil to this, heat it up a little. You will massage your leg with this medicine every morning and evening until the pain is gone.'

'Or perhaps I could add a little salt to it and use it as an accompaniment to my fufu,' Ayonchugu said teasingly.

'Goats do eat this herb, and so can you,' Mengen replied. 'It's a powerful laxative. Eat your fufu with it but don't start bleating for a costive when your bowels start spilling forth.'

They both laughed over this, and like a sudden gentle warm glow, they felt a sense of companionship flooding the room. He came over and sat by the hearth. They chatted light-heartedly as she scooped up the greenish paste and put it on an earthenware platter. She then placed the platter on the fire and added palm oil. She stir-fried it using a wooden ladle.

'The medicine is ready. These broad leaves are *ifumimbuo*. They are for your headache. You will warm them over the fire like this...and press them onto your forehead like this...until the pain subsides. Eventually you will stop having any discomfort up there.'

'Is that what Nyarong said or is it what you believe?' asked Ayonchugu.

'That's what is,' Mengen stated.

'And should these leaves run out? Can I harvest some more and continue my treatment?'

'No. Your leaves won't work,' she declared unequivocally.

'Why? They'll be the same leaves. I know them.'

'These leaves were harvested by Nyarong at a particular time and place. That's what makes them potent.'

'If I harvested the same leaves at the same time and place as Nyarong, would they not work?'

She paused for a while before saying, 'They may work. But you need to know the place and the time. He alone can tell you that. You should know about these things. Don't you have medicine-men where you came from?'

'We have. But they mystify everything.'

'Every trade has its secrets. Who knows what Tachum puts into those rocks that he transforms into knives and axes?'

'Just selected rocks or pieces of discarded metals and lots of heat. Everything else is a charade.'

'That's what you think.'

'I have seen a medicine-man put sputum on medicine before applying it on an incision. Was saliva part of the mystery of the medicine?'

'I doubt it. He could have as well added a few drops of water to it.'

'You speak truthfully and reasonably this time.'

'Every time,' Mengen corrected.

She was getting ready to leave when an idea occurred to Ayonchugu. 'Perhaps you could help me with today's massage?' He saw a hint of reluctance on her face. 'I'm sure it would make the medicine work better,' he said, trying hard to sound convincing in his flattery.

'You're just being lazy or mischievous. Well, I'll do it. Stretch out your leg.'

'Thank you. I'll remember not to tell your father about this,' Ayonchugu said, hoping she would find his words funny.

'He'll know anyway. He knows everything,' Mengen said indifferently.

Before she left, he made her promise to come back and see how his leg was doing. She was knowledgeable in her occupation and exuded a primitive innocence and frankness which he found appealing. Most women kept their mouths shut in the presence of men, but not this one. When she did speak, it was not to challenge but to state exactly what she thought. But even just stating one's mind was way too daring for a woman, especially one her age. She was Nyarong's only child. She spent her time working with him or with Nwenmufu, her father's assistant whom she had known all her life. Perhaps that was why she was the way she was – more matter-of-fact than other women he knew. She was a bit more like the women he met on his travels in the army. Just a bit like them.

Ayonchugu waited for one week before Mengen came. The leg was indeed greatly improved, and he told her it would have been completely cured if she had shown up earlier. She giggled at this and asked if she was a remedy. He said, 'Yes, for bad eyes.' She laughed again. Before she left, she again promised to come back as soon as possible. She did come back the following day, bringing along not only an additional treatment for his ailments, but some food in a basket.

'I'm sorry I could not risk carrying much *njaniki* in a leaf,' she said. 'The meat is also very little.'

'That is no problem at all,' replied Ayonchugu. 'I have some smoked meat right here. Would you mind making some more sauce?'

'No,' Mengen replied.

He reached up onto the low ceiling and brought down a hard-dried leg of a wild animal. He chopped off generous portions of it and popped them on hot embers. The meat sizzled.

She dropped the chunks of meat in a pot, added salt and

set it on the fire to boil.

'I like the smell of that,' Mengen said. 'What's it?'

'It's a squirrel.'

'I can't believe it. It looks big for a squirrel.'

'This particular one has been feeding fat on my palm shoots. I tried catching it for over a month but it kept eluding me. It took me quite some antics to finally win the battle last week.'

'Give me my due,' said Mengen. 'My medication did the trick. You went to battle a four-legged squirrel with one leg. No wonder that you had to lose for so long.'

'You sure brought me some luck because I caught it shortly after you came and left,' said Ayonchugu.

'How do you know it's the same one that has been eating your shoots?' she asked.

'I've not seen any more of my shoots eaten since I caught it.'

'You have no regrets then. The squirrel was on a fattening course for you,' said she.

'No, for us,' Ayonchugu said and they laughed.

She undid the leaves from a bundle of achu, cut off half of it and dropped it in another pot. She added some drops of potash to the achu and stirred the combination smooth with a bamboo pestle. She then added palm oil and stirred further until the mixture turned a smooth yellow. She added spices. The meat was already tender. She diluted the sticky paste with water from the boiling meat and stirred again. The sauce was ready.

They ate together and chatted some more. 'You know, the best accompaniment to achu is frogs,' said Ayonchugu.

'You mean the really tiny hairy ones from the lake, don't you?'

'Oh, sure. Who wants to eat those horrible bitter-head tadpoles children catch in streams? I'm talking about the real *mishugu*.'

'Unfortunately they're very rare. Like every nice thing.'

'I wish I had asked Ndamgu if he still had some. He gave me a basketful, and I ate it all within a month. You know they're caught only once a year, and by only initiated members of select families.'

'Why is it so?' Mengen asked. 'I always wondered if it would not be fairer to allow everyone to catch them.'

'I guess the idea is to limit how much is taken out of the lake each year. Somehow, everyone in the village gets to eat some during the harvesting season.'

'Sure. Isn't it a wonder that they are found only in that particular lake?'

'It sure is a wonder,' Ayonchugu agreed. 'But then there is so much that is a wonder all around us. I saw even more wonders when I was in the army.'

'Please, tell me about them,' Mengen pleaded.

'It would take me a month to tell you half of what I saw. When you're ready to listen, I'll start telling you.'

'How else do you want me to be ready? I'm ready to start listening today.'

'Oh, no! I'll need to get your father's permission first,' he said.

'He never stops me from going out when I want to,' she said matter-of-factly.

'You don't understand then?'

'Understand what?'

Ayonchugu was now sure she was playing the game women play instinctively when they smell a romantic flare in a man's speech.

They enjoyed each other's company without overtly acknowledging this fact. When Mengen was leaving Ayonchugu put what was left of the smoked meat in her basket to take along. She protested, but he insisted. 'I know your father has more than enough meat, but this one is from me to a special friend.'

She thanked him. He made her promise to come back soon.

Mengen did not show up for the next two weeks, during which time Ayonchugu tended to be restless in his sleep, and distracted when awake. He strained his ears in the mornings, longing to hear her singing and approaching his house as she had done the day she first brought his medication. He imagined what it would be like to have her around the house, cooking his meals and sharing them with him and a brood of kids. His imagination took them together to the farm, and then to the market, carrying wares, and chatting about the day's happenings on their return home.

Ayonchugu dreamt about the British nurse who cared for his wounded eye at the Imphal hospital; only this time, the nurse was Mengen and ministering turned into caresses. A man should be man enough not to dream childish dreams, he told himself. He was, nevertheless, sure that being a man also meant confronting the truth about oneself.

CHAPTER EIGHT

More than just another patient

When Mengen eventually showed up she was less chatty than on previous occasions. She was carrying a basket of varied herbs and bundles tied with strings made from a banana plant.

'Why did you stay away for so long? You promised to come back soon,' he chided.

'I only stayed away a few days,' she said, setting down her basket.

'Two market days is not a few days,' Ayonchugu said. 'I thought you'd come back sooner.'

Mengen studied his face steadily before replying. 'Perhaps you should have asked me to come back on a specific day. I've never broken a promise.'

'Do you promise me to come every day?'

'You know that is not possible. I have other patients to attend to. You can see how full my basket is.'

'Am I just one of your patients then?'

'You have been absolutely nice to me, but beyond that you've not given me reason to think you're but one of my patients.'

'I want to be your patient forever. Does that say how I want us to be?' Ayonchugu asked.

'That's not a healthy thing to wish for,' Mengen replied.

'I want you to be mine,' Ayonchugu said.

'That's not good enough. My father will not allow that.'

'I can sort out that with him one of these days.'

'As you wish,' Mengen said, her eyes flickering down to her feet.

Ayonchugu came over to her and held her close for the first time, their scantily dressed torsos aligning in a warm trembling embrace. The top of her head was just below his chin. Her uncertain arms went up and lingered around his powerful shoulders, but they became weak and hung limp, and she stood as if she was not too sure of what to expect or do next. His hands slid up and down her smooth back and came to rest on either side of her hips. When she felt an unusual prodding around her navel, she began to feel her head turn and she thought she would swoon. She began wiggling her way out of his arms, and looking a bit panicky she said, 'I'm afraid I can't stay any longer.'

'Why not?' he whispered, a bit breathless.

'I have work to do,' she said hurriedly.

'Can't it wait a little?'

'No. I have appointments to keep.'

'Will you come back tomorrow?' he inquired in a cracked voice.

'I'm not very sure.'

'The day after?'

'If my father allows me,' she said evasively.

'I thought he never stops you from going anywhere you wish?'

'This is no longer anywhere,' she said.

'I want you to live in this house and be my children's mother. Will you do that for me?' Ayonchugu said, and was relieved it came out so effortlessly.

'I'll have to think about it,' she said. She disengaged herself from his embrace and edged towards the door. She picked up her basket.

'Please, do not panic. I only intend us a lot of good,' he said reassuringly.

'I understand, but you must see my father first,' she said, and with that, she was gone.

Ayonchugu was calmly possessed by Mengen and his every being told him she was meant to be his wife. He knew that what he was feeling was 'love' because he had read things about Europeans 'being in love', and during the war he had talked with love-stricken white youngsters who were fighting to stay alive just in the hope of seeing their beloved one someday. There was the nurse who loved him. And of course, he had been in love with Ngelem, although he had not given whatever he felt for her a second thought or looked for an exotic word to qualify it. His personal experience of love was a nuance of feelings, which he knew ensconced passion that could uplift or bring one down to the verge of perdition.

Love was not the determinant when he made up his mind to marry Mengen. He gave himself to the emotion in a practical manner, following the lessons he had learned from the nurse. How many people he knew married for love in his society, anyway? People married to have a family because they had reached the age of having one of their own, and loving one's wife and children came as the duty of a mature man. Had his father been alive he would never have by-passed him in making his choice, be it in the days when he courted Ngelem or in these. His maturity would have been measured in his ability to negotiate, and if need be, impose harmony among his wives and children.

From what he knew about Mengen, she was a wild thing who went about her duties totally unaware of her own femininity. She had very little time to play the games of girls her age, and she matured in a way that could have pleased a father were she a boy. Young men often saw her as an extension of her father and associated her with the mysterious power that surrounded medicine men. She did not have the bearing of a husband-woman, but having grown up with two men as her closest family, she lacked a certain delicacy that rounded off the sentimental edges of womanhood.

Mengen had never seriously considered getting married because she thought the relationship between men and women was replete with the kind of distasteful issues that came up during consultations, when she did her duties as Nyarong's aid. She knew the kind of things he did, but she had since her childhood been programmed to accommodate his actions without feeling revulsion for them. She held her father in awe and regarded him as one for whom lots of inordinate things were permitted, so long as people got satisfactory results from his actions. And so, without sanctioning his abuses, she lacked the abstraction and cultivation that could have made her to revolt against him. Had it not been for the somewhat redeeming humaneness brought into her daily life by Nwenmufu, she could have descended into the abyss of evil without giving a second thought to her actions. Nwenmufu treated her with a paternalistic touch which was unlike the quasi-indifference she got from Nyarong. Consequently, she felt more attached to the former than to the latter. She was capable of deep feeling, which, nevertheless, skipped the unnecessary hurdles of sentimentality and went straight to the heart of things.

Ayonchugu had very scanty information on Mengen's family background. This did not stop him from feeling a sense of oneness with her which made him unwilling to think of the information void as an impediment. During the short time he had come to know her, he had seen in her the ingredients it took to model a good wife. He had been through the toughest challenges in life and believed there could be nothing so unpalatable in her background that he could not face up to. He reasoned that if he could lose Ngelem, his first wife, who came from the best of families, then perhaps a leap in the dark could turn out for the better for him. He was going to go by his instincts, heeding unreservedly the charm of the affection that he had been deprived of for such a long time.

Ayonchugu went to talk to Ndamgu, his Ngonibi mentor. He met him reclining on a two-piece wooden seat in his yard, with his hands supporting the back of his balding head lest it rub on the plank. Ayonchugu sat on a carved stool across from him.

'I wish to get married,' he announced.

'I've been looking forward to you saying that sooner,' said Ndamgu, nodding generously. 'Do you have any woman in mind?'

'Yes. Mengen.'

'Do you mean Nyarong's daughter?'

'Yes.'

Ndamgu looked a bit surprised and even a trifle disappointed. He brought down his hands and sat forward. He was thoughtful for some time before answering Ayonchugu. 'My brother,' he said, 'I'm truly happy that you've made up your mind about marrying again. A man must be complete in his manhood. I have nothing against your choice because you aren't a child and your eyes are open. It's just that Mengen never crossed my mind as the marrying type.'

'I had the same impression until she started coming to give my medication and I understood that she's like any normal woman,' Ayonchugu said, looking at Ndamgu and willing him to grant his approval.

'She should be. She's not a priestess. Still, she is shrouded in the same mystery as her father,' replied Ndamgu.

'Do you know Nyarong's family?' Ayonchugu asked.

'The man is a healer. He says nothing about his family. People like it that way.'

'Someone must have an idea about where they came from,' Ayonchugu said.

Ndamgu shook his head. 'Not anybody I know of. My wife talked to Mengen once, and the girl remembered very little about her life before her father and Nwenmufu brought her to this village. I remember she was just about half the age of Nebongo when they first came here. He was not married and we understood she was his only child. He said his wife died many years before and he never remarried. There's a presumption that Nwenmufu is a relative of his late wife.'

Ndamgu sat in recollection for a while, and then told Ayonchugu about his experience of Nyarong. 'When Nyarong first came here, everyone rushed to him for treatment. I went there too. I told him about some worrisome dreams I'd been having. Without casting *njoh*, Nyarong told me to go back home and have a good rest. He was very entertaining. We shared some kola nuts and hot palm wine; he told me interesting stories about the feats he had performed over the years. The one thing he never mentioned was where he had lived before.'

'You know, I've lost one woman, and I'm not ready to lose another,' Ayonchugu said. 'After what happened to me in Libah I never thought I would ever want to remarry. But I'm ready to marry this woman.'

'I can't go against your wish if you're convinced that's what you want. I wish you well. Still, I suggest we do a little investigation on her family before engaging in any talks.'

'Can I count on you to do that?' Ayonchugu asked.

'That, naturally, is my duty and I'll be giving you feedback,' Ndamgu replied.

CHAPTER NINE

The loss of the bag-of-evil

News of Ayonchugu's interest in Mengen spread from hearth to hearth, livening evening chats between neighbours, and lightening the burden of work among groups of women as they gossipped away while tilling their cocoyam farms. Ndamgu talked to many people, including the village fon; folks volunteered to give information. But no one could say with certainty whence Nyarong had come. Although he was said to have lived in a number of villages on his itinerary to Ngonibi, his trail got lost in a blur of many versions about the man's origins. He was a polyglot, and this made it hard for anyone to tell his tribe from his language. At a time when individual migration was still common, people had long stopped bothering whether Nyarong had come from North or South.

Nyarong hid his real self behind an entertaining tongue, and the ordinary Ngonibi resident did not know to what extent he could be unscrupulous. His patients could have denounced him, but they tended to condone his actions, when they were not being his accomplices.

The case of Sona and Atemnji was not known to these people because the web of events at the centre of it was spurned some years before Nyarong's appearance in the kola nut forests of Ngonibi.

Sona and Atemnji had been married for three years and had no child yet. They spent more time making the rounds of local medicine-men than trying it out harder in the privacy of their bedroom. They heard about Nyarong and trekked forty miles to Kanke to get his treatment. He listened to the history of the couple's struggle to have a baby. Most men in similar circumstances would take a second wife. Sona was a cautious fellow though; he let his wife take the pressure. Nyarong gave her some medication to take for a length of time. Nothing happened. When the couple reported back to him he told them he had to undo a curse that had been placed on Atemnji; the woman was in need of special treatment that required him to battle with spirits day and night.

Sona decided to return home, leaving behind Atemnji to be treated. Nyarong prepared various medicines for the lady, and she was shocked when he told her that he would have to insert them himself. For some days she pondered the ethics of the treatment and the pressure that was on her from her husband and her in-laws; she had to choose between having a baby and a bitter marriage. Finally, she grudgingly allowed Nyarong to administer the treatment.

Within a month Atemnji returned to her husband, and shortly after, found out that she was pregnant. Sona felt elated, and sent an unsolicited goat to Nyarong. Overnight, Nyarong, best known for treating epilepsy, also became one of the best fertility medicine-men in his region, and women flocked in for treatment with a commendable rate of success.

The downside came when Atemnji gave birth to a boy who resembled Nyarong. It was a most disagreeable embarrassment for Sona. He kept silent, hoping his eyes were deceiving him and that the child would look different as the days went by. Instead, the child's defining features sharpened. Sona could not tell whether other people shared his impression about the child. No one ever made him feel they thought the child might not be his. He finally put all worries to the back of his mind and went about the business of bringing him up.

A few years afterwards, Atemnji started coming more frequently into his bedroom. For some months nothing happened. Then she proposed going to Kanke for treatment. He did not object. So the cycle began all over, and a second pregnancy led to the birth of fraternal twins. One of the babies could be his by the look, but the other clearly was not. When you saw him Nyarong seemed to stare back at you. Sona did not have the courage to face himself and acknowledge the truth. He and his wife accepted the title of Tanyi and Manyi and partook in the honours that were bestowed on all parents of twins.

Unfortunately for Sona and Atemnji, their peace was shattered by an incident that began with an invitation by a friend for a calabash of palm wine on a market day. They were in one of many crowded market sheds which doled out corn-beer and well-fermented palm wine – the type which women never drank. As they sat merrily gulping down horn after horn of the drinks and feeling increasingly wiser, their voices grew equally louder. Ligibi, a rascally fellow who always went home drunk on such days, kept extending his horn to be served wine, but never bought a round. Eventually, a young man told him to buy his own drink or go home. There ensued an exchange of uncouth words that were harmless enough, until someone said that the man could not be asked to go home to his mother that early on a market day. Everybody burst out laughing.

It was an unfortunate thing to say to Ligibi who still lived in his mother's house, and seemed to have no plans of moving out. He looked around and saw Sona laughing and said, 'When people are laughing you too are showing your rotten fangs! They call you Tanyi and you answer! Give me that wife of yours for just a night and I will pour in triplets! All truly mine. Your children will grow up to be like the old crook in Kanke.'

Sona jumped up and went straight for the young man's gut, but strong hands held him back. No one was laughing any longer. The rascal was ordered by many voices to leave immediately, and he did so without further ado, for he knew even in his near-stupor that he had touched on taboo. The drinking continued in a rather subdued atmosphere. Someone started talking about how the dry season had lasted three months and everyone immediately took up the topic, and pretended not to notice when moments later, Sona collected his fibre bag and left, head bowed.

That same evening his wife returned with some ingredients from the market and prepared him his choicest dish. He barely touched it. In the night he lay for a long time waiting for sleep to come. When the fire that warmed his room was dying out he heard her come in.

'Manyi, turn around right now and let me see the back of your head!' he ordered curtly.

She hesitated for a moment. 'My lord, err...I have some good news for you,' she stuttered. He was silent. 'I'm expecting a baby.'

'I'm not surprised. Is it not three months today since you went to get Nyarong's treatment? Go and inform him.'

'My husband, I don't understand you at all....'

'All these years you've taken me for a dumb sheep, haven't you?'

'My....'

'Leave before I get up and strangle you!' Sona hissed.

She peered at him in the blur of the dying embers and saw murder in his eyes and knew that it was time to call off the mutual self-deception. She turned quietly around and crept out of the room.

For a long time Atemnji was under duress from her man. Every day she prepared a delicious meal and put it in his basket, which she placed on the bamboo shelf where his food was normally kept. In the night she would come for the basket and find the food untouched. When he was not out working or chatting with friends, he sat brooding, and nursing a horn of hard palm wine all day, barely acknowledging her miserable existence. The more her belly distended, the more he abhorred her and became irrational and irritated in her presence. She came up with strategies to keep away from him, but somehow their paths always crossed and she would feel shivers of fear crawl all over her body when she saw the silent rage in his eyes.

One morning, Atemnji was passing behind Sona's house on her way to the toilet when she heard the searing sound of a file at work. Her first child was with Sona and asking questions as always. She overheard him ask, 'Tata, why can't I have a machete as big and as sharp as yours?'

'What would you do with such a big machete?' he asked.

'I would help Manyi cut up pumpkins in the kitchen,' replied the boy.

'You don't need a sharp machete to cut up pumpkins. A blunt one would be just as good,' said Sona, concentrating on the task of sharpening the machete.

The boy looked on with interest as his father stopped sharpening, studied the sparkling blade, and then tested it by using it to trim the nail of his left index finger. It cut as smoothly as a razor blade.

'Why are you making this one so sharp?'

'I have a swollen-bellied nanny-goat in this house who takes me for a sheep. I'm going to chop it into tiny pieces.'

'We are going to be eating goat meat then?'

'No, son, you don't eat that kind of meat. It is poisonous. You let it rot in a wooden box in the ground, while gunshots are fired in celebration.'

'Rot in a wooden box? What a waste. Why not give it to the dogs?' the boy suggested.

'Why not...?'

Atemnji did not wait to hear the rest of the scheme. She quickly rushed to her hut, picked up a few items, flung them into a basket and disappeared from the compound using the back tracks. By the time it was nightfall she was very far away from the village, with each step, taking her like a desperate ghost in search of a lair, closer to Nyarong's shrine.

It was dusk when Atemnji collapsed listlessly on Nwenmufu's door-step. She was very weakened and emaciated by the long journey and the stress of the preceding months. Only the prominence of her stomach seemed to have withstood the odds she had been through, and even as she lay prostrate on the bare bamboo bed Nwenmufu had placed her on, she felt the life inside her moving and reminding her she had to stay alive.

Nyarong came to see her and was not impressed by her sudden appearance. He had done what he had to do and had not expected the situation to turn into a personal matter. Did she not see that he was a medicine-man and was not in a position to accept responsibility for fathering children for women he treated? He had done her husband a favour! If all the women he had treated turned up like her, there would be enough women to form a dance group! Ha! He was certainly not going to allow her to stay on his property! No one was going to know she was here – unless she had exposed her own anus like a hen in the wind.

Atemnji explained in a weak voice that she had told no one about where she was going; she had taken the back tracks to come to Nyarong's and had gone straight to Nwenmufu's hut.

Satisfied that things had happened discretely, Nyarong ordered Nwenmufu to make sure she stayed out of sight. He returned to his quarters and started thinking about how to get himself out of the fix. By morning he still had not worked out a solution. He did the day's work without letting the unwelcome developments distract him. In the night he went to bed determined to cause the problem to disappear. Nyarong was lying on his mat cooking an evil scheme when he heard Nwenmufu calling him urgently to open the door. He felt his way through the darkness to the bamboo door. He unlatched and pulled it back. Standing in the pale moonlight were Nwenmufu and a man.

'Ligibi has something really important to tell you,' Nwenmufu announced.

Ligibi launched immediately into his story. 'All the young men of my village are on their way here. They plan to kill you. They will burn down this place and all your medicines. They say that you've made a mockery of the men. They say this time you've gone too far by actually taking the woman Atemnji from her husband. He plans to finish you himself, and then finish her.'

'Why are you telling me this?' Nyarong asked.

'I started a discussion about you and this woman in the market. I never meant any harm. I wish to avoid bloodshed.'

'What about your own safety?' Nwenmufu asked Ligibi.

'I'll hide around until they're here. Then I'll join them in the destruction. They will be none the wiser.'

Nyarong pulled Ligibi's ear as he spoke. 'If this is a trick you are playing on me, I swear by thunder and lightning that your head would be blown to pieces this time tomorrow. Out of my sight!'

As Ligibi retreated, Nyarong dove into his medicine room and went straight for his two medicine bags. In these bags lay the secret to the feats he performed. Unknown to him, one of the medicine bags had been swapped by Ligibi, who had dared every spirit known to be lurking in Nyarong's shrine and had broken in, before going over to knock on Nwenmufu's door.

Nyarong, Atemnji and Nwenmufu set out hastily, and in the course of the next eleven days, the fugitives travelled through thick tropical forests and crossed perilous waters. Sometimes the going was painstakingly slow. They were forced to take detours, or skirt around settlements. There was no shortage of food in the bush, but harvesting or hunting took time, and Nyarong's goal was to put as great a distance as possible between himself and their likely pursuers. Atemnji, in spite of herself, was tugged along mercilessly like the carcass of an insect in the mandibles of a giant ant.

As Nyarong stormed on, indifferent to the duress under which he was placing the woman, he was silently pining at the loss of his wizard-bag. The chameleon he used for sending thunderbolts was gone. The wand that cast darkness in the eyes of people and permitted him to manipulate them was gone. The rain-making brooms were gone. The bee that invited a swarm to the kill was also gone. He was not half as powerful as he had been a few days before. But so long as no one knew about his predicament he hoped to remain the great medicine-man and sorcerer he was reputed to be.

Nyarong became increasingly angry with Atemnji by the day. She was the cause of his present predicament; and here she was lagging behind all the time. He twisted his face into an ugly grimace and said in his most derisive voice, 'Do you have to get one leg to ask permission from the other before taking a step each time?' He could have reached back and strangled her for good. The only reason he had not done so was that she was carrying his child, and he was determined this time to keep this particular baby. This was not so much out of any paternalistic sentiments as from the desire to curb his losses.

On the twelfth day of their weary march, Atemnji collapsed from exhaustion near a hamlet and would budge no more. All too suddenly she went into labour. Nwenmufu wanted to go into the hamlet and get a mid-wife or whatever help, but Nyarong stopped him. Atemnji suffered through the throes of labour, while Nyarong hung around, as concerned as a vulture waiting for its prey to breathe its last before moving into action. Nwenmufu gathered some herbs and crushed them in his hands. He squeezed a few drops into Atemnji's mouth and her pains eased a little. Shortly after, she gave birth to a baby girl who uttered a short cry and kept silent as if she knew that was what everyone wanted of her. Nwenmufu took charge, wrapped up the baby in one of its mother's wrappers, and tied the umbilical cord with fresh fibre.

Nyarong disappeared that same night and only returned in the morning, pulling along a nanny goat and its nimble kid. Atemnji looked more recovered, although exceedingly cold from sleeping rough in a makeshift tent with only a fire as her sole comfort. Nyarong ordered the party to move on. Atemnji gave him a forlorn look, picked up her bedraggled self from the ground and trudged on after the men like a cow being led to the slaughterhouse. In spite of Nwenmufu's protestations and her utter helplessness, they walked until midday, at which time Atemnji collapsed and begged the men with what remained of her energy to go no further.

Nyarong took the baby from Nwenmufu's hands and started leaving, tugging along the goat, with its exhausted kid trying to keep pace.

'She can't move any longer,' said Nwenmufu. 'We have to rest here for a while.'

'I'm not waiting,' Nyarong replied.

'What would become of her?'

'Kill her!'

It was an order. Nwenmufu had never disobeyed Nyarong. When he saw the evil look in his eyes he knew that the man was mad, but serious. He had to do what he had to do.

'And what would become of the baby?'

'She is already provided for,' said Nyarong. 'Kill her now!' he ordered and walked on as indifferently as ever. Without looking back he added, 'Also kill that miserable kid. There's enough milk for only one mouth.'

Nyarong was gone along the narrow track for some distance when the woman screamed. And then she was silent. Nwenmufu caught up with him shortly afterwards. His hands were still stained with fresh blood.

'Clean those hands and take the baby,' said Nyarong. 'There are seven rivers ahead to cross.'

Nwenmufu did not dare to look at his master in the face.

CHAPTER TEN

Palm wine and a lot of cash
Ndamgu and Ayonchugu tried to peer from a vantage point at
Nyarong's compound. All they saw was thick foliage that rose
above the surrounding greenery. The dwelling was flung deep
in the heart of the forest where nobody ventured without a
cause; it was the kind of place where neighbours never stopped
by unexpectedly for an evening chat. It was perched on a
hillock that suddenly protruded in the middle of a disorder of
giant tree trunks and thick undergrowth. There was no visible
thoroughfare by which the divination-seeker accessed this
hermitage. The pair knew their way in the wilds, and so going
up to Nyarong's residence did not present any major difficulty.
They followed a tiny track which snaked about, dodging major
obstructions for half a mile, before bringing them to their
destination.

Ndamgu noticed that the place had changed much since
he first came there. Whereas there were just two huts on that
visit, the dwelling now had expanded considerably, and
consisted of seven huts built in a circular form, one of which
was bigger and stouter, and located in the middle of the
compact habitation. The dwelling was hemmed in by a natural
fence of seven huge mahogany and kola nut trees which
silently brooded over the huts. The naive wayfarer would think
Nyarong had planted the trees; that was not the case. He had
actually expanded his territory to meet the trees. Nyarong was
known to claim that the trees had eyes and communicated to
him news of the approach of any person. He told daunting
tales of the magical feats he was capable of performing by
summoning the seven spirits which dwelt in the trees. As
questers approached Nyarong's residence they had the queasy
impression they were being watched not only by the all-seeing
trees but by the animals dwelling therein as well.

Nyarong kept seven monkeys which were reputed for
playing pranks on visitors. They would suddenly snatch a
visitor's cap from an overhanging branch and prance off with it

in a cackle of jubilation. It was common to find a reptile lying about, curled up, undisturbed and insouciant of any intrusion. Whoever came to Nyarong's knew that his were not animals like others, but spirits.

The divination-seekers therefore bore themselves with reverence for their surroundings, lest they be charged with desecration of sacred grounds and called upon to cleanse themselves of malediction. Cleansing took seven chickens and seven grains of *alakata pepper*.

Nyarong's followers were aware of his special mystical penchant for the number seven. He had seven divination cowries, seven earthenware medicine pots, seven seats; on the walls of his temple, supported by seven poles, hung seven skulls which looked more human than animal. Often he would boast, 'I work with seven spirits! Cut up a chicken in seven parts and tell me whether you are left with anything edible!'

When the two men arrived at Nyarong's, he was in the process of performing a healing ritual. They placed the calabash of palm wine they had brought in a tree shade, and sat on a large log of wood which had been polished smooth by hundreds of other bottoms. They watched and waited for the medicine-man to complete the public rituals.

Ayonchugu studied more closely the look of the man who was probably going to be his father-in-law and about whom he had always had some subdued misgivings. Nyarong was an ageless man. The colour of his skin was darker than usual. He was huge, with the compact muscles of a man who ate and exercised well. He must have been too old to be recruited to fight in WW2, but he probably fought on the home lines in the Great War. And even if that had not happened, Ayonchugu was absolutely certain he had done *Njogmassi*. For an elderly man who did not spend time working on the farms, his physical aptitude could only have been boosted by manual tasks he performed in his earlier days. His hair was unkempt and cascaded down his shoulders in entangled locks. His eyes were huge glaring balls that seemed to read into the depths of the souls of his clients. Nyarong's feet, like his hands, were large, flat and bare, and as he did the ritual dance, they hammered on the ground with great momentum. On each arm were strung amulets and charms, and around his neck was draped a bracelet of slates of copper and bronze, not unlike the ones Ayonchugu had earned in the war. He had a circle of a different colour around each eye, and from his nose hung the incisor of a lion.

Ayonchugu had met him a few times going about collecting herbs, and it was only a few months ago that he had stopped by his house and spoken about his leg. That visit was a turning point for him. Sometimes he had the feeling that he was falling for a master scheme designed by Nyarong, but he brushed this aside, preferring to go by the passion that burnt within, and which he felt could only be assuaged by his marrying her. His destiny was entwined with Mengen's; any other path he imagined for his life seemed to be rather elusive.

Ayonchugu and Ndamgu watched as both sick-looking and able-bodied men and women submitted reverently to Nyarong's theatrics and athletic nostrums. There were those who were ill and wanted treatment and those who were physically healthy but had worries about being vulnerable to the evil ploys of enemies, both visible and invisible. Some wanted to find out the cause of their misfortunes and how to reverse them.

Towards midday he was done with the public rituals and went into his consultation room. The two men made themselves more conspicuous. Nyarong came out after some time and approached the guests. Ayonchugu noted that most of the amulets were gone, as was the paint. He now looked more like any elderly man you could meet on your way, although his body still exuded the inevitably strong smell of the powders and mixtures that were the trademark of medicine-men, and his eyes still had a penetrating glare.

They all moved over to the building which served as his private quarters and sat down on low stools hewed out of logs. After greetings and some light-hearted conversation about Ayonchugu's leg, Ndamgu placed a *badi* of palm wine mid-way between Nyarong and themselves.

'When you hear the buzzing of bees in a tree, you don't have to look up to know that the tree is either their home or that there are bound to be flowers blooming up there,' Ndamgu said. 'I will rather spare us many words and state the goal of our mission promptly, if you permit us.'

'Ndamgu, treat this house as yours, and speak from your heart,' Nyarong said, while breaking kola nut. 'I'm listening to you. If you say something that is unbecoming, it is what is said that is unbecoming, not you.' He held out kola nuts to his guests. They each picked a lob and waited until Nyarong threw one of the last two lobs into his mouth, then they too ate theirs.

'Thank you for your kind words and for welcoming us at no notice,' Ndamgu said. 'My brother and I have seen a hen in your pen, and would like to take it along and make it multiply in his home.'

'I'm honoured to have you choose my humble home of all places to look for a hen,' Nyarong replied. He ran his tongue over his yellow-stained teeth and in all angles of his mouth and swallowed. 'Still, I would rather not be too presumptuous. Could you make your meaning clearer?'

'I wish to ask the hand of your daughter in marriage to my brother here,' said Ndamgu, gesturing towards his companion.

Nyarong sat back and half closed his eyes for a while. 'The people of Nambem are discontented with their fon, I understand,' he said.

Ndamgu understood. Nyarong was not trying to be impolite. One did not respond to a request for marriage to one's daughter as if he were responding to his neighbour who had come over to ask if the big girl of the house could come and help with the children for a day. Although Ayonchugu had hinted how Nyarong had only just fallen short of throwing Mengen at him, the fact remained that it was one thing for a father to titillate someone's interest in a maiden and another handing her over for good through formal courtship. And since no father would agree to marry off his daughter at the duration of a market haggling, Ndamgu obligingly went in the new direction the conversation was taking.

'They always seem to be discontented with their rulers too soon,' he replied. 'They are on their third ruler in twelve years. Two of them are on exile.'

'One was beheaded for being too good,' said Nyarong. 'He should have been like his subjects. A beetle, no matter how large, can't rule over soldier ants.'

'What's the problem this time around?' asked Ayonchugu, trying to show interest in the trend the conversation had taken.

'The same old sin,' Nyarong replied. 'Apparently, his subjects think he is too compromising because he has allowed a handful of nomads to settle on the hills for far too long.'

'Why would anybody have a problem with that?' Ndamgu asked. 'The nomads never bother anyone. They have the wandering spirit in them, and before you know it, they would be on their way again.'

'Seemingly, not these ones,' Nyarong said. 'They have been on the hills for some years and do not seem to want to move away yet. Instead, new families have joined the ones that came earlier and they are now building a few solid huts. They even started a market of their own, I hear.'

'I would be surprised if they stayed. These people are as wild as the beasts they herd and no single place can contain them. They would go in search of fresh pastures before long.' When Ndamgu finished talking, he emptied his second horn of palm wine and set it aside, indicating that he wished to talk about something else.

'They have discovered wet salty slopes on the rocks of Adjintse, and this is very suitable for their cattle. I think they have come to stay,' continued Nyarong, who seemed intent on carrying on about the nomads.

'It won't be such a bad thing if they settled down in a village of their own, and let the cattle and the herders do the roaming,' said Ndamgu.

'That, my brothers, is exactly what the Nambems don't want to see happen,' replied Nyarong. 'And you seem to forget that they are all herders anyway.'

'Were it not for the largesse of the surrounding villages, would the Nambems have had land of their own? Perhaps, they should be reminded about that,' said Ndamgu.

'Gratitude, my brothers, has a short memory,' said Nyarong.

Ayonchugu cleared his throat and was about to remind the others about the onerous mission that had brought them to Nyarong's. He turned and looked at Ndamgu inquiringly, and the latter discretely indicated to him to hold his patience.

The medicine-man sat in thought for a while, and then continued talking. 'I won't blame the Nambems too much though, for wanting them to leave. Those people are good for the hills only. A Nambem man who was brought to me for treatment two weeks ago had been stabbed by a nomad just because he greeted a woman from their ethnic group.'

'That was probably the husband or a relative defending his honour and that of the entire ethnic group,' opined Ayonchugu. 'I saw thousands of wilder-looking nomads in East Africa, and they were indeed the lords of the savannah. There, they owned the hills and the plains, you know – the ones that were not productive enough for the plantations of the British farmers – and the Bantu knew how to respect them.'

'Respect! I won't respect those blood-thirsty, knife-wielding *ganakoh*!' Nyarong spat out.

'You know, these people are more than just herdsmen. Ayonchugu said. 'They are herd owners. All the meat we will one day buy will come from them. That will make them very rich.'

'Who would want to give up bush meat for beef?' asked Nyarong, who was sceptical about Ayonchugu's far-fetched theory.

'We trap bush meat every day, and no one replaces what we consume. One day there would be no more bush meat and we will all resort to cow meat,' Ayonchugu explained.

'You see my young friend, bush meat has been caught in these bushes since the days of our early ancestor, and there has since always been enough to last every generation,' said Nyarong.

'I agree with Nyarong,' Ndamgu said. 'But I also think that some delicacies like the buffalo and the deer are a lot rarer to come by today than when we were youths. The good thing is that these bushes are teeming with rodents, and perhaps hunters should start hunting them and allow the big game to regenerate.'

'The hunters in these bushes would laugh at that. They hunt not only for meat but also to show their bravery. Rodents can't earn you a red feather, can they?' Nyaron turned his cup up-side down, tapped on it with his forefinger before laying it on a bamboo shelf by his side.

Ndamgu moved on to the business at hand. 'My brother and I came with a full calabash, and would leave with joy in our hearts knowing that you drank our wine.'

'I will not refuse your wine because I know it comes from the best sources in this village. Ayonchugu, you are welcome to fill my cup.' Nyarong retrieved his cup from the shelf and held it just in front of him.

Ayonchugu felt relief wash over him. He stepped up and took hold of the stringed handle of the *badi* with his left hand, supported its base with his right hand, and poured wine directly from it into Nyarong's out-held horn. He placed the calabash gently on the floor and returned to his seat. Nyarong gulped down the contents of his horn in three smooth sweeps and held it out again for a refill.

'I taste no sharpness in this wine. It is in fact the best wine I have drunk this year. How do you manage to have this quality of wine?'

Ndamgu held out his cup to Ayonchugu to fill it as well, while he explained the secret of tapping good wine. 'You know, sludge is caused by a build-up of dregs. This leads to fresh wine fermenting in an unhealthy condition. The result is the sharp taste which slaps your jaws from within. Twice a week my son goes with me on my tapping rounds. He carries a container of water and some pebbles for washing the receptacles.'

'What you do is no magic,' Nyarong said, 'but very few tappers are willing to do the same. They get people to drink poison in the name of wine.'

Nyarong pointed at an *ndong* at one corner of the room. It was a smaller calabash with a long curved neck, a tiny hole on its tip and a bigger hole on its shoulder. Ayonchugu took it and filled it with wine using the bigger hole, and then set it in front of Nyarong, making sure it was just a bit to his right, with the curved neck facing forward. He then put the bigger calabash out of the way. Ndamgu held out his cup and Nyarong poured a drink for him. Ayonchugu went towards Nyarong, stooped, and held out his cup in his right hand, his left palm supporting his elbow. Nyarong filled it in one smooth flow, and he sat down and sipped. The main matter of the day was thus successfully accomplished and they were now socialising. All they needed to know next was a date on which to return and continue the delicate negotiations with the future father-in-law and the people he would want them to see.

Three weeks went by before Ndamgu and Ayonchugu decided to send word to Nyarong asking if they could come and continue talks on Mengen. The reply was positive and a day was chosen. Ayonchugu sent word through a mobile trader in refurbished lamps to his brother in Libah to come for the occasion. Ndi came, looking visibly changed for the better. But the real gladdening surprise guests were his uncles, Teneng and Kwende, who came uninvited. Ayonchugu could have used them to pull off a good deal with Nyarong, but he already had commissioned Ndamgu, who was equally apt in negotiations. The three men were going to make a formidable combination if Ndamgu opted to let them into the talks.

On the appointed day the men were joined by Manyi, her youngest son - Ndeh, who carried a calabash of wine, and a couple called Bishwing and Nawain, who were neighbours to Ayonchugu. Nawain carried a large basket of achu on her head, balancing it precariously at an angle. Her left hand was behind her supporting a baby that was strapped onto her back with a well-worn wrapper which looked like it could give way any moment, but which surprisingly lasted the day. Each man had a fibre bag slung over his left shoulder, a sheathed knife on his right side, and dangled a *badi* of palm wine in his left hand.

They arrived at Nyarong's home just after midday. He received them cordially and had them settle down in his big room. When Ndamgu judged the moment appropriate he cleared his throat and spoke in a formal tone.

'We are grateful for your hospitality. These people you see here are all my family. You might have met some of them before, but not Ndi, who is Ayonchugu's big brother, and Teneng and Kwende, his kinsmen from Libah. Whatever I say, I say it for them all, and since I'm no stranger to you, they should be no strangers to you either.'

'When one receives august guests in his home it is an

honour,' said Nyarong, nodding. 'When the same guests come back bringing along their kinsmen and women, it shows that they mean business. My house is your house.'

Ndamgu nodded generously and said, 'We say thank you for the kind words that come out of your mouth. It takes a good tongue to build the kind of bridge we are here to build. Some weeks ago we came to this house and expressed our desire to marry your daughter. As you know, one cannot buy a chicken in a basket. My family is here today to know who their sister is.'

'Ndamgu, I'm pleased to see you are all here. I'm reassured that my daughter is going to end up in a family with many people to support her. Yet, it seems to me that you have swallowed your kernel before chewing it.'

'There is no situation that can't be fixed by the power of sensible words and appropriate action,' replied Ndamgu. 'I can't pretend that I know all the customs. Tell us how you want us to proceed.'

'I'm glad I'm dealing with serious people here, said Nyarong. 'The bride-price is the foundation on which a lasting marriage is built. I'm not being greedy, but that must be sorted out before we proceed with other formalities. Again, you are all welcome, and may your stay here be peaceful.'

'I thank you again from my heart for the words of welcome,' Ndamgu said. 'I won't take into my family a woman on whose head questions about bride-price are still pending. We'll sort out that question as soon as it is time to do so.'

'That is the correct thing to do,' said Nyarong. 'The time for that is now.'

Ndamgu turned to the men and said, 'Can you join your heads with mine outside?' Ndi, Teneng and Kwende stood up and followed Ndamgu. Once outside and beyond earshot, Ndamgu said, 'This was expected. But I'm a bit surprised he brought it up so soon.'

'He did not even offer us kola nuts or drinks,' remarked Teneng. 'Not even from what we brought.'

'I smell greed in that man. Since when were questions about bride-price mentioned in public?' wondered Kwende.

'And in the presence of women?' Ndi chipped in.

'I guess we would just have to discuss the bride-price and

have it done with. When you turn away the devil, send him off for good,' said Ndamgu.

'That is right,' said Ndi.

'You should join me in the haggling.'

'I think my uncles should do it with you,' said Ndi.

'Tell Nyarong we are waiting to hear from him,' Ndamgu instructed.

Ndi went back inside. Mengen was in the room greeting the guests under the scowl of her father, who had not invited her yet to meet them. She avoided Ayonchugu's eyes as she went towards the men and greeted Ndi with a courtesy. She reached out to Nawain and took the baby who had just woken up and sat down to chat with the guests. Ndi talked to Nyarong and he went outside to meet the men. He invited them into another room. When they had seated themselves, Nyarong addressed them.

'The man who hunts into the night soon starts hunting ghost game. Are you ready to talk serious matters on the head of your future wife?'

'Yes, we are,' Ndamgu said. 'We are listening to you. You have the first and the last say.'

'You shall put here on the ground forty pounds. That's the money on your woman's head.'

Ndamgu cleared his throat very slightly and spoke. 'You have spoken. A man who does not know the value of his own wares probably stole them. Your daughter is very dear to us, but forty pounds is an outrageous amount of money to ask for bride-price.'

Teneng lost his verve for diplomacy and went straight to the point. 'Your daughter is not an article for sale. She is coming into a family to be a sister and a wife.'

'Gentlemen, I feel affronted. What are you driving at?' asked Nyarong.

'We value your daughter more than any amount of money,' said Kwende. 'But we can't dip our hands into a place where we can't take them out.'

Ndamgu nodded at the men's input, and then spoke. 'The fact is that you have named an amount so high that we are at a loss for words. Rethink what you have just said, and tell us what you truly desire as bride-price for your daughter.'

'Gentlemen, are we a bunch of market women? Or did you travel all the way here for sight-seeing? I'm now doing my best not to feel insulted. I'm not a man of many words. I have said my well-thought-out say. If you people are not serious about your mission, then you can return on another day.'

Ndamgu saw no possible benefits of insisting that their mission was a serious one. He said, 'The presence of the most important people of my family here tells you just how seriously we take this mission and the respect we have for your person. We hope to soon see the people you shall designate us to see. We have the two marriage ceremonies to do. Your daughter and her husband would be left with nothing to live on if you set the stakes so high.'

Nyarong was adamant. 'Where I come from, we do these things differently. You don't have to see anyone but me. I will see my family myself.'

'We acknowledge that customs differ,' said Ndamgu. 'I have travelled quite a bit in my life-time. This is the first time I have encountered this kind of situation. You can't possibly be the only person to marry off your daughter.'

'A man gets married to a family, not just to a woman,' Kwende chipped in. 'We won't feel comfortable not seeing at least your wife's father, who we all know, is a very important person in these matters in every custom.'

In the face of these weighty arguments, Nyarong got into the explanatory mode. 'As you are aware, I come from very far away. I lost my wife many years ago. I have here only Nwenmufu and my daughter. I will take you to see the rest of my family in the future, so that you understand I did not fall from the sky. I will let you know when that journey is to be. What I ask for is on behalf of every member of my family that is absent. When you eventually meet them, I'll be the one to sort things out with them, not you. Put what I ask on the ground here, and the bundle is tied.'

'I will have a word with my brothers outside,' Ndamgu replied.

The three men went outside. Ndamgu called Ayonchugu and Ndi from the adjoining room and explained the developments to them.

'Nyarong's approach and demands are unprecedented,' said Ndi.

'But not inconvenient for us,' said Ndamgu. 'I think that seeing just him saves us from the trouble we would go through if we had to see the rest of his family.'

'Will that amount to real marriage?' asked Ayonchugu.

'Sure. The father of the bride has the final say in these matters, and if he prefers to take everything on behalf of his family, so be it. We would have done our part on our wife's head. Is that not what we came here for? The short-cut and the long road lead to the same destination.'

'I think I see Ndamgu's point,' said Teneng. 'As for the forty pounds, that is a life-time worth of savings. I think it is out of the question to consider giving him such an amount.'

'We must get him to bring it down,' said Kwende. 'Leave it to me. I know what to say to him. We'll try fourteen, twenty-one, and then twenty-eight. If he is still adamant we'll tell him forty has nothing to do with seven.'

The men laughed at this, and agreed to try the strategy. They went back inside the house.

CHAPTER ELEVEN

A secret investment

Two days after the bride-price on Mengen's head was paid, Nyarong stepped out of his shrine and set forth towards the hilly range, whose mist-covered face and splitting falls were barely visible in the distance. It was a cold and slightly foggy morning. He kept a determinedly fast pace, and with his pipe fully charged with rare lung-warming herbs, he was already at the foot of the hills by the time the sun peeped over the summits into Ngonibi. He began the tedious ascent, slackening his pace somewhat, but never pausing for a breath. By the time the sun's rays had licked up the dew from the grasses, he was on top of the hills, and had he looked back, he would have seen the village lying serenely beneath his feet; he would have seen a spiral of smoke here and there marking the location of houses, canopied by the evergreen kola nut trees that were characteristic of the enclave below. But Nyarong was not the type to look back either at his deeds or at what lay behind him.

He tore through the tall elephant grass for some miles and finally came to the green turfs on which cattle grazed. He arrived at a paddock, where the only sign of human habitation was a tiny ramshackle hut. A naked little girl popped her head out of the door, saw him and ran off in fright towards her mother, the talisman around her tiny waist playing from side to side. The woman came out to meet the visitor, carrying the child.

'Salam alekum, baba.'

'Alekum salam, dada.

'Awarina?'

'Ei. Noi?'

'Jam. Salifu has gone over that hill there with the cattle. Here's a seat. Here, have some butter and roasted cocoyam while I call for him.'

'Thank you,' Nyarong said. 'I'll eat after seeing Salifu.'

The woman glided across the green field in experienced steps and came to a vantage point from where she called out to her husband in a smooth voice that could have been heard over two miles around the empty hills. Within minutes the man came hurrying over the hills. He was a tall, lanky, light-skinned man dressed in ragged garbs and wielding a long staff. He was like a bamboo that had withstood many tempests, marked by wear and tear. His curly beard, which seemed to have known only his fingers for a comb, bobbed up and down as he chewed endlessly on a herb or a nut, which kept his teeth strong and stained brown to the admiration of his wife. His skull-cap had holes in it so big that Nyarong wondered silently why the man bothered at all to wear it. His long bare feet knew every undulation on these hills, and gripped onto the green slopes like the claws of a cattle egret.

'Salam alekum, Nyarong,' he greeted cheerily.

'Alekum salam, Salifu. How are you today?'

'Insha'Allah, fine.'

'How are the cows'?

'By Allah, fine.'

'And the dogs?'

'By Allah, fine. And you?'

'Fine.'

'And your health?'

'Fine.'

'And your compound?'

'Fine.'

'And your daughter?'

'Fine. What about the taxes?'

'By Allah, all paid.'

On and on went the exchange at so fast a pace that it took virtually no time at all.

'My babies are doing fine, I believe?' Nyarong asked.

'Yes, more than fine. There is a lot of pasture this season. They're very happy.'

'Where are they now?'

'Ali has taken a hundred to the salty waters at Adjintse. Bouba and his boys have taken a hundred to the Fujua valley. Saibou has taken fifty cows to cross in Alhaji Fodjo's stock. The rest are with me down in the valley, just across the stream.'

Salifu moved nimbly over the turfs, his staff slung across his shoulders. He led the way to a point where the hill sloped into a lush valley. There was a herd of long-horned cattle grazing peacefully down there. Nyarong watched them for some time, their moos of satisfaction music to his ears. Salifu kept chatting excitedly.

'Cattle thieves tried entering the paddock three days ago but the dogs and the spell kept them away. Wardo's boys had spied them earlier in the day and passed on information to everyone. They came from Kekwini. All daggers were sharpened and waiting for them. It wasn't their day. Insha'Allah, we would have done them in! And they're not the only thieves. There's a man called Angabill who steals under cover of clouds he casts. He hits a cow of his choice with a cane and it follows him. But he's a loner and causes little harm to us. You see that hill over on the horizon...over on the other side is the Pond plain. It has become a no-go area. Malam Dulaihi has appropriated the plains. Ever heard of such a thing? If individuals start owning grazing land, cows would soon all die of famine.'

'How many have you got down there? Nyarong asked.

'Seventy-two. Two cows foaled today and we are expecting two more next week.'

'You are doing a fine job. Here's some money.' Nyarong handed Salifu a bag of coins. 'Buy us more stock.'

'I'll do so tomorrow,' replied Salifu, doing a quick count of the money. 'Malam Adamu is selling some healthy calves. It's a long way to Nyos but the trip is worth making. I'll leave this same evening.'

'Good. Do you know where I can find the ackee plant?' Nyarong asked.

'Yes. Over at Mbomushong. We don't let the cows go there lest they get poisoned eating that horrible plant. Do you want the leaves or the fruits? I'll dash over and get some for you.'

'Don't you bother. I'll get them myself on my way back.'

CHAPTER TWELVE

Tears and smiles of a bride

'You hurt me again,' complained Mengen, managing to hold back tears. 'You promised to be good. Why do you hurt me?'

Ayonchugu raised and supported himself on one elbow. He looked at Mengen's scantily clad form lying by his side on the straw mattress and a wave of pity hit him.

'I'm sorry,' he said.

'You've said that before. I was beginning to like it. Then you spoilt it again.'

'I did not realise how much I was hurting you.'

'That is the point. I'm not firewood you are splitting.'

'I'm truly sorry.' He felt guilty, vacuous and stupid at the same time. His outward serenity hid a rage which surfaced at odd times. He had to make Mengen understand what he was going through, he thought. He was not sure about where to start. He guessed if he just talked he would soon make things clearer for her and for himself. 'It's the war. It keeps following me. It makes me mad.'

'I think you are bewitched. You should see my father.'

'I'm certainly not bewitched. What I'm going through is beyond Nyarong's understanding.'

'You need treatment,' Mengen said with the conviction of someone speaking within her specialism. 'Sometimes you are simply impotent. At other times you rage on like a mad man. Do all the warriors in Libah treat their wives like you do me?'

'I don't know.' Ayonchugu thought for a long while, and then resumed speaking. 'The loss of my eye was nothing compared to the pain of seeing people die on the battlefield. The machines of war were gigantic and precise in killing. The first time some comrades and I came face to face with a tank in action we were so frightened that we actually started running away. You know the bulldozers used by PWD. A tank is like a chained-foot bulldozer carrying a very big gun. I couldn't hear anything for some days. I thought I had seen it all until I witnessed a flamethrower setting fire on an entire storey building with a single puff of fire from its nozzle. The building which was full of screaming people was reduced to ashes in minutes.'

'I know nothing about war machines,' said Mengen. 'You were trained to be a soldier, weren't you?'

'My training was tough. Yet it did not prepare me enough for what I met on the battlefield. I was not well prepared for the mowing down boom of the tanks which defied rugged terrain and bore down on humans with a merciless thirst for blood. I was not adequately prepared for the dirge-like drone of planes that came spitting death in conical balls falling from the heavens. I was not prepared to face the dismembering blasts of mines in otherwise peaceful-looking fields. I was even less prepared to see and sometimes taste – yes, taste – the charred, flying bits of human flesh, shredded by explosives. Those cries from the wounded! They tore right into my heart and tested my sanity more than the impassive silence of the dead.'

Ayonchugu started shivering as if he had suddenly caught a cold. His teeth chattered and his lips trembled. He lay back and culled himself up like a baby. Mengen looked worried. She pulled up the blanket and covered him. She moved closer and cuddled him.

'My senses became numb; I felt nothing, tasted nothing, saw nothing, and smelled nothing; I only half heard, and that was enough for taking orders and for staying alive. The more I lost feeling, the braver I appeared. My comrades called me Number One. I earned medals for exceptional bravery. I felt invincible and took more and more risks. Now, memories of the war are besieging me. They haunt and taunt me day and night, testing the last strings of my sanity. I'm terrified.'

'I think you need a lot of rest, my husband.'

'Resting makes things worse. I have to keep doing something. Have you forgiven me?' Ayonchugu asked.

'What for, my husband?' Mengen replied.

Even with her limited experience of the world of intimacy between the sexes and her total obliviousness of what a modern war was like, she was indeed convinced he was different from most men of his time and clime. She understood why his experiences toughened him, but never could understand why they also made him alternately so wild and so vulnerable.

'Why did you refuse the offer of a job with the PWD?' Mengen asked. 'That would have kept you very busy.'

'How could I accept to work as a labourer?' Ayonchugu asked. 'As a volunteer, I've been assisting the overseer supervise construction work on four bridges over the streams that flow across this village and even one in Pond. The PWD people told me I couldn't be overseer because I did not have a certificate. I'd rather focus on my coffee farm.'

When the sun rose, Ayonchugu and Mengen went out to work on their farm. A party of friends including Bishwing, Nawain, Ibonge and Nibonge joined them in harvesting ripe coffee beans, which they carried, bag after bag, on their heads and on a wheelbarrow to the local cooperative for decorticating. Back home, they had the coffee washed in a nearby stream until it shone white. They then spread the beans on mats in their ample yard to sun until they were cackling dry. They next bagged the crop and took it back to the cooperative where it was groomed, weighed and carted off in a big lorry. Ayonchugu was given a date to return to the cooperative for payment.

Ayonchugu was in high spirits the day he received his payment. He stopped by a provision store and bought some rice, a tin of Ovaltine, a packet of sugar, and a bottle of Maggi. He fitted his shopping by the side of a machine in a wheelbarrow and pushed it home.

'Thank you for the things, my lord,' said Mengen. 'And this machine? It looks like you've spent all your earnings.'

'The cooperative loaned us this hand-wind decorticator. Don't even worry about the cost. The repayment is spread over five years from debits to be made on the proceeds of the sale of our coffee. As for the things, you deserve them in your present state.'

Mengen smiled. 'This is the first time you have said something about my state. Since when did you notice it?'

'I felt the changes in you even before your pregnancy became visible,' Ayonchugu said. 'Don't you see how I've been in very good spirits for some time now? I go to work with renewed hope for the future.'

As he gently ran his hand over Mengen's body that night, he again marvelled at the rejuvenated hue and feel it had taken on. They both delighted at the prospect of seeing the new being that was growing within her. Life took on a new meaning for Ayonchugu, and he had fewer nightmares about himself buried alive in quicksand in North Africa, or a shallow grave in the sun-baked, cracked soil of the Sahel of Northeast Africa, or the swamps of the jungles of Burma, or the leached cold red earth of Libah. He felt a sense of worth he had not known for a long time, and wished they could make a baby for every friend he lost in the war.

He was whistling a war-time song when he did the following morning's palm wine tapping and trap inspection routine. While on the back roads, he heard the hoofs of horses coming briskly behind him. It was rare for horse-riding nomads to go through the village in that direction at that hour. He stepped out of the way and waited for the riders to approach. The lead rider came by and Ayonchugu could make out his stunted form perched on the back of the horse. He had an enormous head and bulging eyes. His greying hair was covered in a tropical helmet. Visibility was not very good, but he still made him out. It was G. H. Ashamba. The massive man with a scowl on his face who was behind him was probably his guide or servant. They trotted by in silence and took no notice of him.

Ayonchugu continued on his tracks in the opposite direction. He could not help but wonder what such a man was doing in Ngonibi at such an hour. It was unlike him to be anonymous. G. H. Ashamba was a well-known and influential political figure who never went anywhere without the people coming out, usually at the behest of the fon, to welcome him with fanfare. He had been educated both locally and abroad. After the first year of WW1 he returned from Germany, and although he was fit to fight, the Germans chose to use him to organise the drafting of soldiers from the Kamerun Grassfields.

All day long Ayonchugu thought about G. H. Ashamba and sought reasons he was in Ngonibi so early in the morning. He talked about him to neighbours and friends, but no one said they had seen him. From the look of things, he was either passing through, or he had been somewhere for a secret meeting. These were delicate times in the political life of the people; the struggle for self-determination was going on and politicians were making in-roads in the hinterlands, mobilising people and seeking political ground. That evening he sat across from Mengen by the hearth and talked about G. H. Ashamba.

'Are you sure he was indeed the one you saw?' she asked.

'Of course he was. I can never mistake the man. His eyes were as prominent as ever. I even noticed the warts on his neck. I've known him all my life, remember?'

'He is from your village, of course.'

'And he inspired my father to send us to school,' Ayonchugu said. 'I wonder what it would have been like if I had become a government official or a teacher.'

'I would have been just a bush woman to you,' said Mengen, and they both laughed. 'How did he inspire your father?'

'It's a long story.'

'You don't have to ask my father's permission to tell me this time. So out with it, soja!' Mengen said.

Ayonchugu closed his good eye and reminisced for a moment. He smiled and started speaking. 'For the people of Libah in the old days, schooling was meant for the likes of the Atumebetas, who could be allowed to indulge in the pastimes of Europeans. Young men from noble families had better things to do. They had crafts to learn from their parents. They had extensive farms to cultivate; they had wives to inherit and children to produce. Especially, they had the art of war to learn from the elders.

'A misfortune of birth played out for the better for G. H. Ashamba. You know he has Atumebeta blood, but he grew up in Libah. Many families of Atumebeta lived a life of serfdom in Libah. Peonage was rife. When missionaries came campaigning for children to be sent to them to be educated, G. H. Ashamba was sent off to school as a sign of spite to his likes.

While his peers were savouring the pride and pleasures of being groomed to local grandeur, he was in the classroom, heading for an uncertain future in the hands of foreigners. He might have been about fifteen when he was recruited to work as a clerk and a translator for the local German administrator.'

'That must have been embarrassing for your people,' Mengen remarked.

'It was,' Ayonchugu concurred. 'He wore European clothes and sat behind a desk in the room adjacent to that of the administrator. He stood beside the administrator and took down notes in German, and was not obliged to perform all the rituals others did in the presence of the fon and the elders of the clan. So he was spited. His relatives were persecuted during traditional ceremonies or rituals. German administrators were usually unable to help.

'G. H. Ashamba spoke many native languages, fluent German and even English. A good orator, he made use of his understanding of the lore, mores, and susceptibilities of the people to get the desired results for his masters. Ashamba rose fast within the ranks of the colonial administration and became an envoy. He was quick to realise his indispensability to his employers. He set himself up independently of them and went on to provide paid services. He negotiated with tribal leaders for them. He collected taxes on a commission. He liaised with a chief called Atangana who already had ample experience in that area, and the two and their militia set out to exact from the people the payments they would otherwise have evaded. By the time Ashamba was in his mid-twenties, he was very rich, powerful, feared all over the land, and hated by the nobility in my village, who in spite of themselves, were obliged to do him homage.

'His success was an eye-opener to the people of Libah who did everything to send their children to school, and frustrated as much as they could the efforts of the Atumebetas to do the same. In my case though, G. H. Ashamba personally advised my father to send us to school. He said the Germans would leave one day and Kamerunians would rule. As I said, his story is long. I've given you only a summary.'

'He sounds amazing. We do not have any big government

man from this village. Your village is far advanced.'

Ayonchugu nodded in agreement and said, 'It is not as advanced as it should have been.'

'Can you count how many clerks and teachers you have?'

'Oh yes. There are as many as thirty teachers and perhaps twenty clerks, according to my brother,' he said proudly.

'My mother! Those are huge numbers!' exclaimed Mengen.

'There could have been many more if the best of our young men had not become soldiers, and had many of the young girls not left school to get married to the teachers and clerks,' Ayonchugu said.

'So do that many women go to school in your village?'

'Yes. I was in class with a girl called Nah. She was one of three girls in my class. My brother told me she is a teacher in the village school. She is married to the headmaster. The two others are in Ibadan in a big college.'

'Those must be exceptional women,' Mengen said.

'Mm. Nah was quite brilliant and used to answer all the teacher's questions and this angered the boys.'

'But how could you boys allow a woman to be smarter than you?' Mengen asked, her voice conveying her incredulity.

'She was simply very clever,' Ayonchugu replied. 'I met even smarter women when I was in the army.'

'White women, of course?'

'Many White, Indian, and African women too.'

'Did they also fight?' Mengen asked, eyes widening.

'No. They were mostly nurses. They treated wounded soldiers. Women treated my eye.'

'Black or white?'

'Some white, some black. An English eye doctor did the operation to take out a piece of metal following an explosion. Another woman attended to me three times a day.'

'Were you that special?' Mengen asked.

'Every soldier was supposed to be special. We were fighting the same enemy. One soldier less made a difference in the jungles of Boma.'

Mengen pondered for a while and then said, 'I'd like our male children to go to school. One day they will all become teachers like Moka. He is a real gentleman.'

'And what about our female children?' Ayonchugu asked. 'They can become nurses.'

'I'd rather they help us on the farm and get married,' Mengen said.

'And what if we have no male child to send to school?'

'Your other wives will have male children. You can send them to school.'

'There will be no other wives,' Ayonchugu stated.

'Even if I do not give birth to a male child? I don't believe you.'

'Wait and see.'

'I hope you are not wishing I shouldn't have a male child so you can prove me wrong.'

'No, that is not my wish. I want you to have male and female children. If you can't have male children, I will be sad. But I won't marry another woman ever,' Ayonchugu insisted.

'I will get you one when the time comes. I can't grow old in this house without a co-wife,' Mengen said adamantly.

'As you wish. But I will not love her,' Ayonchugu declared.

'Who was talking about love? I never wasted time thinking about it until you started going on and on about it.'

'Love is important in everything. Without love there will be nothing worth living for. That is why providence brought me to this village - just to find you and love you.'

'You are now embarrassing me again, silly man,' Mengen said, looking away as he came over and held her two hands and brought his face closer to hers. 'Don't kiss me again, soja. I'm not your white nurse.'

'But you like it,' Ayonchugu said.

'No, I do not,' Mengen replied.

'No, you did not,' he corrected. 'You do now, don't you?'

'Don't you see my state?' she asked, looking down at the bulge that prevented their bodies from aligning.

'And how does that stop you from accepting the attentions of a gentleman?' Ayonchugu asked teasingly, his lips caressing her cheek and going lower and lower.

Three weeks to the time the village midwife had estimated

Mengen was going to give birth, Ayonchugu, Manyi and Nibonge set out for Shisong hospital in Kumbo. The village mid-wife and Nyarong considered it a waste of time and energy. Ayonchugu insisted on going to the distant modern facility. They went on foot because Mengen said she could not stand being jostled in a Land Rover. They each carried a big basket and flour sacs containing enough supplies to last some days. Ayonchugu carried a straw mattress in addition to his old military carryall. It was a tiring walk for the women in the baking heat of the dry season, bedevilled by the harmattan which blew so hard that it sometimes nearly plucked the luggage off their heads. The wayfarers had to stop frequently by the many brooks spilling from the mountain sides to have a refreshing drink. There never was lacking along the way somebody willing to invite them in for a little rest and a bite, especially when they saw Mengen's distended belly.

They arrived at Shisong late at night and met the night duty nurses who did a brief assessment of Mengen, and being satisfied that it would be yet a long while before the baby was due, showed them to a nearby shack. There, Ayonchugu spread the mattress and the three women lay down, with Nibonge sleeping the other way round to the older women in order to gain more space. Ayonchugu sat on dry banana leaves, leaned backwards on his bag and promptly fell asleep.

Shisong hospital had one doctor. In his absence, consultation was done by experienced nurses, who did virtually everything, including emergency surgery. It did not matter to the villagers whom they consulted; they only looked forward to seeing someone in a white uniform carrying a stethoscope to call 'doctor'. The young ladies who were clearly not doctors were 'sisters' or 'misses'.

The following morning when Mengen went to consult, Ayonchugu was called in to translate for her. She was examined by a European 'doctor', given vaccines and advised on her hygiene and nutrition. She was required for the duration of her pregnancy to see the 'doctor' once a week. It was agreed that the women stay with her; Ayonchugu was to do the journey back to Ngonibi and return frequently until the birth of the baby.

For the next three weeks Ayonchugu was to be seen every two days boarding the Land Rover from Ngonibi to Shisong. Twice, when the vehicle broke down, Ayonchugu did the journey on foot.

And so it was that on one of his trips Ayonchugu was shown in to see their first baby lying peacefully asleep in a makeshift cot. It was clothed in knitwear that had been supplied by the sisters. He looked at the baby for a long while. All he could see was a messy tiny face, frowning like an unfriendly doll.

'Is it a boy or a girl?' he asked.

'It's a boy,' Mengen whispered weakly.

He smiled broadly, and started moving towards her. She looked around her. The only person present was Manyi.

'Don't you dare kiss me!' Mengen warned.

Ayonchugu smiled even more. 'No, I won't,' he said, and patted her arm.

'Where's the umbilical cord?' he asked.

'Here it is,' said Manyi, taking it out of Mengen's handbag and handing it over to Ayonchugu. It was wrapped up in fresh cocoyam leaves.

'Are you taking it to Libah or to Ngonibi?' Mengen asked.

'Ngonibi. I will bury it right behind our house.'

'The doctor says I have to stay here for one month. They have to make sure the baby is healthy before we leave.'

'That's a long time, but I guess it is a good thing.'

Even as Ayonchugu was speaking, two nurses came in and made a fuss over the baby, tickled its feet, held it up, took its weight, temperature and samples of urine and blood, all the while taking notes in a large register. Thereafter, they invited Mengen to join twenty other women with wailing babies for a demonstration on how to bathe a baby. When Mengen returned from bathing the baby, the nurses oiled its navel and bandaged it. They squeezed medicine into the baby's eyes, dressed his wound and administered vaccines and injections.

When the nurses finally left, Mengen turned to Ayonchugu and asked, 'Why are they doing all this? They visit the baby three times a day. Are you sure he is fine?'

'I think he is fine. They do this to all babies, I believe.'

'Did you see the needle they were using? I was afraid it would go right through him,' Mengen said.

Nibonge and her mother made sure that Mengen got everything she needed, including abdominal massages. She was on her own only when she did her private hygiene. When the baby's stomach started griping, it writhed and cried all the time, causing distress to everyone. The doctor told them not to bother much because it was going to be over soon. But it did not. Mengen brought out a black powdery substance from her moth-eaten handbag and gave it to Manyi. She mixed it with some *manyanga* and massaged the baby's stomach with it. Sister was mad the next morning when she saw the dark tell-tale oil stains on the baby's clothes and on the navel bandage. But the baby was calm and sound asleep for the first time in two days. Later, Sister secretly asked Mengen to give her some of the black powder.

The hospital gave Ayonchugu a delivery certificate without a name which he took to the nearby civil status registry, to have a birth certificate drawn up. Ayonchugu named the child Nkahfi. The following day he came back and picked up the birth certificate and scanned it. The child's name was written as Kafi. Ayonchugu protested.

'The civil status registration clerk is the most able person to decide how names are spelled,' said the office messenger he met. 'And by the way,' he added, 'the child has to have a name that teachers can pronounce when he goes to school.'

Ayonchugu left, shaking his head.

On the day of their return to Ngonibi, Ayonchugu bought a wide umbrella, a Tilley lamp, a water flask and some utensils from the traders who gathered in front of the hospital every Saturday. He bought Mengen a special gift of three pieces of English Wax material, two blouses, a pair of copper earrings, a colourful head scarf, a large bathing towel and her first ladies' sandals. The gifts were laid out on her bed in her new room at home.

CHAPTER THIRTEEN

A silver lining on black clouds

The birth of Nkahfi brought new life to Ayonchugu and Mengen. He shared with her the reality of a dream he had every day, when he prayed to survive the war and return home to Ngelem. He woke up each day with a renewed zest for life and worked on his farm with little help from others. He was already putting aside the resources he needed to build a stone house. First, he volunteered his services towards the construction of a new Catholic Church, which was an opportunity to polish his stone-masonry skills.

Ayonchugu watched over Mengen and Nkahfi in a way that was unusual for men of his standing. She confessed that she had never known the love of a mother, although she had never lacked adequate care from a succession of female patients who were glad to nurse her during their stay at her father's. Some of them had stayed on for many weeks while her father worked on them, and had welcomed the opportunity to be foster mothers to her, as no blessing for a barren woman surpassed the one obtained from nurturing a motherless baby. Ayonchugu was her man, and she felt fulfilled, while still dreaming of the day her household would be teeming with people. She found some time to prepare herbal remedies for people, but her duties as a full-time aid to Nyarong were over.

Late one afternoon, seven weeks after the birth of Nkahfi, Ayonchugu opened a wooden trunk he kept in his room and pulled out an old military kit. He dug into it and brought out a plastic bag in which he had stashed away his war memorabilia, and started sorting its contents. He found his medals and held them up. They had lost their lustre, although the ribbons looked as good as new. He took out a piece of charcoal from dead embers and used it to scrub each medal. He wiped them with a piece of cloth and they glittered. He nailed a piece of plank on the wall and strung them up. He stepped back and looked at his work. Then he looked around him, shook his head and mumbled to himself, 'This is incongruous.' He took the medals off the wall and returned them to the plastic bag.

He took out his Army Pay Card, a little booklet which was the equivalent of the Labour Card. It identified him as Corporal Yoncho of Libah. Date of birth: Around 1922. Date of engagement: January 1941. Army Pioneer Corps. Height: 5.8 feet. Salary: 1/-6.

Ayonchugu dug out a faded piece of paper lodged in the middle of the pay booklet. He peered at it and could still make out some addresses. One was a Gold Coast address belonging to Kafui Gifty. The second belonged to Kelechi of Onitsha. These two and Ayonchugu were the surviving three of the Fearless Five, so named for their daring feats on the war front. The two other men had died from a combination of typhoid and multiple infections which penicillin could not treat. There was a third address belonging to Jack Terry, a Briton. He had bonded with these men in the most treacherous of times. They had exchanged addresses and agreed to keep track of one another after the war, if they were lucky enough to survive it. He had given his address as care of the fon of Libah. He wondered if any of them had written to him and if his letters might be in the custody of the fon or even Ajong. He put the addresses in a side compartment of his fibre bag and made a mental note to get some writing material from the Headmaster and write letters to these devoted friends-in-arms of yesteryears.

He pulled out some rare newspaper clippings he had collected about his contingent's performance in the war. He would have had a lot more, but most of the clippings had got wet and been destroyed when his unit swam across flooded fields during the monsoons. He liked reading newspapers. He read them over and over, memorised whole reports, not only because the stories were often inspiring, but also because he liked the language; it was very different from what was in his school books.

He ruminated over the clippings and dared to dwell on unsavoury memories of the war. His concentration was intruded upon by the voice of his neighbour.

'Iyeuh!'

'Iyeuh!' he answered back, looking up. 'Come right in!'

Bishwing, Tachum and Niba came in. Niba was a sensible but reserved and deferring young man who was well thought of by many an elderly man. They had their caps on, and all displayed bare torsos. The lower part of their bodies was draped in *ntum*. Their large flat feet were bare and well powdered with dust, giving the impression they could have been trampling on mud to produce sun-dried bricks.

Ayonchugu had told them he was expecting the headmaster and his wife. These neighbours were coming to keep the house warm for the esteemed guests. They each carried a *badi* of palm wine.

'Father-of-baby, how is it today?' asked Bishwing.

'Fine. There are stools under the table in the corner,' he said to Niba. 'The table chair is for the HM.'

'Hold on to this *badi* for the occasion,' said Tachum, setting down the specially designed calabash. Bishwing and Niba did the same.

'I thank you all,' Ayonchugu said to the men. He called out to Ndeh, Ndamgu's youngest son who had replaced Ibonge in his household. He came in and carried the calabashes to the wine storage room – the *atege*. He returned with wine in a new container and served the men.

'I see the HM is not here yet,' said Tachum.

Ayonchugu looked at his wrist watch. 'He said five. It is still four twenty-five. Trust me, he will be here at that time.'

'He is a punctilious one, that HM,' said Bishwing. 'I see, *Tamboo*, you must be enjoying the born-house. Your forehead glitters with palm oil.'

'The women are enjoying it you mean,' Ayonchugu replied. 'I've bought a large tin of palm oil every week since Mengen and the baby returned home. I'm down by three goats and countless chickens.'

'Boys are costly commodities,' said Bishwing. 'You spend more when they are born and they never bring in a bride-price.'

'And next thing you know, they lay claim to your property, even while you are still alive,' said Tachum.

'With your happy complicity,' said Bishwing. 'That's the price you must pay to have someone succeed you.'

'At the first go the man already has a successor,' said Tachum. 'It took me a third wife, after the birth of eight girls, to get my first boy.'

'And ever since, your wives have gone on a boy-making spree,' said Bishwing. 'Soon the boys will outnumber the girls and there goes your profit evaporating into the air.'

'Bishwing, must you always speak in terms of commerce?' Ayonchugu asked. 'Maybe you should stop making drums and start trading.'

'Life is commerce, isn't it?' replied Bishwing. 'I consider myself a trader anyway. The only difference is that I never have to take a drum to sell in the market because I work only on orders. A good medicine-man needs no advertisement.'

'How come the new drum you made for the *mangisa* got burst on its second outing only? It was such a disgrace for the dancers who had to then beg for a drum from the *waniboh* dancers.'

'You see, Tachum, everything we do involves buying and selling, and we always want to sell for a profit,' said Bishwing. 'If you pay me well, you will get a good drum. You don't pay well, you get a goat-skin drum and don't you blame me if it disappoints you in the middle of a celebration.'

'The thing is, when a drum bursts as it did, it does not speak well of your craft,' said Niba. 'That is bad advertisement for business.'

'Was it not clear to everybody that the drum actually got burst because the juju house had not protected it?' asked Bishwing.

'You made the drum and you knew the best charms to ward off attacks from rival dance groups,' said Tachum. 'An article never leaves my smith unless it is complete in all senses.'

'I made the drum and the juju house had to reinforce it with charms,' said Bishwing. 'The contract we had did not include my making it foolproof against witchcraft. Leave your door open and the devil walks in.'

'Maybe you have a point there,' said Niba. 'But the people always ask, "Who was the lousy craftsman who made that drum which got burst?" and never, "Who was the lousy medicine-man who protected that drum from being bewitched by rival groups?"'

'Oh yes, thinking people do ask about the medicine-man,' said Bishwing. 'There is no *tamukum* who is ignorant about preventing spells on their musicians and equipment.' He lifted the *badi* in front of him, looked up and asked, 'Where's that boy?' Ndeh stepped into the house. 'Please, put this away for me.'

'Not so fast, Ndeh,' said Ayonchugu. 'Refill the *badi* and serve the guests.'

When a full *badi* was placed in front of him, Bishwing licked his thick black lips and smacked in satisfaction. 'The teacher and his wife must be on their way now,' he said.

'Sure. It is a long way from the school to here,' said Niba.

Just then they heard a man's voice greeting the women in the kitchen adjacent the main house.

'Didn't I tell you?' asked Bishwing. 'That is the man speaking.'

'What did you tell us?' asked Tachum.

'That he is coming, and here he is.'

'You said he and his wife must be on their way. That was no news to any of us, or was it?'

'Not at all,' agreed Niba.

'What are you asking credit for?' asked Tachum.

'Keep talking. The mouth that loves a drink, have this one on me!' Bishwing tilted his head backwards and took a long noisy sip from his cup. 'Whoever gave man the intelligence to hack into the vaginas of raffia-palms and bring out this inspirational milk, may he forever be blessed in the land of our ancestors. May he not look upon you juju-heads with contempt.' He smacked his lips loudly.

'I think we should not waste our breath on your effrontery and language,' said Tachum. 'Only watch your slippery tongue when the teacher is here.'

'You don't want him to use his whip on you,' said Ayonchugu, who had all the while been going in and out, making sure all was set to receive the guests. A big cock had been slaughtered and Ndeh was busy plucking the feathers in front of the kitchen, where the women were busy with cooking chores while making a fuss over the baby and pampering its mother.

'He is smarter than you dumb-heads and knows how to appreciate a joke,' said Bishwing.

'Sure, when the joke is funny, unlike yours which are sometimes irritating,' said Niba.

'Look at who is talking. Refill my cup lest malediction befall your milk-filled mouth.' Bishwing held out his cup nonchalantly, and Niba picked up the *badi* and refilled it.

Ndamgu appeared at the door and called out a greeting as he came into the house, holding a pod of kola nuts. 'Someone told me he saw the teachers coming. Ayonchugu, here's kola nut. Share it with the guests.'

'Thank you. I can tell this is from the tree directly behind your house,' Ayonchugu said.

'It is,' acknowledged Ndamgu, taking a seat next to Tachum.

Moka came into the house, followed by Atewele. The two men were best friends, as were their wives Matalina and Enanga, who had come with them but had stayed with the women. The two men sat on straight-back chairs at the table and after surveying the people in the room, Moka greeted in Binibi. 'Have you men gone ahead?'

'Mm, teachers,' the men replied. 'Have you followed?'

Ayonchugu brought out a packet of new glasses and placed two on the table for the teachers. Niba served them from the badi. Ayonchugu picked up a pod of kola nuts and took off the shell. He took the skin off the three nuts that he found inside. He broke the nuts. With the lobs in his open palm, he moved over to Ndamgu, who picked up two lobs and threw one into his mouth and crushed on it with an appetising crunching sound. Ayonchugu held out his palm to Tachum, then to Atewele, Moka, Bishwing and Niba. He then threw a lob into his mouth and chewed it.

'I have not tasted kola nut this good for a long time,' said Moka. 'It is dry and crunchy. It is hardly bitter at all.'

'It has a flavoured bitter-sweetness which blends perfectly with palm wine to give a smooth savory experience,' said Atewele.

'It comes from a tree in Ndamgu's compound,' said Ayonchugu. 'It is indeed of very good quality.' As he said this, he washed down the kola nut with a generous gulp of palm wine.

'Unfortunately the harmattan blew away most of the pods. It left me just enough to last a few weeks. I should be able get some for the teachers, though. Ndeh!' Ndamgu called his son in a loud voice, and he came hurrying in. 'Go and find out if there's still one or two pods of kola nuts in the tree behind my house; harvest it for the teachers.' The boy left, having understood his father well.

'Where did you get the seed for this kola nut?' asked Moka. 'I wager it is not from around here.'

'I got it from where you won't imagine at all,' Ndamgu said. 'It was left by someone at the *mitiee* in the market.' Everyone's eyes widened at his answer. 'I know that you must be wondering how come I took something which did not belong to me from the *mitiee*. The thing is, the kola nut had lain there for a long time and had germinated. I saw it and thought it would be a terrible waste if the market sweepers weeded it out, so I took it home and planted.'

'It can't be said that you stole from the mitiee,' said Moka.

'No, Ndamgu did not steal,' said Tachum. 'He won't be sitting here with us today if he did. He rather did a good thing. Just look at the results - the best kola nut tree in the whole village.'

'It might not be the best though, because the tree from which the seed came must be somewhere in this village and probably producing a better quality of nuts,' said Atewele.

'Perhaps Ndamgu took very good care of his tree,' said Ayonchugu. 'The parent tree may actually be producing nuts of lower quality.'

'I agree with Ayonchugu,' said Moka. 'We just have to look at human beings to see sense in what he says.'

'Teacher, I can't see the comparison you are making,' said Niba.

'You see, not all good fathers have good sons, and good sons are not always begotten of good fathers,' said Moka.

'I think that good upbringing accounts most for the

character of a child,' said Ndamgu.' 'As for the kola nut, I tended the tree really well. It was Ibonge's job as a kid to water it two times a day during the dry season. For many years I threw droppings from my wife's chickens under the tree.'

'No wonder then that this kola nut has a flavour – chicken droppings!' exclaimed Bishwing and the men burst out laughing.

'There you go trying to spoil my appetite,' complained Tachum.

'Am I?' asked Bishwing. 'Gizzard, not to talk of chicken's anus, smells of chicken pooh. I'm waiting to see the day you give up your share because of loss of appetite. I guess you have as good a sense of smell as I do. So don't even try to argue.' He carried his horn to his mouth, and as everyone expected, smacked his lips.

Tachum looked at Bishwing steadily for a while, then he turned and spoke to Ayonchugu. 'I bet you missed eating things like this when you went to fight in the white man's land.'

'I did very much,' Ayonchugu replied.

'You must have been eating rice and stew,' said Bishwing. 'Imagine having Christmas meals everyday in hell! Huh huh huh!'

'Rice in Boma, yes. Some of it was growing in the fields there. But that's not what we ate in the army. We had K rations handed out to us. Each ration was some biscuit and corned beef sealed in a packet just a little bigger than a clove of kola nuts or large Maths Set box.'

Bishwing burst out laughing again, nearly choking on his wine. 'How many Maths Set boxes of Queen Biscuits did you have to eat to fill your stomach?' he managed to ask. Queen Biscuits were the only biscuits they all knew well because a mobile salesman sold them on market days in Ngonibi. 'Queen Biscuit di go round! Go round brother go round! Go round sister go round!' chanted Bishwing in imitation of the trader.

'They were not Queen Biscuits and were not meant to fill the stomach. The combination tasted horrible at first but strangely enough, it provided the energy to keep us going during long tortuous marches, which in the early and later days of the war seemed to be the purpose of our going out there.'

'If I don't have a full stomach I feel hungry. Biscuits are good for the white man perhaps, but I won't have survived on that if I had had the misfortune of going out there,' said Bishwing.

'You see, different foods have different calories,' Moka said. 'Calories give strength. It is not so much the quantity of food that goes into your stomach that gives you energy, as how good a source of energy what you eat is.'

'I totally agree with the teacher, although I have never seen the calories he is referring to,' said Ndamgu. 'Take honey for example; it must be teeming with the so-called calories. I have stayed for seven days in the forest with a hunting party eating just some honey and perhaps a piece of roasted meat a day. Our challenge was to take along no food. We all fared quite well.'

'Tell me, soja,' said Bishwing, nearly choking on wine. 'Were biscuits and corned beef the only food that King George of England could afford for you boys?'

'Oh no, it was not K rations every day. At our base we nearly always had enough to fill our stomachs. In Boma, where we got trapped in thick forests while pursuing retreating Japs, we had some bread and sardines and stuff without names dropped from planes. On Christmas Day in '44 we even had some chocolates and sweets as well. Interestingly enough, the Japs were sometimes so close to us that they shared in our manna from heaven, as our General Wingate once called it.'

'So Japs were eating your food and shooting you! Ungrateful devils!' Bishwing exclaimed, wiping the tears off his eyes with the back of his hands.

'But are you saying for all those years you ate only white people's food?' asked Niba.

'We had some wonderful African cooks and they often came up with some corn-fufu which our white friends called mealies. Funny name. We had it with the usual okra and meat from cans. The meat was horrible – just like mashed up stuff to be fed to a baby – not a single bone to exercise your teeth on. Once in a while, we secretly caught wild game and had a feast. At our base we had lots of tea to drink. Sometimes without milk or sugar, but who cared? There are places in Boma where the plants are exactly like here. On one occasion we happened on mango trees in a village and I remember this boy from Kano called Ali who ate so many mangoes that they made him sick. They also probably saved his life. He was supposed to be a member of a special reconnaissance team that was assigned to survey and blow up a bridge which the Japanese were using to hit our base. When he took ill he was replaced. The five men who went to do the reconnaissance never returned. Two days afterwards, we found their mutilated bodies hanging on stakes like scarecrows in horror-land, not far from the bridge. They had been strung up by retreating Japs. Everybody started calling him Mango Alive.'

'What a name!' said Tachum. 'He certainly was alive because of mangoes.'

'So what did you miss eating most?' asked Niba.

'Drinking most, you mean. I missed palm wine most.'

Bishwing nodded generously. 'That is a man talking. Whoever does not miss this inspirational milk when he's away from it, even for a few hours, is better off dead. The mouth that knows what is good for itself, have this one on me!' He drained his cup into his mouth and ceremoniously held it out for a refill.

'About those bodies, did the Japs have to hang them up?' Niba asked. 'I mean, they were dead. So why not just leave the bodies on the ground and go away?'.

'To create fear in the enemy camp, I suppose?' asked Ndamgu.

'Yes. They wanted to discourage us from chasing them as they retreated.'

'From what I know about the Japanese, it was never part of their culture to treat captured soldiers as war prisoners,' said Moka. 'They saw no reason for that kind of civility. They were said to do horrible things to prisoners, including using them for target practice. Am I correct, soldier?'

'Definitely. We were always reminded that Japs didn't have the culture of taking prisoners of war. There are things you see and hear at war that you cannot repeat to anyone. They stay with you and haunt you all your life and bog you down. You can't say what you did yourself, and you keep asking yourself, for example, if you should have shot that man or let him stay alive.'

Ayonchugu placed his elbows on his knees and supported his head with both hands. His facial muscles contorted. Everyone including Bishwing was silent.

'By the time the big rains came in '44 the Japs were losing the war. They were short on supplies and the roads were bad. The rivers were full and they were getting drowned in them. We dared not drink water from the rivers, so they gave us tablets to put in all water before drinking it. We were shooting down their remaining planes; their over-ambitious and foolhardy Janar Sokomoto had abandoned them. Their best exit routes from the Imphal were cut off.'

'What's Imphal?' asked Bishwing.

'Did you ever listen to the BBC?' asked Tachum.

'Well, the Imphal is the place where we beat the Japs decisively. Some of their troops were left behind to carry out suicide attacks on us, while the bulk of them were retreating. They had respect neither for their own lives nor for ours. We happened on Japs sitting in hidden holes dug along the highway, carrying bombs to detonate in a suicide blast when our tanks rolled above them. They treated their own exhausted soldiers like animals. Instead of letting them die, or letting us capture them alive, they bayoneted them to death.'

'At least, it saved them some bullets,' said Bishwing.

Ayonchugu shook his head vigorously, as if doing so would get some of the horrible memories to fall off like drops of water from his hair.

'Crucifixion Day was one of the worst days I witnessed. Terrible! Terrible! What a day!' exclaimed Ayonchugu.

No one dared to ask him what Crucifixion Day was. They knew vaguely about one Crucifixion Day, and the happenings of that day were chilling enough.

'You boys were surely better off than other soldiers, at least in one aspect,' said Atewele. 'The climate in Boma is similar to the one here, isn't it?'

Ayonchugu shook his head in disagreement. 'It was similar perhaps to that of the forest region, which we from the highlands find quite unfriendly. We spent a lot of time in the heart of the jungle, hacking our way through it. There was no better definition of a jungle than the one in Boma. It was thick, impenetrable, dark and treacherous. It was as nauseating as life in a can of rotten fish and made breathing a revolting act. Stagnant black water teeming with vicious life was everywhere underfoot. It could rise by the hour and drown you if you were unlucky to be at the wrong place in the heart of the rainy season, when the gloomy skies opened and poured an unabating avalanche of warm tears from one dawn to the following dawn for weeks.'

Ayonchugu paused for breath. His good eye was half-closed, like the bad one. His mind was thousands of miles away. 'The jungle in Boma breeds mosquitoes the size of butterflies. They swarm over you and sink their wicked fangs deep into your skin. And the leaches! They are long and love sweet fresh African blood!'

From the women's side of the compound came the sound of singing and dancing. The only accompanying instrument to the music was the *pfeng*; a powerful puff of air sent into the bamboo cylinder produced a deep hooting sound.

'Why are the women singing that twin song?' asked Atewele to no one in particular.

'Sometimes they do that to invite twins into the family,' said Ndamgu. 'Did Nyarong tell you he'd seen twins coming?'

'No. I'll go over and see what they are up to,' Ayonchugu said, brightening up as he left the room.

Everyone relaxed in relief when they saw Ayonchugu get out of the mood the recollections of the war had brought upon him.

'He's a strange man,' said Moka. 'I've met some ex-soldiers and all they do is brag about their exploits. You would think they were out there on an adventure trip.'

'He rarely talks about the war,' said Ndamgu. 'You should have seen him when he first walked into me one cold morning. I said to myself, well, I've never heard of a ghost killing someone. It took me all my manliness and the sound of his boots not to run away.'

'He must have looked quite frightful then?' Niba asked.

'He did. But the moment he talked to me, I realised that

he was not a ghost but a despondent young man needing some warmth and shelter. I invited him home.'

The singing had lost some of its coordination and the women were heard laughing louder and louder.

'I think we should go over and see the baby now,' suggested Moka to Atewele.

The two men drained their glasses, got up and left the room. They sauntered over to the room where the women were dancing. Ayonchugu was at the centre of the amusement that was consuming the room. He was standing in front of two women who were each carrying a baby. One was Mengen's and the other was Matalina's. The women were teasing him because he was not able to say immediately which of the children was his.

'Hey hey hey!'

'Hooey!'

'Hey hey hey!'

'Hooey!'

'What's his fine, women?' Manyi asked aloud.

'He shall not go near baby's mother for five years!' suggested Matalina.

'He shall baby-sit for one month!' said Enanga.

'He must place here in front of us a big calabash of palm wine and a live chicken!' Nawain decreed.

Ayonchugu scratched his head and smiled comically. 'The wine you will get now. The chicken...can you ladies wait until the next market day?'

'No! Now!' said Manyi, who obviously was the spokesperson of the women. 'And here comes the HM! Let him help his friend. Tell us HM, which of these is yours? There's a fine if you can't tell immediately.'

Moka stared from one baby to the other.

'The HM is taking longer than he should. Women, what's his fine?' asked Manyi.

'Wait a moment, please,' said Moka. 'This is my son,' pointing to one of the babies.

'He got it right, but he must pay for taking too long. His fine, women?' asked Manyi in an up strung but merry voice.

'Hey hey hey!'

'Hooey!'

'Hey hey hey!'

'Hooey!'

'He shall not undo Missis' wrapper for three years!'

'He shall change baby's nappies for one month!'

'He shall place here in front of us a crate of imported beer!'

When the fines were paid, the women let the men go. They returned to the men's room. Food was about to be served and the men were washing their hands. The taboo-bearing parts of the chicken were placed in front of Ndamgu.

CHAPTER FOURTEEN

Letters across borders

That night Ayonchugu's mind was invaded by memories of the war. He got up from the bed and sat down by the Tilley lamp and thought about his closest wartime comrades. In the sands of Northeast Africa and in his short stay in the Middle East, he had formed bonds with men of all climes, but he had not held on to them in the fore of his heart as he had held on to the bonds that were formed and nurtured in the puerile, unpredictable battlefields of the Arakan, the march on the Imphal, and later, the pursuit of retreating Japanese forces. He had tried to bury deep down the memories of the war. This day, a hole had been drilled through his mental amour, and everything was vivid again, and he felt like he had just returned from the battlefield. He picked up his pen on an impulse and started writing.

24th May, 19..

My good friend Gifty,

I greet you! When you receive this letter I am very happy because it means you are alive and me too. Who else is there alive with you who was at the war in Abyssinia and Boma? What about those brave boys Koffi, Kwaku, Yaba, and Govina? Did they all return well to home in Gold Coast? I have so much sorry in my heart for Ada, Ekaw, Kwame, Mustapha and Afia who died in front of us in Naga Hills. The bullet they received from Japanese enemy was for us to stay alive. I remember them every day with pain in my heart.

Some of my people played tactics against me and said I died at war. Then a prince Ajong took my wife and killed my child. They took my land. My people say that evil things always happen in twos. To me evil happened in fours and fives. Enemy set fire to my house and it all burnt. I knew the people. I could fight them, but for me the war was finished. I went to a small village far away and started another life. But peace is hard to find anywhere. I fought another short war with neighbour village. We won, but I nearly lost my leg because of arrow wound. My leg which bullet did not touch in the big war!

My people say that plenty time, even bad things can lead to good things. The girl that put medicine on the leg to make it well is now my new wife. She is a good woman and we have a boy baby. His name is Nkahfi. That mean new light in my language.

I am not sure where my country is going. My papa worked for German with no pay. Now for English, we work. We fought. But it was bad market. The French are just over the mountains on the other side where I have my mother, a brother and cousins I don't know if I will ever see them again. They are crying every day because they have built many-many prisons and the gendarmes and DO's are wicked. Those Vichy people sold the war and the world to the enemy. Just think what would have happened if our brothers did not support Free France! And if many sojas from French Cameroun did not fight with us in Boma! The pay our brothers get is prison and gendarmes and hard labour. We on this side are not real British Nigeria, but we go where British Nigeria go. On which day will we have our own country? They have turned us to sheep goats and pulling us away with rope. Is that not how it has been since many hundred years?

Reply my letter please. Are you alive and strong as the bull that fought and won the war for King George?

Your obedient servant,

Ayonchugu

Ayonchugu's letter to Kelechi was shorter. It read thus:

Dear Kelechi,

This is Ayonchugu. I greet you from the Cameroons. Kelechi, son of Igkoegba, the Eagle of Onitsha! The terror of Japs! How are you?

If I get reply to this letter I will be very happy. I have many things to remember about you at war. I remember our small unit. I was our commander, but you and the boys gave me the courage to keep fighting. I could not fail you. So I showed plenty courage like you. I faced Japs I should run away from because I had Fearless Four with me.

Do you remember Crucifixion Day? The thing that those retreating Japs did was worse than Jesus Crucifixion. I sleep and cannot sleep. I scream because I see Crucifixion Day in my dreams. I see the cross Japs made on the ground with human bodies buried upside-down with legs in the air. They wanted us to stop chasing them. But we were angry and followed and wiped out them many. Now, what can I do to forget that day? Tell me please. Should I drink and drunk all the time? I did not go and fight and come back to drink and drunk. My wife she thinks that I am a craze man some nights. But if she was in Boma with us like those nurses she would understand. I want you don't suffer like me.

I live in a quiet village. But sometime is not very quiet even here. I have a new wife and a new-born boy child. My first woman left me in wartime. I am not in any political party. I just work for the village and for my farm. I helped the village to build some bridges like the ones we build sometime in the war. Cars have even passed through my village to the other far side this year.

I want to read your reply. Bye bye Boma warrior!
Your obedient servant,
Ayonchugu

The following day Ayonchugu handed the letters to Moka, who gave them to a visiting priest to post for him in Abakwa. A month later, the headmaster gave him the reply to one of his letters. Ayonchugu was indeed excited, but he was in no mood to read the letter in a hurry. He folded it and slipped it into his raffia-palm fibre bag. That evening he pumped oxygen into the Tilley lamp until it glowed in a warm, gently hissing brightness. He sat on a stool next to the lamp and took out the letter and read it:

12ᵗʰ June, 19..

Dear Number One!

I was overjoyed when I saw your letter. I had dreamt two days before that something good happened to me, and when I saw that envelope from the Cameroons I knew that it was good news from a friend. How glad I am to know that you are fine! It's a pity about your wife and the poor baby. Your story, touching as it is, is reminiscent of a hundred others here in the Gold Coast. Your wife was probably not a bad woman, and only bowed to pressure from the so-called Ajong. I can assure you that she is not happy where she is now.

I remember telling you about the beautiful girl in my class at Achimota College who had promised to be my wife no matter how long she had to wait. She was indeed true to her word. Her father tried marrying her off to a rich illiterate businessman but she refused and stood her ground. In her town, she became an example of how headstrong educated girls could be, and caused many a man not to want to send their female children to school. Unfortunate, isn't it? We are a very happy family. Like you, we have a son, and are expecting a second baby.

Ah! Those brave boys we fought with! I mourn for them and their families every day. I made an effort to contact the families of those I could. I managed to trace Afia's family and went to visit his parents in a town some 300 miles from Accra in January 1947. I met his mother. She was sitting at the entrance to her compound and looking up the road, waiting for the return of her son. Afia had been an only child. She had had complications during delivery and had been unable to bring forth more children. Being a devout Christian, her husband had vowed never to marry another woman. When I introduced myself and said I had known her son closely during the war, she was beside herself. She held me tight and cried for a very long time. Thereafter she sat down and wanted to know every detail about her son. Was he a brave soldier? I told her about the exploits of our company. Did he talk about his family? I told her he did talk about his family all the time, especially about her. She went berserk. Her lamentations shattered me as much as the deaths in the war had done.

I sat there wishing I had never come, although I knew I had done the right thing. She asked me to describe how he died. I told her he was mowed down by Japanese machine guns which we were confronting with Crimean War rifles and bayonets. She asked if we gave him a decent burial. I could not tell her he was ripped into unrecognisable bits by Japanese snipers and left to rot in the jungle, until weeks after, when his scraggy skeleton and maggot infested uniform were scooped and dumped into a shallow grave. I lied. I told her a catholic priest-soldier prayed over his body, which was then buried in the Htaukkyant Cemetery. I gave her Afia's belt buckle and his rosary. She was silent for a long time. Then she said she was absolutely sure he was in heaven. Then she got up and prepared a feast for me. His father who had been absent during my visit came to see me in my new office a few days after. He asked me to tell him the facts as they happened in Burma. When I told him he was indeed horrified, but soon regained his composure, and said it was important for him that the truth, no matter how painful it was, be known, and even cherished.

Since then I have been to see them a number of times and I must say they always treat me like their own son. The mother has stopped expecting to see Afia. She can even afford to smile again.

We were more than 100,000 of us from the Gold Coast who fought Germans, Italians and bladdefaken Japanese. We returned to an exploited and tortured land with a lot of expectations. Yes, the British had promised us better pay. They had promised us decommissioning pay. They had promised us pensions. They had, above all, promised us self-governance. When we won the war, promises had served their purpose. Who were we to hope that those promises made in the heat of war were going to be kept? Yet, we had this blind trust that somehow the powers-that-be were going to listen to us finally and do something for the famished soldiers. For four years we wrote a succession of petitions to the government. It would seem our cries never reached London, or that London was deaf or indifferent, or too busy reconstructing.

Well, I am sure you have heard about what happened in Accra some time ago; the BBC reported it. When we could no longer stand the chasm of being ignored, we decided to take our petition to the Governor General ourselves. I can tell you that although all was calm and orderly, I personally had this ominous feeling that that day was going to end badly. For one thing, it was a daring and unprecedented move. But we were soldiers and ex-soldiers and had guts, and guts are what it took to win the war. A short distance from Christiansborg Castle some of our bravest comrades were shot and killed. Adjetey was among them! Even as I write, the tears are falling from my eyes for his wasted life, for his despondent widow and orphaned children. The Gold Coast lost a great person.

As your people rightly say, misfortune can beget some good. I thank the gods of our beloved but bleeding land that this nation has many valiant sons, and that Kwame Nkrumah rose to the occasion, and even as I scribble you these words, the CPP is winning elections here under a new constitution that recognises our right and ability to govern. I conjecture he would emerge from prison to continue the fight for self-rule.

This brings me to you. In the military we learned that you must keep fighting with all the weapons at your disposal, with all your might, until you understand that you have definitely lost a battle before giving in to the enemy. In my opinion, you gave up what was yours too easily – without a fight at all! You sound so unlike the Ayonchugu I know. I won't let someone take my wife. I won't give up my home and flee to the comfort of the hinterlands. I won't give up a square foot of my land to land-grabbers.

Our continent is fighting a formidable enemy called colonialism and that fight should be led by us. After three hundred years of slavery, I won't sit still and see my country complete a hundred years of subjugation. You have wielded the gun against enemies we once thought were invincible. When you retreat to find your personal comfort among the simple-minded, who is going to fight for the freedom of your people? From what I know, your people are not faring well within the commonwealth of Nigerian provinces and the Cameroons. Simply put, I doubt that you would ever be accepted as Nigerians, who themselves are still struggling to define who they are. You do not have to go where Nigeria goes. You do not have to go where the Colonial Government wants to take you, if that place is not an independent nation where the shackles of colonialism – the despicable remnants of the faeces that slavery was – are still allowed to hang onto your anus.

When you and I were about to face Japs and renegade Burmese, De Gaul announced the so-called 'new deal' for French colonies. It now turns out this was only window dressing to get your brothers 'on the other side of the mountain to fight. Today, while Senghor is still mourning beneath the rainbow of peace, it is scandalous that the corvée labour and the despicable Indigénat are still carrying on there, in a disguised and repackaged form, albeit. In strict legality, Kamerun has never been a colony of any nation! When will you come together to fight the good fight? Will Kamerun remain a divided and weakened people because a whimsical shuffling of papers at the League of Nations refused to acknowledge your right to single nationhood?

I loved you like a brother. We owed our lives to the sacrifices made for one another. Wake up from slumber! We made the sacrifice of blood to win that war. Now is the time to take freedom to our people. There is no war back home that you can't fight. I am sorry, but your war is not over yet!

I wish to read from you telling me how far your nation has gone towards self-determination and that you are living up to the meaning of your name and shaping history rather than letting it take an uncharted course.

I remain yours-in-arms,
Kafui Gifty

Ayonchugu read the letter slowly many times over. He sat back in his chair and closed his eyes. After some time, he reached into his military bag and dug out a pencil and started underlining parts of the letter.

That night Ayonchugu slept badly. He heard every cry of the baby next door and the lullabies its mother sang to make it sleep. Gifty's letter had provoked further memories of the war, and they came welling up, threatening to drown him in their swell.

He dozed off for a brief spell, only to be besieged by nightmares. His mind was playing games with him. It took him back to the thick forests of Burma, where every step ahead was a possible step towards death and staying on the spot was not any safer; he was transported to the wide expanses of the North, where the sands of Ethiopia, Libya and Egypt were as treacherous as the stormy seas of the Pacific, and where the spectre of Rommel and an inspired Afrikakorps supremacist army repeatedly awed the allied troops until their demise at El Alamein. His mind whisked him into a trench in an unknown location, where he felt suffocated by the acrid odour of gun powder and smoke from shelling and mortaring and revolted by the raw, nauseating smell of blood. His head was exploding from the noise of heavy artillery and the rattling and crackling of machine guns. He looked around and saw only death, not a single soul stirred in the knee-deep mud. His ghostly hand tried feeling for his head but it was not there. He felt light and drifted up and out of the trench as if his spirit was going out of him to take an astral walk in Armageddon. He floated like an invincible bird over the battlefield, taking in the spoils of the day in a daring flight. He saw white limbs hanging on black bodies, and then white, black and brown hands holding out to one another in the last spasms of death from bullets which knew neither race nor continent of origin. He swooped down fearlessly on enemy lines, bringing death with him, and felt an intense excitement as he sprayed bullets into their shattered ranks, while the survivors responded ineptly with fire that zipped harmlessly through his insuperable spirit.

He was getting even more worked up in a display of hypnic jerks when his mind told him dead men do not fire guns, and he suddenly felt heavy and crashed onto the ground like a parachutist whose gear had not opened on the drop-down.

He opened his eyes and peered at Mengen standing beside him. She was rocking the baby gently and looking at him with sleep-deprived eyes.

'You are making noises again in your sleep. The baby can't sleep.'

He mumbled a few unintelligible excuses and yawned widely and loudly without bothering to cover his mouth. As she returned to her room, he got up and made himself a cup of tea.

Outside, there was a raging windstorm which threatened to uproot every plant in its wake. He could hear at least five banana plants going down in heavy heaps in spite of the precaution he had taken to support them with bamboo poles. Why did storms rage only when crops were half-way through the growth cycle? He knew what he would find outside in the morning – uprooted plants and plants tilted in diagonal positions, plucked immature fruits strewn under avocado, mango, orange, pawpaw and kola nut trees. Homeless bedraggled animals would be crouched in nooks, drenched and shivering, waiting for the rays of the sun to revive their dampened spirits. The devastation would be the morose subject of conversations. Women would be out on the rugged and slippery paths leading to their farms to see how much of their labour had not been in vain; there would be talk about witches having been on the rampage. There might even be a few outright accusations, which the likes of Nyarong would confirm or refute.

'The skies of Burma must be cramped with vicious witches and wizards who cause the monsoons,' thought Ayonchugu and gave a burst of solitary laughter, cut short when he remembered the baby in the next room.

He lay in bed and thought about some of the things Gifty had written in his letter. *I would not let someone take my wife.* Should he have gone out to retrieve Ngelem? That to him was out of the question. But was it not rather strange that she had been able to face up to her father in her choice of a husband, and then given in so easily to his adversary later on? Should he have investigated the circumstances under which she caved in to Ajong? *Your wife was probably not a bad woman.* News about his death came later when she was already carrying on with Ajong, as the story went. That definitely made her a bad woman. Did he consider just how much power the fon and his son held over the people and how abusive they could get in the use of that power? Would he have fought to get her back if he had found out that she had indeed been manipulated into marrying Ajong? No. No? A bothersome tiny voice kept hinting that he had been brash in his judgement of Ngelem.

And what about the land issue? The utter helplessness of his people was disarming. Land traditionally belonged to the village as a whole. But it was under the custody of the fon, whose messengers on his orders, doled it out to men who were deemed deserving of it. Traditional land was never bought and sold because, like humans, it was widely available and yet priceless. On many occasions the fon had refused to share land, and had instead cultivated it for his own personal profit.

He was in a dilemma over the land issue. The disputed land was handed down from his grandmother. Her spirit would not rest peacefully until hearthstones had been set up and used in a kitchen dedicated to her on that land. Ayonchugu knew too well toward whose side the Colonial Government was going to lean if he started a fight with the fon and Ajong. That very Colonial Government had made it clear that they were not going to support ex-soldiers on matters of land confiscated from them during their time at war.

No, he did not fight to retrieve what was his from Ajong. At the time, his disillusionment had been so total that he felt inept. His brother's drunkenness had not only disheartened but had also disgusted him; he had felt heavy-hearted at the deprivations in which his extended family was living. Thereafter, his anger rose until he felt a rage that could only be assuaged by blood. And he would have spilled blood the day his house went up in flames. A man's house was sacrosanct. Thankfully, the war had taught him to keep his calm and listen to orders and react sensibly when under fire.

Military discipline had deterred him from using his gun; he knew he would end up in the rotten dungeons. He wanted a life after the years of war. Ngonibi was his home now, and he was happy with the way things were going for him.

Gifty's words ran through his mind. *When you retreat to find your personal comfort among the simple-minded, who is going to fight for the freedom of your people?* Was he satisfied with the way things were going in his nation? He had a soldier's mentality, which required him to keep away from frontline politics. He was not politically indifferent, though. He could have militated in the KNDP, which had a cell in Ngonibi, but he was not inspired enough to do so. He preferred staying open to ideas and to voting for candidates who presented the best programmes in his judgement. At that moment, apart from the Communists, there were very few differences in what politicians stood for anyway. The quest of the day was devolution.

More than one hundred thousand men from the Gold Coast! An entire generation! How many of those men made it back alive like him? That information, thought Ayonchugu, would be available with the Catholic Mission School headmaster, who knew everything that could be known.

CHAPTER FIFTEEN

A friend in need

The Catholic School was nestled in a flat piece of land that had been carved out of a flourishing forest of kola nut and acacia trees. The block which housed the headmaster's office and the adjoining storeroom and workshop was built of stone and roofed with corrugated metal sheets. It sat apart from, and adjacent to, the classrooms. The rest of the school was a single six-room structure built with sun-dried mud bricks and roofed temporarily with thatch. The building was plastered with white clay, which gave it a light-grey hue and exuded a semblance of modernity within the surroundings of virgin vegetation. In front of the classroom block was an open field, wide enough to contain two football pitches. Where the field ended was a beautiful hedge of marigold, behind which loomed the roof of the inevitable Catholic Church building, and behind this, the new graveyard.

Behind the school building was a large garden tended by pupils. A little path by the garden led to the homes of the headmaster and the catechist. Trees covered the rest of the back of the property, extending to the nearest houses which were located about a mile away.

Ayonchugu came to see the headmaster towards closing time. The school was dead silent; not a single soul was about. He found him in his office, seated in a straight-back chair behind a simple wooden table, and poring meticulously over registers. Ayonchugu entered the office, stood and waited for the headmaster to acknowledge his presence. Mr J. Moka looked up briefly, adjusted his glasses and pointed to one of two seats that had been squeezed into the narrow office. Ayonchugu sat down and took out Gifty's letter and started looking over the words he had underlined. The school bell, which was a discarded piece of metal hung from a pole and hit with another piece of metal, sounded the end of the day, and in a chorus all the children shouted out 'Closing!'

Ayonchugu looked outside as the pupils spilled forth from their classes onto the open field, screaming, chasing and taunting one another. Less than half of the pupils were in the prescribed sky blue shirt for boys and gowns for girls. One of the bigger girls who was scantily clad in what remained of a colourless worn-out dress, was having a tough time with a handful of boys who were persistently pestering and trying to touch her. She made desperate efforts to ward them off but her agitation only spurred on the urchins. A teacher carrying a cane appeared, and the boys took to their heels. One of the boys produced a football made from freshly-tapped latex and kicked it high up into the air. A bare-footed crowd of excited pupils chased it and the lucky one caught it and equally kicked it as high up as possible. The chase went screaming out of view, and Ayonchugu, whose mind had been transported back to his own school days, returned to his list of words just as the headmaster finished working on the registers and gave him his attention.

'Thanks for waiting. Are your baby and its mother fine?'

'Yes, HM, they are quite fine, even though he keeps us awake all night. He never seems to have enough milk. He only stops crying when breastfeeding.'

The two men had a good mastery of the local language and conversed alternately in English and Binibi.

'That's a really good sign that he's healthy,' said Moka. 'It's bad when they refuse to breastfeed and cry for no apparent reason at all.'

'I'm getting used to his cries, though,' Ayonchugu said. 'Bishwing says a sleepless night is the prize I pay for having my wife in an adjoining room.'

'He would be shocked to learn that my wife and I and the baby sleep in the same bed,' said Moka. 'The little man has a cot but never wants to sleep in it.'

'I suppose he and his mother are fine too?' Ayonchugu asked.

'They're very fine. Is there anything I can do for you today?'

'Oh yes. I have been reading the letter you gave me

yesterday. I wish to find out the meaning of some new words I came across.'

'That would be fine. Do you wish to use the dictionary or discuss the words?' Moka asked.

'I think it would be better if we discussed them. But I don't wish to take up your time. So I'll go for the dictionary.'

'Don't speak like my former Schools Inspector,' said Moka. 'You don't have to worry about taking up my time.'

'Here, read the letter. I have underlined the parts that are not clear to me.' Ayonchugu handed the letter to Moka.

'Are you sure you want me to read it?' asked Moka.

'Yes. It's from a friend of mine in the Gold Coast. We fought together in the war.'

'I see,' said Moka, who adjusted his glasses and started reading the letter, giving away not a single reaction until he finished reading. He sat back and took in a deep breath. Then he looked at the letter and read aloud from it. "Your story, touching as it is, is reminiscent of a hundred...." He is saying that your sad story is similar to those of many ex-soldiers.'

'Understood. There was this Lancashire boy in our regimen who shot himself because he learned in a letter from his wife that she had left for America with another man. He had filled a whole exercise book with poems about how he liked her.'

'You mean how he loved her,' said Moka.

'It is the same thing in my language.'

'In mine too, but I'm afraid not in the English language,' said Moka. 'Love is stronger than like, and between a man and a woman, it is passionate.'

'Let me tell you a story. I met a nurse – a sergeant by rank – during the war. Well, I was on board a ship from Mombasa to Colombo when I first met her. She treated me for sea-sickness. I happened on her again in Colombo, a beautiful seaside town from where things were put together for the Southeast Asia Command. We were waiting for transportation to the front, and I had some weeks to spend as I liked. In Colombo, I happened on the same nurse on the beach and she recognised me. Whatever a lady like her was doing alone on the beach only she knew. I was very excited when we got talking and she said that she liked me. The following day I spent a whole evening hanging around the beach. She came too. We met a number of times on that beach, although the unspoken agreement was that no one knew we were meeting there. One day she said she loved me. I was exhilarated. I told her I would like to marry her and take her to my country at the end of the war. She asked if I would like to be a polygamist. I told her that polygamy was the norm in my village; my wife would be so proud to have a lady like her for a companion. She said that it was so sweet of me to want to marry her for my second wife. That evening we consummated our union on the beach. We met a few more times and she kept telling me she loved me. And then all so suddenly, she stopped showing up.

'I hung around the beach for four days. Finally, it was time for us to move to the war front, and I decided to go to her hospital and talk to her. When I arrived there and asked for her, she sent a Kenyan soldier to tell me to drop her shopping at the usual place. I went down to the beach that evening and there she was. She told me in a voice I hardly recognised as hers never to come to the hospital again. I said I would never have gone there if she had come to the beach. I told her I was heading to the front, and she said that was fine because she too had been transferred to another hospital in Ragama. Then she asked me to leave. I said we still had our future to talk about. She ordered me to leave immediately. I heard a noise behind me. I looked over my shoulder and saw three navy boys approaching. Next thing I knew she was screaming that I was stalking her. The men came on me like bulls. I could have taken out two, but not three. I only regained consciousness at midnight and managed to crawl back to meet my company. To think that at the time I thought she loved me and wanted to marry me! For a long time afterwards the word made me sick!'

'It must have been very painful for you. There was so much you did not understand. You surely learned your lesson the hard way. Back to your friend's letter. He writes: "Her father tried marrying her off to an illiterate business man." The man could not read and write.'

'Oh! Oh! I thought illiterate meant he was suffering from an illness,' said Ayonchugu, laughing at his own ignorance.

'Actually, illiteracy is an illness, isn't it?'

'Indeed?' said Ayonchugu.

'Let's look at it this way,' said Moka. 'When you are ill you are suffering from a physical disability. When you are illiterate you are suffering from a disability in your head, an intellectual disability. And like physical illness it can be cured.'

'Through learning at school?'

'Through learning. At school and out of school.'

Ayonchugu shook his head in accord and said, 'In a way I'm ill right now and you are my doctor.'

'As you say, in a way, yes.'

'And of course you are also a doctor for all the children in this school.'

'Yes and no.'

'How is that?'

'I believe you understand the "yes" part. I impart knowledge to them. "No" because they are young and in school and are following the normal developmental route they have to follow in order to acquire learning. I will describe your friend Bishwing as an illiterate, but not his seven-year old son who just started Infants One and can't yet read and write beyond his ABC. He will get there when the time comes.'

On and on went the explanations and discussions thereof. When they got to the part about the Crimean War rifles, Ayonchugu said, 'I never heard of those kinds of rifles in the war.'

'I think what he means here is that you were fighting with outdated weapons,' Moka explained. 'The Crimean War was fought about a hundred years ago. It was the last ancient war, or the first modern war, depending on how you look at it.'

'Well, we used Lee-Enfield rifles. I used to think ours were the best guns until we confronted Italians with their M38 Carcano bolt-action rifles fitted with bayonets and discovered that the man behind the gun counted even much more than the gun he was carrying.'

'That was in Ethiopia, I suppose?' Moka asked.

'Abyssinia,' replied Ayonchugu.

'It's the same place,' Moka said. 'The real Abyssinia was by far larger, though.'

'Was it? And I hear it had a civilisation older than Egypt's?' Ayonchugu asked.

'It not only had a very ancient civilization; in fact, it was a world power in biblical times. Haile Selassie whom you boys returned to the throne was from a dynasty that had ruled uninterrupted for over a thousand years.'

'I didn't know that,' Ayonchugu said. 'I now see why the British wanted him back on the throne so badly.'

'Not *so badly*,' Moka said. 'I would say in spite of themselves. They could have gone fighting sooner. There were issues related to the Suez Canal and Germany's threat to the entire Empire.' The headmaster stopped talking, took a deep breath and returned to reading through the letter.

Ayonchugu closed his eyes and leant back in his chair in recollection for a few moments. 'We were lucky Italian troops faced us with only guns and bombs. They had sprayed poison gas on whole villages and wiped out settlements. We found thousands and thousands of skeletons baking in the hot sands, behind endless miles of barbed wire. It was the same scenario in Libya as in Abyssinia. Whom were they going to rule after the extermination? Sands and date palms?'

'Italy wanted to boost its national ego. Armed with lessons from the First World War, Mussolini and his butchers had their opportunity to take revenge for Adowa. Can you imagine what a disgrace it had been for them to be beaten hands down by Abyssinian troops? They were taking no chances this time.'

'It was horrible,' said Ayonchugu, shaking his head.

'Libya had to be subdued by whatever means before they could take on Ethiopia,' Moka explained. 'In spite of modern weapons and savagery only equalled in the dark ages, it took them sixteen years.'

'The League of Nations opposed that war, didn't they?'

'The League of Nations was a sham,' declared Moka.

Ayonchugu's knowledge about what the League of Nations did or did not do was limited mostly to its role in the dismembering and parcelling out of his own fatherland and he did not dare an opinion lest it be flawed. He knew a lot about guns, so he talked about them.

'When we finally beat the Italians, it was not just the

guns,' said Ayonchugu. 'It takes much more than guns to fight a war. It takes a spirit behind the gun. It was our determination and the genius of our commanders.'

'And the officials who drew up strategies far away from the battlefields, don't forget,' said Moka.

'Yes, officials in London. The Italians never had real control over the entire territory, you know. I was happy when we got the Mafiosos – twenty thousand of them surrendered to three thousand of us in Beda Fomm.'

'I remember hearing about that on the radio. At first I thought it was just propaganda.'

'Commonwealth troops hemmed them in on their retreat from Benghazi. They tried desperately for three days to break through our lines, but we just held on until they gave up.'

'That was a feat indeed.'

'That was in just one instance. In another, the 11th Army overcame eleven thousand Italians and took five thousand guns. I wanted to put my bullets in them but our commander forbade us.'

'There was no way they could, even with the support of Rommel, beat the combined forces of the Commonwealth. Italy thrives on the glories of ancient Rome. Look at this map of Europe on the wall.' Moka used a long ruler to point out Italy. 'The country looks lame. A lame bird's leg.'

Ayonchugu wondered silently how a country could look lame. Well, he thought, it was a quality of the highly educated to see these things. That Lancashire boy who wrote a lot had a hundred ways of saying how he liked or loved his wife. At one time when he was really exalted he read out loud one of his lines in which he said although he was so far away from home facing raging desert storms, to not love her was as inconceivable as saltless ocean water....

'When it comes to military prowess, Italy has never won a war except by use of the utmost cruelty against poorly armed villagers. Fascists!' Moka sighed, shaking his head and twisting his mouth in distaste.

'You should have seen the 11th Army when we marched into Addis Ababa to reinstate Emperor Haile Selassie,' Ayonchugu said, a proud tinge in his voice. 'Rommel's army was in tatters in the desert. Wingate was with us. Everything was grandiose and colourful. We knew for sure that day that colonisation would soon end everywhere.'

'Your victory was worth celebrating,' said Moka. 'I have not learned the history of ancient Abyssinia. I guess it has the same hidden mysteries as Egypt.'

'Egypt, ancient or modern, to me is forever mysterious. After reinstating Haile Selassie we travelled there for a short holiday, and what did I not see! It was a thrill to see the tombs that those ancient white men built for themselves. You know, some were nearly as big as the rock from which Ngonibi got its name.'

Moka sat back in his chair and studied Ayonchugu. 'You know, I envy you a lot for having seen such places,' he said. 'When you looked at the pyramid with a human face what did you see? African, European or Asian?' Moka asked.

'African,' Ayonchugu said. 'The guardian of the tombs, we were told by our guide.'

'He is not the sentry that they would make you believe he is. He is a divinity. We pray to our ancestors to watch over us. That's what that spirit is doing there – representing ancestors. Inside those tombs lay his kinsmen. The human make-up of Egypt has been muddled up by interracial breeding, migrations, extermination of the true natives and thousands of years of pillage. Researchers are keeping the facts hidden. Their history books have done the rest.'

'Hmm. I never stopped wondering what happened to the spirit's nose,' said Ayonchugu.

'That appendage was probably too large and too broad to withstand the forces of distortion,' said Moka, knowing full well Ayonchugu did not understand him. There was so much clse he did not understand, and he was not going to learn everything in one day.

All so suddenly a crash of heavy rain-drops pelted the corrugated roof and a gusty wind sent leaves flying in through the open door; papers flew off the HM's table, and the wall maps flapped about.

'The rains this season are falling on a violent note,' said Ayonchugu. He got up and partly closed the door, but as soon as he released it, the wind pushed it back and it banged loudly against the wall.

'I'll have to rush home before the downpour,' said Moka, retrieving the dislodged papers and putting them in a drawer. 'I'll spare Magdalena the trouble of bringing me an umbrella. Come home with me. There's a basket of something waiting.'

'Thank you. Can I come tomorrow?' Ayonchugu asked.

'Yes. Here, have your letter.'

'It will get wet in the rain. Give it to me tomorrow.'

'Come at closing time,' Moka said. 'We are having a meeting tomorrow with the School Inspector.'

Ayonchugu stepped out of the HM's office and tarried under the eaves, undecided whether to go home in the rain or wait. The children were still screaming after the football from one end of the open field to the other, not giving a care about the rain. Ayonchugu thought about the long waits in the wet mosquito-infested forests of Burma. In comparison, this was going to be a leisure walk; better get home wet and sit beside a warm hearth with a cup of steaming palm wine than stay here waiting indefinitely for the rain to cease. He stepped into the rain and walked briskly home.

CHAPTER SIXTEEN

To school or not to school?

The inspection was still not over. Ayonchugu hung about the grounds and waited. In spite of its modest buildings, the school was always well kept. On this day it was impeccable. Ayonchugu went around the buildings admiring flowers and taking in their beautiful smells. Not a dot of weed could be seen in the flower beds, and the blossoms danced brightly in the transient rays of the sun which preceded heavy rains during this season. He tried to remember the names of the different plants. There were lantanas, marigolds, gentians, daisies, lilies and white and red roses. At his school in Libah children loved eating the rose buds just before they exploded into delicate chubby flowers. That was until the school administration got wind of, and staved off the practice by giving twenty strokes of the cane on the suspended bottom of the first pupil who was caught in the act.

He came to a bed of plants whose names he did not know in English. It amused him that these plants which were found normally in the wild and better known for their medicinal value than for their decorative presence were being grown in the school as 'flowers'.

He came to the lone *ananah* tree at a Y-junction, the tail of which was the path that led out of the rear of the campus. This was a sacred plant. It was not an eye-catcher. Its leaves were a dull green and its rough-skinned aubergines were uncomfortable to the touch. It was to be found at road junctions leading into the village and in all places considered sacred. He could still see traces of the medicine that was sprinkled around the tree and across the roads three times a year to neutralise evil forces that were up and about or attempting to enter the village. This was the *mitiee*. Little baskets containing pupils' lunch were hanging from the branches of the *ananah* tree like large birds' nests.

As he went about the school, nostalgia set in. His life as a village farmer was eventful and productive enough, but not very fulfilling. The one thing that worried him was that he was older than most of the teachers in Ngonibi and felt it would be ridiculous to go back and sit in Standard Four or Five with children. He planned to get advice from Moka.

Ayonchugu wandered towards the school farm. He stood behind a hedge which was reinforced with bamboo fencing, and admired plants flourishing within. He saw several varieties of vegetables competing to outgrow one another in the well-tended garden. The farm was irrigated by a network of well-channelled rivulets of sparkling water that dribbled ceaselessly. On all corners of the garden were massive heaps of compost manure formed from the abundantly available grass and leaves the children heaped together during gardening time. Ayonchugu stood there for a while, remembering how in such a school farm he had learned to take an interest in growing crops.

'Are you taking a stroll?' a female voice said.

Ayonchugu came out of his reveries and turned to look at Matalina, who was carrying a basket of vegetables on her head.

'I came to see your husband but he's still at work. I'm hanging about waiting for him to finish.'

'Then come over to the house. I will send someone to tell him you are waiting.'

'Thank you, Missis.'

Apart from her husband, everyone else called her Matalina or Missis, appellations imposed upon her by village women. As they walked leisurely towards the house Matalina said, 'Inspection day is a very important day for the school. The new inspector is even more critical than the British one who came last year, I am told.'

'Really? Where's he from?' Ayonchugu asked.

'He is from Libah. I hear he checks right down to the number of pieces of chalk used by each teacher. He will also come over to the school farm.'

'I may know him if he's from my village. I'm sure he'll give a good report of the school. It looks really tidy.'

'I am sure he will. My husband has always received the best commendations. You know, this is his third year as HM. Since he came here things have only been getting better and better. Did you see the number of children that came to Infants One this year?'

'Yes,' Ayonchugu answered. 'Bishwing who was a sceptic even sent his son to school. The other day, he said that he sent him there because the boy was too lazy for anything else.'

'Don't mind him. He was just trying to be funny. Do you know that he encouraged so many others to come here too? Do you know Taghen?' Matalina asked.

'The disabled man at Ntah who weaves bags?'

'Yes. That's the one. He brought in his two children last week. Then there's Beri the widow, who keeps refusing to remarry. She brought in her only daughter too. Atewele says she already can count to a hundred after one week only.'

'She must be a little genius,' Ayonchugu said.

'Well, she already knew how to count to any number in Binibi. I guess she just had to put English words to what she already knew.'

'You must be right about that. But wouldn't it save her a lot of trouble if she just learned to read and write in Binibi?'

'And where would that take her? English is the language used by all educated people in their work.'

Ayonchugu walked on silently with her, wondering about what it would be like if schools taught Binibi and government conducted all affairs in Binibi.

'And do you know that the drop-out rate has reduced?' Matalina asked. 'In the last two years only eight girls have left to go and babysit. Three have left to get married in the Coast. That girl...mm...Lembi, left just three days ago. I tried to talk her out of it but she said her parents had already taken their decision. She was carrying around the man's photograph. She kept talking about the gramophone and the radio that were on a table beside him.'

'She had never met him before, had she?' Ayonchugu asked.

'No. He left the village to work in the rubber plantations just after the war,' Matalina said.

'I pity her already,' Ayonchugu said. 'She will be an unhappy bride when she discovers that the things in the picture belonged to the photographer.'

'I even told her about friends of mine who ran away from the Coast and returned to the village because life as a plantation labourer's wife there was unbearable. But who has ever known a girl in love with a fancy man to be reasonable?'

The HM's house was a rectangular three-bedroom house built of sun-dried earth bricks and plastered both inside and outside. It had a metal roof and the ceiling was made of bamboo. They arrived home and Ayonchugu sat on a wooden reclining chair outside while Matalina went into the kitchen. He heard her instruct the babysitter to take information to her husband that Ayonchugu was waiting at home. She came out with the baby and sat down on a low stool and started breastfeeding him.

'It is indeed a wonder how God does things,' said Ayonchugu. 'The resemblance between my son and yours is so striking.'

'I think people are exaggerating a little. I guess all babies resemble one another. Let's wait and see how they develop in a few months.'

'You are right. Let's wait and see.'

'For how long have you been married?' Ayonchugu asked.

'Five years. I understand you were married before?'

'Yes. Before I left for the war. She left me for another man when I was out there.'

'That must have been very sad for you,' Matalina said, looking at him sympathetically.

'It was,' Ayonchugu concurred.

'It's a good thing it happened sooner than later. A woman who can't respect herself in the absence of her husband will not do so even when he's there.'

'I'm glad that I'm married to a good woman who has sealed the mouth of the wounds of my past. You know, I never imagined for once that I could remarry.'

'Indeed? Was it that bad?' Matalina asked.

'It was,' Ayonchugu said. 'Apart from the fighting and killing, I was hurt by my women both at war and after.'

'You knew women at war?'

'I knew one woman. British. In my naivety I thought she loved me. We were going to get married, but she stripped me, got what she wanted and set loose some vicious men on me. I'm lucky I survived their bashing.'

'I am sorry to hear that,' Matalina said.

'That was a long time ago. About ten years ago, I think. The things youth do.'

'How did you meet Mengen?' Matalina asked. 'There is a rumour in the village that her father used charms to make you fall for her.'

'Do you believe it?' Ayonchugu asked.

'Knowing you, I think it is all rubbish talk.'

'Thank goodness if he did charm me. I'm satisfied with her.'

'That is the answer of a balanced-minded man. A man who has been given a love potion would never acknowledge what happened to him.'

'You tell me, how did you meet the HM? Did he charm you?'

'He did not have to at all. He shocked me by choosing me for his wife.'

'Were you that unattractive?' Ayonchugu asked, smiling.

'I will show you something,' Matalina said, getting up. Holding the baby onto her breast with one hand, she went into the house and returned brandishing a picture which she handed to Ayonchugu. He looked at it closely but recognised no one.

'You see this picture of a happy family.' Matalina pointed out the people in the picture as she spoke. 'There is of course the father, and there is the mother of all these ten children. He and Mama were staunch Catholics, and had walked a hundred miles on foot to get married in the twenties in Bojongo. You see all these children, I babysat five of them. He was a modern man. His children wore clean clothes, even on ordinary days, and shoes on Sundays. The day this picture was taken, I was there. Guess why I'm not in this picture.'

'You were not allowed to join in,' Ayonchugu said.

'I was naked. Believe you me, stark naked. Not even a sack cloth on. The big boy in the house treated me like dirt. Don't look so alarmed. He never laid a hand on me because I was too dirty to touch. Guess who the photographer was.'

'Moka, I suppose?' Ayonchugu said.

'Yes,' Matalina said. 'He was standing in for his father, who had taken ill. I could not hide because I had to dress the baby and bring her to the photo session. He took a look at me even as I kept hiding behind the loin cloth with which I had strapped the baby to my back. When Mammy took away the loin cloth to use for this large head scarf you see her wearing here, I once again was stark naked. I have never pitied myself and the plight of my lot more than I did that day. I cried everyday for a long time. Can you imagine how I felt when my father sent for me one day and told me that Moka wanted me for his wife? Foolish and excited as I was, I ran back in a new floral dress to tell my family you see here. The only person who was happy was Papa here and these three children.... The big boy spat on my new dress saying "That is your parting gift!"'

'Your story touches my heart,' said Ayonchugu. 'Moka is indeed a good man. An intelligent man too. I must add that he is a man of good taste.'

'Oh, thank you,' said Matalina with a broad smile. 'You know G. H. Ashamba wanted him to join the KNPP party and he refused. He disagreed with him on his party's stance on the question of the future of the Cameroons.'

'Do you mean the same G. H. Ashamba of the pro-Nigeria movement?' Ayonchugu asked.

'Yes. The man has been here twice to see him,' said Matalina.

'You don't mean it! Right here in this village?'

'Yes. And it's not too long ago when he last came.'

'Aha! I see. It was indeed him that I saw one early morning. What did the HM say?'

'He said neither G. H. Ashamba's, nor Foncha's or

Endeley's parties stood for what he wanted,' Matalina replied.

'And what does he want?' Ayonchugu asked.

'He supports the split from Eastern Nigeria and wants immediate and full independence for the Cameroons.'

'That is a strong stance,' Ayonchugu said.

'It is. G. H. Ashamba thinks that we are too small and too poor to be a country on our own. He thinks it's a choice between joining French Cameroun and Nigeria. And to him, the better option is Nigeria.'

'The KNDP is very strong. It brings together the hinterlands and the coast. What makes him think the people will buy his idea?'

'He says he has a lot of support from the North,' said Matalina. 'He says the disagreement between Foncha's party and Endeley's is proof that there is need for an alternative approach. When he sat there preaching to the HM, I was only thinking about the horrible Igbo traders in Abakwa. When you ask for the price of an item, they force you to buy it irrespective of whether you think the price is good or not. Who wants to be bed partners with them?'

'Apart from him, probably not one reasonable person I know of. He owns many lorries and *mammy wagons* which go to Kumba, Lagos and Onitsha. He is said to have lots of other investments over there. That man can sell his own head for money and power.'

'And for young women. Is his new wife not from Kaduna?'

'He has a new wife then?' Ayonchugu asked.

'Yes. She is said to be younger than his youngest daughter by his third wife.'

'She must be very young then.'

'She's a teenager,' Matalina said. 'She calls him *Baba*. I hear she was a gift from the Sultan of Sokoto.'

'People do say all sorts of things. I'm not surprised that he sees the future of our people only in terms of wealth.'

'He is indeed a sell-out. Just a moment, please. I have to check the pot on the fire.'

'Let me carry the boy,' said Ayonchugu, extending his hands to take him.

Ayonchugu sat carrying the baby and thinking about the politics of the day. Some years after the war, the well-beloved Endeley, whose name was now on the radio every day, had returned from school abroad and become a shining beacon for the people. He had fought an honourable fight to get the people's voice heard in the National Council for Nigeria and the Cameroons. The fight for devolution had started soon after. The result was a government in Gbuea. The Leader of Government Business was now being sung in the lore of the people from one smoking hearth to another, from the creeks of Bakassi right to the mountains of Yola....

'Food is ready,' said Matalina from the kitchen, interrupting Ayonchugu's thoughts. 'Come in and eat something while it is still hot.'

'I think I will wait for the HM. The mouth that eats alone is like the devil's – it never knows the joy or virtue of sharing.'

'True. I hope he returns soon,' Matalina said.

She came out of the kitchen and went about tidying up the already neat but sparsely furnished parlour. She switched on the Hi-Fi radio, and it bailed out High Life music from Radio Calabar.

'You know, your father-in-law came to greet the baby the other day. We were at your house at the time.' She was speaking at the top of her voice so he could hear her.

'Did you say something?' Ayonchugu asked.

'Sorry, I will take down the volume. I said your father-in-law came visiting while we were at your place the other day.'

'That's wonderful. He's not the visiting type. Did he come fortune-telling?'

'No. He brought a gift for the baby. A goat. Just a kid.'

'Ha! He must have a special liking for you or the HM. He hardly comes to my house. Instead, he asked for his due when he was informed that Mengen had given birth to a boy.'

'Has he not been to see your baby?'

'No,' Ayonchugu replied. 'Mengen took the baby to him.'

'Why did he not come to your place?' asked Matalina.

'I don't know. All is settled between us. He only seems to be a bit off-handed. He has always been a strange man, and

Mengen long learned not to expect too much from him.'

'Poor motherless thing. But she's got a good husband.'

'There you go. So Nyarong brought you this kid.'

'Mm. My husband wanted to send it back to him. He said he does not touch things associated with fetishes. I have managed to stop him from returning it. But I'm not so sure he will keep it.'

'You did well not to send it back,' Ayonchugu said. 'It would have been very discourteous.'

'The HM does not seem to understand that quite often. People used to bring lots of chickens to him. He kept refusing to take them. That did not endear him to the villagers.'

'People are very happy when you receive their gifts. After all, they are not bribing him, are they?'

'He says he does not sell his friendship either. They no longer bring him things, though, and he is friendly with everybody.'

'I wish that could be true of that inspector who came in today.' Ayonchugu turned in surprise at the sound of Moka's voice. Moka had overheard Matalina as he and Atewele appeared around the bend from the school. 'Good to see you, Ayo. I'm sorry I kept you waiting.'

'Good to see you, sirs. I think it was not a good idea for me to come today. Has the inspector left?' Ayonchugu asked.

'After he had seen every bit of stray leaf in the school, he chatted for some time, hopped on his bicycle and took off,' said Atewele.

'And did he like the school?' Ayonchugu asked.

'Yes, but he was a very tough customer,' Moka replied. 'He asked to see everything: handicraft workshop, school farm, drinking water source, toilets, and you name it. I thought he was even going to want to see where my wife keeps her firewood.'

'I was hoping you would all come here for a meal,' Matalina said.

'When he was done with the inspection, we spent the next one hour disagreeing on the type of secondary school the mission should open if and when we get the authorization to do so. He thinks that we need colleges that produce very educated people to eventually take over the positions the British are holding.'

'I thought that is exactly what we need?' Ayonchugu asked.

'Yes,' Moka replied.

'What was the disagreement about then?' Ayonchugu asked.

'Have you heard about Lugard and the White Papers on education in the colonies? Of course, not. We have been jumpstarted in Western civilisation, and it will take more than educated men and women to bring about development. It will take innovative thinking, scientific invention, and independent action to bring about meaningful development. Today's education shall be the cause of tomorrow's woes.'

'I'm sure the HM knows best what is good for our people,' said Ayonchugu.

'I'm sure you have a good idea too,' Moka said. 'You were out there in the world. You saw many things. You saw buildings, machines, weapons, medical equipment. The kind of schools we need should be able to educate people to build those same things from scratch. Present-day practice trains us to use things, not make things. We need competent people, not people who are full of a lot of inapplicable information.'

'I see. You have a point,' Ayonchugu said.

'It's so clear that anyone should understand, anyway,' Moka said. 'I don't know why he refused to see my point. Just tell me this. How many former pupils of this school have you seen living in this village?'

'I know the catechist and a few gardeners,' Ayonchugu said.

'Two of our teachers as well,' Atewele chipped in.

Moka nodded and spoke. 'Yet every year so many of them have their GSSC. They then move off to Abakwa, Kumba, Mamfe, Victoria, other big towns and even to the Colony of Lagos.'

'But that's where the jobs are,' said Ayonchugu.

'Agreed,' said Moka. 'They work as house-boys, cooks,

lorry drivers, carriers, gatemen, you name it. A good number remain jobless. Our schools have not taught them useful skills. They can't stay in this village because they can't weave a fibre bag like Chi.'

'Or make a gun like Tachum or Tangang,' Atewele said.

'They can't decorate a calabash like Awemu, or make a better drum than Bishwing or Afunke,' Matalina added.

Moka nodded at the input of the others and carried on. 'They can't tap excellent palm wine like Anwanwen and Ndamgu. The essence of education should be improvement and innovation on existing practices and standards. Education today takes away youth from the village, and does not prepare them for the town.'

'You may find it ridiculous, but I have been thinking about returning to school,' Ayonchugu revealed. 'I may one day have to move out of the village myself.'

'Where would you wish to move to?' asked Atewele.

'Abakwa. I do not want to be too far from my farms.'

Atewele smiled at Ayonchugu's words, but Moka looked at him with interest and said, 'If you really want to have your GSSC, I'm sure you can. Matalina had hers only last year. She studied for three years at home.'

'I started from scratch,' Matalina said. 'From learning how to hold a fountain pen to a-b-c-d, one-two-three, and telling the time.'

'That must have been a feat to perform in three years,' said Ayonchugu.

'Had she taken longer than that, I would have started doubting the HM's credentials,' said Atewele.

'He was very tactful,' Matalina said. 'There were times I was learning without knowing he was teaching. It was amazing how things unravelled once I got the basics. Every day I was learning volumes. I'm still learning. Once my English gets really good, I will go to the teachers training college.'

'That would be one special case where a woman got into marriage to go to school and not the other way around,' said Ayonchugu.

Matalina set out food on a small table by the wall and the

145

three men sat down to eat.

'How soon do you want to start schooling?' Moka asked Ayonchugu.

'As soon as possible.'

'Have you thought this out very well?'

'I've spent years thinking about it. For an ex-soldier, it has taken me rather too long to make a move.'

'And you reached Standard Four when you went to school?' Moka asked.

'Yes.'

'I think you should go into Standard Six now,' Moka said.

'Is that a wise idea?' asked Atewele. 'He has been away from school too long.'

'It would be unwise to have Ayonchugu in as a pupil. If he comes in as staff he should be able to learn while working.'

'You are thinking about recruiting him then?' Atewele asked.

'Yes,' Moka replied. 'But nothing formal. He pays no fees, he receives no salary. Only the staff will know he is a pupil. He comes to school dressed like us; he stays with the staff, and assists us in the classroom with slow learners, giving them the opportunity to achieve. Meanwhile, he's learning all the time. Soldier, what do you think?'

'I like it,' Ayonchugu said with enthusiasm.

'The manager may not like it,' Atewele said. 'He is nearly as fussy as the inspector.'

'He is a new priest. He is British. I will talk to him. I'm absolutely sure he will understand. I've been talking with Ayonchugu. This man is a wealth of resources. Our pupils and our teachers could learn something about his travels and the war from him.'

Atewele nodded but said nothing. 'My idea about teaching,' Moka explained, 'is that experienced people in various fields be brought in as often as possible to teach pupils first hand. These children should be able to learn how to make drums from Bishwing, and pots and spoons from Tachum.'

Atewele did not look impressed. 'You seem to have forgotten the reprimand from the former manager when you brought in the palace historian. You really want to be fired this time around!'

'His reprimand was to the effect that I did not ask his permission before bringing in the old sage,' Moka said.

'Do you think he would have accepted that you invite an old, haggard illiterate who delves in the fetishes of the palace and tells unwritten stories in the name of history to talk to the children?' Atewele asked.

'So you see why I did not bother asking,' Moka said. 'These children may never know the stories we knew when we were their age. They may never sing the songs we sang.'

'Independence will change all that,' said Atewele.

When they finished eating, Matalina cleared the table. Atewele left, and Ayonchugu and Moka continued discussing Ayonchugu's plans to return to school, how he was going to organise his time around his family, farm work, school, and responsibilities in the village.

'I will talk to the manager and get back to you,' Moka said.

'Thank you very much, HM. I thought you would consider my idea ridiculous.'

'Not I,' Moka said. 'I have plans of my own. It's because of my wife and this school that I'm still here. As soon as I'm sure she has what it takes, we are leaving this village to chase our dreams. Independence will happen sometime soon. I look forward to fitting in at the right place to contribute to building the nation.'

Moka pulled out from his fibre bag the previous day's letter and a new one which he gave to Ayonchugu. 'The inspector brought this letter from the Parish Office.'

'How can I thank him?' asked Ayonchugu, looking at the return address. 'It is from Kelechi. We fought in the same unit in Burma.'

'I see.'

The discussion they had thereafter was reminiscent of the one the day before. As they shared and learned from each other, the two men felt for each other empathy they could not explain, but which surely lay in the craving of the one to share in what the other knew. Unknown to them, the bond that existed between them went beyond the mutual hunger for knowledge and understanding to the very essence of who they were. It was a family bond, at the centre of which was a woman – a wife and a sister.

Before leaving the HM's, tugging along the kid the HM prevailed upon him to take along, Ayonchugu opened the letter and read it out in hesitant English. It went thus:

Dear Warrior!

I am delighted to read from you. My letter comes with the best wishes to you.

I thoroughly admired your bravery and that of all those boys from the Cameroons. Fighting side-by-side with you boys made me to understand why it took so much trouble for the Allies to take Kamerun in the First World War.

My mother died while we were in 'Boma' (smile). The woman I call my mother is from the Cameroons. I can't remember how she came to be my new mother.

Believe me when I say I personally regret the departure of the Cameroons from joint administration with Eastern Nigeria. But I equally acknowledge your right to nationhood. The presence of your delegates here had created a political imbalance whereby the East was becoming too strong. We have redrawn our political map, and can now forge on realistically in our struggle for unification of the regions and independence.

Before the war, vested power was in the hands of Warrant Chiefs such as Okugo, who had no place in our traditional society. Naturally, they were hated. Today, things have changed. Authority is in the hands of Village and Clan Councils. Educated people and ex-soldiers are managing our local affairs through these Councils. So-called Indirect Rule is no longer the leeway for the Northern leaders to run tyrannical emirates and sultanates, although I doubt that they would stay out of politics. I am one of the councillors for my village.

Many of our former comrades continued in the army. Some are business men, and others have gone on to be teachers, doctors and lawyers. There are even a few studying abroad. I am now working for Highways Department as a clerk and I hope, if my health permits, to become chief-clerk for transport in my area.

We have an association called Burma BOA, meaning Burma Boys out of Action. But the association is fragmented over so many issues. Now, there is Ibo Burma BOA, Northern Burma BOA, Eastern Burma BOA, Christian Burma BOA, Moslem Burma BOA, etc. Each Burma BOA is fighting for dominance and each one is claiming to be the real Burma BOA. We can't get as much from the Colonial Government as we should. Discordant as our voices are, our message has been reaching them somehow. Independence must be immediate!

I remember nothing about the war front. Absolutely nothing. Do you believe me? Three weeks after my return from the war I suffered a horrible pain running from my head right down my back. The pain rendered me helpless for two days. Then I went into a deep sleep for a long time. When I woke up I could not remember who I was, who my relatives were, where I was. I could not understand my native language. I could understand and speak English quite well. At first no one believed my condition was real. I was lucky that a British army doctor was called in. He diagnosed and started treating me. I am still not completely recovered. I have had to relearn my language, but I am still not fluent in it. Villagers call me Kele the Gentleman or the Englishman!

So how come I remember you? Because you have written and talked about Crucifixion Day. Anything you mentioned, I see it. When recalled by others, I remember things, but I do so in picture form, or in flash episodes. Beyond that, I see nothing else in my mind from the war.

Please write me again as soon as you receive my reply.
Good luck.
Your obedient servant,
Kelechi

PART TWO

OUT OF A BAG-OF-EVIL

CHAPTER SEVENTEEN

One grain of a son

Mengen was restless. She had been restless for the last two years, and recently her disquietude had been increasing by the day. She had always hungered for the warmth of people she could call her own and had dreamt of building a very large family around her. Nkahfi was close to five, and she was yet to get pregnant again. The boy was well beloved and even a trifle spoilt by his doting parents. But having a single child was a far cry from what was needed to bring Mengen the contentment she so craved for. She consequently applied all her mind and body to her quest to conceive; but her efforts proved futile and left her feeling like a moving hollow tree. While in the past she had found solace in her husband, recently he was becoming the very source of her anxiety because he seemed to be indifferent to her plight. On whom else could she vent her frustrations?

She was sitting by the hearth preparing the evening meal, an aura of deep preoccupation clouding her otherwise plain face. Ayonchugu had just returned from his evening wine-tapping rounds. She peered through the blur of the kitchen smoke across the yard towards the wine storage room and saw his movements by the light of the torch he was whisking about. She could tell he was alone in the *atege*. Her heart skipped a beat. Where was Nkahfi? She could have gone out to look for him immediately, but it was not wise to do so at this stage of dinner preparation. She could have called out for him, but it was already dark and she could not shout out his name to the spirits. She waited impatiently for Ayonchugu to come over to her kitchen as he usually did when he returned from his evening chores. Instead, he came out and took off in the opposite direction.

'Ngembale *tiemuo!*' she called out to him.

'Just a moment,' he said.

He walked a few paces away, then changed his mind, turned around and came over to the kitchen.

Mengen stopped stirring the food and asked, 'Where is my son? I thought you took him to your tapping rounds?'

'No. I just realised that the goats have still not been returned to their pen. I was going to get them.'

'Are you going to get your son first or your goats?' she asked, her eyes flashing with accusation of negligence.

'I thought he was with you,' Ayonchugu said, trying to sound casual.

'If he were with me I won't be asking you where he is.'

'Take it easy, Megemuo. He is surely at the neighbours'. I will get him.'

'Before the goats. Thanks.' She resumed stirring the food.

Ayonchugu sighed as he walked out of the compound, a ponderous frown on his face. When was his wife not in a bad mood these days? He knew exactly what was upsetting her. He was doing what he could to make things fine for her. But it was all going to take time. She wanted things to happen faster. She wanted him to cut corners and people the compound immediately. He judged that it was neither the right time to do so, nor was she going about it the right way.

He found Nkahfi in Bishwing's compound. He was in the kitchen with other children squatting on every bit of available space. They were shelling groundnuts in preparation for the next planting season and were listening with glee to animal tales Nawain was telling them. The children were popping as much groundnuts into their mouths as they were putting into the basket. How else could they be kept on task if they were not allowed to eat the 'bad' grains? Ayonchugu interrupted the session for a few seconds and inquired about the whereabouts of the father of the house, and when informed he was not yet home, he left, promising to come back later. He went to get the goats from a nearby field.

When he had ushered the animals into their pen, he came over to the kitchen.

'I thought you went for the boy?' Mengen asked before he could speak.

'I did. He is in Bishwing's compound.'

'So why did you not bring him home?' Mengen demanded to know.

'He was having a good time and I thought I shouldn't take him just yet,' Ayonchugu replied.

'There were other children there then?' she asked.

'Yes. All his children were there.'

'And his wives too?'

'Yes.'

'Is he coming home or sleeping over?'

'I'm afraid it is over-crowded there. I will bring him over later.'

'So my son now has to go to the neighbour's compound to seek companionship. I feel sorry for myself, and even sorrier for you.'

'Please, Megemuo, don't start it again,' Ayonchugu pleaded.

'Don't start what?' Mengen asked, her voice getting louder. 'My child can't stay at home because you have here a large empty compound to which you are adding a cold empty jangling stone house to people it perhaps with goats. And you stand there and talk about Bishwing's children and his wives! Overcrowded indeed!'

'I will bring him right away if you wish,' Ayonchugu said.

'I don't wish for anything but my son's happiness. He can't have it here. So let him be there.'

She wiped her tears with an angle of her wrapper, but the flow was not yet capped, and her eyes got wet again. Ayonchugu felt a jab of pain in his heart as he watched his wife crying, her face contorted, sorrowful, less appealing, yet vulnerable. He sat next to her.

'Megemuo,' he said, 'I understand what you feel. Would you stop crying now?'

'No you don't understand! This house needs children! This house needs women! Why can't you just show you understand these facts by doing something about them? Why don't you get married?'

'It was never my intention to marry another woman.'

'Well, things are not the way they should have been. I need a co-wife. We need children.'

'I have to get the right wife, not just a baby-maker,' Ayonchugu explained.

'What kind of right wife do you want?,' Mengen asked, her voice as loud and tearful as before. 'How many times have I proposed a decent girl to you and you have procrastinated until another man whisked her away? Three times!'

'You know, after what I went through with Ngelem....'

'Don't even talk about that! What did you go through? A man should be a man. You let someone take away your wife and you tell me about what you went through!'

Ayonchugu was in no mood to discuss the issue further. He looked at his wife for a few seconds as she resigned herself to her fate with a final tearful sniff, wiped her face with the end of her wrapper and started dishing the steaming food she had finished preparing. Ayonchugu felt dazed as he stepped out and hurried over to Bishwing's compound to take Nkahfi.

Ayonchugu and Mengen had enjoyed a harmonious marriage until it gradually dawned on them that she was not the fast-baby-bearing type. Ayonchugu had gone out of his way to please her by accepting to administer the medicines she brought from her father. Her disappointment was infinite when the very emulsions her father used with exceptional success failed her. Ayonchugu had counselled patience, but she was patient about everything except in her desire to conceive.

Ayonchugu wished to see the little man in his son emerge, but Mengen tended to be overly-protective of him. Ayonchugu spurned her protestations and took the boy along on some of his daily chores. He explained that the boy would soon go to school, but before that, he had to understand the life of men in the village.

That night, unlike some bad nights before, Mengen sobbed for a very long time. She punctuated her sobs with words which told of her misfortune at not being able to have more than a single grain of a son. She ceased her lamentations when she felt Nkahfi recoil from her and started silent sniffs of his own. She pulled him to her bosom, and only let go of him when she heard a light knock on the door, by which time he was fast asleep. She got up and left the room, to which she returned only at cock's crow.

In the morning she was quite nearly her old self again. There were no signs on her face to tell of the last night's distress, and her steps were lighter. She started singing one of her old songs, modulating her voice at different pitches and putting in new lyrics in praise of Nkahfi. She prepared breakfast, put a generous portion in his lunch basket and set it on the kitchen bamboo shelf where he could reach it by standing on a stool. She called him endearing names, and made an embarrassing fuss about what a caring and intelligent young man he was when he apologised for staying late at the neighbours' the previous night.

'One of these days your father is going on a trip. You will be the man in this compound. How would you like that?'

He looked perplexed for a moment before speaking. 'I'll work all day on the farm. I'll go wine-tapping. Papa has shown me how to do it. I'll take out the animals in the morning and bring them in in the evening.'

'Impressive. And what else will you do, sonny?' Mengen asked.

'I'll bring in the logs of wood,' Nkahfi replied.

'And what would you do for your mama?'

'I'll fetch you water with the little calabash. No, the big one. I can carry the big one now. I'll make you happy.'

'That's my hero. I know you will, my little man. You will also complete your father's stone house, won't you?'

'Yes. But the stones are too heavy for me to carry.'

'Not for you. You are a strong man. But don't worry about the house. Your father will continue building it when he returns.'

'Where's he going, Mammy?'

'To his first village,' Mengen replied.

'Has he another village?'

'Yes. It's called Libah.'

'I've heard that name before. Why is it Papa's first village?'

'That's where he was born. He was a big man already when he came to live in this village.'

'Is it far?' Nkahfi asked.

'Yes. Very far,' Mengen said.

'Like from here to school five times?'

'Like from here to school and back two hundred times.'

'Huu!' Nkahfi exclaimed, eyes widening. 'Is his village at

the other end of the world where the sun sets?'

'Not so far,' said Mengen. 'If he took a mammy wagon at sunrise, he could get there by midday.'

'I'd like to go there too,' Nkahfi said.

'You will someday. But not now.'

'Were you born there too?' the child asked.

'No.'

'Where then?'

'You will have to ask your grandfather.'

'He scares me. Just like that woman-juju.'

'What woman-juju?' Mengen asked.

'Mammy, I saw a woman-juju one day. She tried talking to me. I ran away.'

'Come on, jujus don't talk. There's no woman-juju and warriors like you don't get scared.'

'It's true. I saw her,' Nkahfi insisted. 'I see things crawling around the room in the night when you are not there.'

'I'm always there.'

'You were not there last night,' Nkahfi said.

'I had to talk with your father.'

'Why don't I have a nice grandmother who stays with us like Ngwa's?' the boy asked. 'I could sleep in her bed.'

'She died,' Mengen replied.

'When?'

'When I was a baby.'

'Did he get you another mother?'

'Yes,' Mengen answered, her voice beginning to tremble.

'Where is she?'

'Eat your food and stop asking questions like an old man.'

'Am I not the man of the house?' Nkahfi asked.

'No, you aren't,' Mengen replied. 'Your father has not left yet.'

'I see,' Nkahfi said in all seriousness.

CHAPTER EIGHTEEN

Mission to Libah

Five days later Ayonchugu dusted his soldier's bag, strung it over his back, and rode purposefully on the main road that ran the diameter of the village. He went past the school, looking at the HM's office as if expecting his old friend to appear at the door with his hands on his waist, brandishing a cane, as he always did when he wanted order to be restored in the school yard. He smiled to himself, thinking about the man thanks to whom he took a round-about route to return to school and earn his GSSC. It could not have happened at a more opportune moment. The very day Ayonchugu went to pick up his certificate Moka told him he had obtained admission and sponsorship to study in the Gold Coast. Matalina was awaiting the results of her interview to enter the Catholic Teachers Training College. Villagers had received the news of the impending departure with a lot of sadness, but had gone on to organise a big farewell ceremony for him at the palace. The fon had honoured him with a red feather, and given him an honorary title: Mbumnwali. Knowledge hunter.

Recently, Moka's name was once again echoing into the village, this time, from government circles in Gbuea, where he held an important office which permitted him, it was claimed, to interact with Foncha, Endeley, Jua and Muna on a daily basis. Ayonchugu smiled to himself again. He was used to his people's tendency to hyperbolise fancifully about the greatness of officials they liked. As with the other political zeitgeists, Ngonibi women had already included Moka's name in the lyrics of their lore.

Unlike the time many years before when Ayonchugu walked all the way from Libah to Ngonibi, he was going to ride only a part of the way to the main road, wait there, and hope to be picked up by a commuting Land Rover, which came by twice a day. That was the luck Ngonibi had. There were villages which were totally inaccessible even by bicycle, unless the rider

carried the bicycle on his head sometimes, to the amusement
of the people, who would poke fun at him for carrying his own
legs. A good rider could have done the journey on Ayonchugu's
bicycle in less than half a day. Ayonchugu knew it would do
him no good to ride for long on bumpy roads because of his old
injuries which resurfaced like bad old friends – just when he
wished to see the last of them. His bad eye watered and itched
when exposed to dust or wind. Even in normal conditions he
needed to dab it constantly. His bad leg would be numb for
days whenever he rode for long.

A grey mammy wagon on which was written THE DAY
WILL COME crawled to a stop. He boarded it and squeezed
himself into a place on a wooden bench. His bicycle was piled
high on top of a mix of items already overflowing the carriage
of the vehicle, which went swaying gingerly with the weight of
its burden on every bend like a masquerade with an oversized
head. Every now and again a suffocating but resilient pig, tired
of squealing in protest at being confined in ropes and bogged
down by luggage, grunted from the top of the vehicle, to the
satisfaction of its owner, an old lady sitting next to Ayonchugu.
The journey could have lasted a few hours, but the bus kept
stopping to drop off or pick up passengers, and on each
occasion it took up to fifteen minutes to get the engine running
again, following a play with live wires by the driver and lots of
cranking by the motor-boy.

Ayonchugu arrived in Libah at dusk. It was a good thing
he did, for he wanted to draw very little attention to himself.
His mission to Libah was a delicate one, needing careful
planning and rallying of people on his side; it was calculated to
culminate in unprecedented changes in the power rungs, and
in his family make-up. It was important to meet his family in
Libah, especially his brother, and be updated before putting
the finishing touches to his master plan.

The atmosphere in Libah was ceremonious when he
landed from the vehicle. At the village square which tripled as
daily market, car park, and rallying grounds, came the blaring
of a voice over a hand-held battery-operated loudspeaker. The
crowd was hanging on every word the speaker was
pronouncing. Ayonchugu remained anonymous in the crowd

and listened.

'Who pulled you and your children and your future generations out of the Eastern Region? We did. Who negotiated with London for our own autonomous regional government? We did. Why can we now boast of our own set of offices in our own natural capital in Gbuea? Because we fought for it. That fight was for you. It was for your future and your children's future. And today, does Endeley's new party want to compromise all our gains by taking us back to where we were years ago? What does our tradition or any in the world say about the man who finds and brings your lost son back to your house? That he be repaid with a slap in the face? Or he be thanked with a pat on the back? If you listen to the KNP, you are giving us a slap in the face, my people. Endeley was with us at the beginning. But he has since back-tracked. We should be going forward, never backwards. Or are we backward-groping nymphs...?'

Ayonchugu had heard it all from other speakers the previous week in Ngonibi. He did recognise today's speaker, who had remained silent in Ngonibi. Judging from the energy he put into his speech he had perhaps been saving his voice for the bigger village. Ayonchugu walked away from the crowd and headed towards his brother's house, using the same road he had taken nearly fifteen years before. He did not have to step upon stones in the stream this time because a narrow bridge had been constructed across it.

Nothing had changed fundamentally in Ndi's house but for the atmosphere which Ayonchugu found too subdued for a compound he expected to be teeming with children and wives and wives' relatives. It was as if the whole compound had gone to sleep early. He knocked persistently on the door to the main house. No one opened it. He turned around with to head towards the women's section and saw his brother pointing a double-barrel rifle at him.

'Have you been hunting?' asked Ayonchugu as calmly as possible.

'Is that Ayonchugu? My brother! Where have you suddenly appeared from like a mushroom?'

'I'm just coming in. Put down that damn gun. By the way,

why is it so quiet here?' Ayonchugu asked.

'You will know in a moment,' Ndi said. 'Come in here through the side door. As you can see, I created this new door. Ha! Dreams don't lie. I saw two new palm tree saplings right in the centre of this compound in my dream. I cut them down because they were out of place but they grew up again right under my eyes. I decided to nurture them. And here you are.'

'I'm alone,' Ayonchugu said. 'You talked about two saplings.'

'Await your surprise.' Ndi knocked on the door to his room and called out. Someone opened the door from inside. 'It's Ayonchugu,' he announced. 'Let's see if he can tell who you are.'

Ayonchugu looked inside the poorly lit room and saw a man who looked vaguely familiar but whom he did not remember meeting before. He looked much bigger than either Ndi or Ayonchugu, but he had features that were similar to those of the two men.

'You remind me of someone. My father. Are you...? You are my brother!' Ayonchugu said in a loud voice.

'Not so loudly,' Ndi cautioned. 'You got it. This is our brother Tongembe.'

'Gott sey dank!' exclaimed Tongembe. 'Ayonchugu! Mon propre frère! Dieu est grand!'

'What?' Ayonchugu looked lost for a moment.

'Gott dey! I glad plenty for see you!' Tongembe said.

'I'm really glad to see you too,' Ayonchugu replied, nearly as loudly as his brother. 'I always wondered if I would ever set my eyes on you again.'

'You were a baby when I left for Nkongsamba,' Tongembe said. 'What happened to you? Dis-donc! You look nearly as old as our big brother.'

'First thing: How is our mother?' Ayonchugu inquired. 'Is she here too?' Excitement and expectation were visible all over his person.

'Fine. Fine. She is in safe hands,' Tongembe said.

'Where?' Ayonchugu asked.

'With friends. There was a lot of fighting in our region. She was taken through Tombel to Kumba. She is fine.'

'And you?' asked Ayonchugu, once he made himself comfortable in a seat by the fireside. 'Please, tell me about yourself, brother. I want to know everything.'

'Where do I start? I fought for *les français* in the '45 war. After that, I fought for them in *Algérie* and *Indo-Chine*.'

'You don't look like someone who has been to war,' said Ayonchugu. 'I mean...you do not even have a scar on your body.'

'My brother,' said Tongembe, 'my scars are deep inside. I will explain later. Know that I'd rather have lost an eye like you, than be doomed to bachelorhood *à jamais*. After the wars, I lived and worked peacefully in Nkongsamba as a carpenter until the UPC party which was asking for immediate independence was outlawed. The militants took up arms. *Au début*, I had nothing to do with the fighting. One day, soldiers descended on my neighbourhood and killed indiscriminately, razing everything, *tout* – homes, my workshop – to the ground. A rival carpenter betrayed me. He said I was a UPC *partisant*. I managed to escape with a handful of *maquisards*. We scaled the hills of Dschang and wangled our way to the Bamenda Plateau. Once we got close to Abakwa, I deserted and sought the way to Libah. *Me voici chez moi.*'

'Ayo, our brother's situation is precarious, as you can see,' said Ndi. 'The Cameroun government is hunting for him. The *maquisards* are after his flesh for betrayal; if he ever lands in the hands of Nigerian authorities he would be handed over to the French. You know what would happen next.'

'He should not be living here,' said Ayonchugu. 'Anyone looking for him would obviously begin by looking here.'

'That person would be dead before going inside to bring him out,' Ndi said, looking every bit as serious as his words. 'Look under my bed. There's another gun. It is the real thing, not my hunting piece.'

'I can see it. Heavens! How did you get this?' Ayonchugu asked, his good eye widening.

'Courtesy of my so-called *maquis* friends,' Tongembe replied. 'They trusted me enough to give me one of these.'

'It looks Russian to me,' Ayonchugu said. 'How did you manage to bring it all the way here?'

'Ayo *mon frère*,' Tongembe, 'you don't give up the last fibre by which you hang on to life. And by the way, that weapon is not *Russe*; *c'est français.*'

Ayonchugu whistled in wonderment as he looked at the weapon. 'Russian or French or American, it blows a hole through anything that it confronts. That is what matters. I still think you would be safer out of this place.'

'It's close to forty years since he left,' Ndi said. 'Not that many people know him. We can count on the discretion of the elderly people. Or have you forgotten how jealous our people are about their self-preservation?'

'Ayonchugu may have a point though,' said Tongembe.

'I suggest we sleep on it,' Ndi said. 'It's not a wise thing to run when you are carrying a clay pot. Ayonchugu, this is your compound, and so I won't ask you why you've come in so suddenly. But I hope all's well with you?'

'Quite well. Mengen sends you greetings. She sends you this.' Ayonchugu handed Ndi a package.

'Thank you,' he said. He used his hunting knife to cut the strings around the bundle. 'Hey, the good woman. She has sent *egusi* pudding. That's a true sister-in-law. My, this is quite a lot.'

Ndi fetched palm wine from his *atege* and poured it in an earthenware pot which he set on the fire. They shared the egusi pudding and smoked unprocessed tobacco. They drank hot palm wine and talked into the heart of the night, catching up with the happenings in their family and their nations spanning a period of forty years. It was a different story each one had to tell.

Ayonchugu was amazed at how Tongembe was remarkably different in his outlook on life; but the brothers found more common ground than differences to share with one another. They had emanated from this very compound where they were now sitting, and had travelled the paths their fortunes had taken them, reacting to and overcoming their travails. Here they were again, mature men, as one family, one blood, pulled back by unbreakable bonds, harnessed by the pulsating umbilical cord their parents had taken the ritual precaution of burying at the back of the family house. They had served different nations and had achieved for them their liberation from fascism and Aryanism. Tongembe had subjugated others in the North and in the Far East in wars to regain the shattered pride of his commanders' nation.

Ayonchugu and his kin knew they had contributed much, and were still contributing to the fight for independence with their blood and sweat. It was now only a question of time, and freedom would come at last, for long after the wars, colonisers had finally started listening to the voice of the people because that voice had become too loud to be ignored.

The three men saw an urgent need to put their house in order. They solemnly vowed to go to every length to bring their mother back home, and if possible, their brother from the mines of Jos. It was time to pull their family together again and make a new start, consolidated in their bloodline.

Ayonchugu said little about his mission to Libah that night. It was not until the following day that Tongembe, shaking his head in disbelief, listened to the whole story of his brother's post-war life.

'Where's this man Ajong now?' he asked.

'I suppose he's in this village,' Ayonchugu replied. 'We'll have to ask our brother.'

Ndi confirmed that Ajong was indeed in the village. 'He has been fomenting one problem after another,' Ndi added. 'Recently he has become even more controversial than in the past. He has been accused of very serious crimes, but as yet nothing has been pinned on him.'

'Serious crimes such as?' Tongembe asked.

'Two assassinations,' Ndi replied.

'*Merde!* Those are grievous crimes,' Tongembe said, shaking his head.

'Unfortunately, none of those who could incriminate him are willing to talk,' Ndi said. 'Some are accomplices and others are afraid for their lives.'

'And this Ngelem woman?' Tongembe asked.

'She's Ajong's woman,' Ndi replied. 'They seem to have had their ups and downs, but she's there. Where the head goes the tail follows.'

'Are they that close?' Tongembe asked.

'I mean that she dances to his tune,' Ndi explained.

'That's normal, isn't it?' Tongembe asked.

'Perhaps not so normal when you think hard about it,' Ayonchugu said.

'Perhaps,' Tongembe said. 'How many children has she now?' he asked.

'Two,' Ndi replied.

'Why?' Tongembe asked.

'I can't speak for them, can I? Everybody has been asking that same question. His other wives have been giving birth. So the woman is probably the problem here.'

'About these *assassinats*, who were the victims?' Tongembie asked.

'King-makers,' Ndi replied.

'Who happened not to have sided with him on some issue, I guess?' Ayonchugu asked.

'Definitely,' Ndi said. 'It's been rumoured for some time now that there's cold in the palace. The fon may soon go missing. You know how succession to the throne in this village has been happening from the time of our ancestors. First, the fon designates a son, usually, but not always from his first queen, as his successor. By queen I mean the woman he marries after he's enthroned. Any woman he married before becoming fon is a wife, a palace woman, but not a queen. Secondly, the son designated for the throne is never the first son, but rather one of his younger brothers. I'm saying this for you, Tongembe. I don't know if it's the same practice where you come from.'

'I lived with the Bamilikes for a while, and I believe the *pratique* is somewhat similar among them. Among the coastal and the forest people, it's whoever the council of elders asks the *Préfet* to appoint that becomes Village Head.'

'You understand me well then,' said Ndi. 'One very important thing, though: All king-makers have to accept the fon's choice, or his candidate would never thrive on the throne. Here then is the problem as I got it from my sources. The fon wants to have Ajong succeed him. Ajong is a second degree prince and he's the first son. Either of these descriptions disqualifies him. The fon is said to have received the support of the District Officer. In fact, it would seem the idea was hatched in the DO's office. I can't confirm anything though. As it is, Ajong has been tipped off as the successor to the fon.'

'That's a far-fetched prospect,' Tongembe said.

'Succession rules have been tampered with in many other parts of the Colonies,' Ndi said. Ayonchugu and Tongembe were shaking their heads as Ndi explained the situation. 'This is an issue which in our tradition is so secret and sacred that it's never discussed except in the inner sanctuary of the king-makers. It is believed that a number of king-makers have been bought over. The two elders who have been assassinated are among those said to have opposed any change in the succession tradition.'

'Ajong has the motive. Anything else?' asked Tongembe.

Ndi nodded and said, 'Recently he has been heard saying he's not interested in the throne. I think he's lying.'

'It might be his way of trying to show that he has no motive,' Ayonchugu suggested.

'He really does not have to say he is interested in the throne in order to get to sit on it,' Ndi said. 'You know how it happens. The king-makers 'hijack' the incumbent and sit him on the throne even before announcing to the citizens that the fon has gone missing.'

'Tell me more about this woman that you married,' Tongembe requested.

Tongembe had an investigative streak about him, and gleaned as much information as he could about just everyone who was linked to the family's destiny. By the following day, the men had, with his input, refined the strategy that would ensure the success of Ayonchugu's mission to Libah.

CHAPTER NINETEEN

Among sojas

On the second day of his return to Libah, Ayonchugu started entertaining wave after wave of family members and well-wishers. So it was that just after mid-day on Ayonchugu's third day in Libah, four men came to see him unannounced. It was a noisy reunion, full of military epithets and foot-stamping salutes. It took a while for the men to settle down and start saying anything constructive.

Fuochu, Saji, Mbah and Niba were ex-soldiers. In the early post-war days the foursome was always drinking and boisterously reminiscing together. People never heard enough of their stories. Their exploits were embellished in countless versions by the people until the lines between fiction and history became blurred. The killings and hair-breath escapades the young soldiers experienced became glamorised in the oral lay and physical gimmicks in men's dance groups.

Now more mature men, they could look back at the war more philosophically. It needed some prompting with alcohol or tobacco to get them talking to 'civilians' about North Africa or 'Boma'. And when they did talk, it was more about the wisdom of Wingate, the resilience of the Japanese, the unpredictability of an ambush, the ingenuity of Japanese human trees and the like, and hardly about how they wielded the gun.

A veteran of the two wars, Sergeant Maama, whom everyone called Saji, was in his late fifties and had been moving on wooden crutches ever since he recovered from injuries incurred in North Africa. His time in the war was cut short one fateful day when thousands of Italians surrendered. An angry soldier who could not stand the humiliation of being pointed a gun at while he carried his hands on his head suddenly attacked him and tried to wrestle his gun from his hands. An awkward new recruit stepped in to help and, instead of taking out the Italian, fired two way-off shots, one of which hit Saji, before a third one hit the right target.

Saji since regretted that he had not been able to go to other fronts. Over the years he became even more embittered about his disability, which prevented him from pursuing other ventures. He drank heavily, and when he was in his darker moods, was known to hit out with his wooden crutches at his wives or whoever dared to cross his path. What he lacked in physical ability he made up for with a loud voice that sent his wives and children sneaking off to the safety of their rooms or appearing promptly to do his bidding. Presently, only the youngest wife and her two kids could still manage to put up with his regime, and there were rumours that even she too would soon run away. Villagers attributed his violent outbursts to vaccines he was given in the army.

Fuochu was into his mid-thirties. He was a rather small man with knock-knees. Everyone apart from the recruiting officer had doubted he would ever make a good soldier. But his thin legs were solid like red wood. He seemed to tap inexhaustible reserves of energy from nowhere, except it be from the large amounts of *achu* he ate, which never seemed to have any effect on his stature. He served in the army with distinction, returning unscathed, either in mind or body. Whenever he donned his military uniform to celebrate Empire Day, the medals lining his breast pocket threatened to pull his little frame down with them. Fuochu always ran errands during occasions or arbitrated between disagreeing villagers. He was the town crier, and for one so small, it was surprising how far his voice could be heard. He was not yet married, and hardly seemed to care about his situation.

Niba was an erratic man who was always in an eccentric military apparel. At the time of his discharge in 1945, he was only eighteen, and had quickly outgrown and outworn his original soldier's outfit. In his ingenuity, he had a tailor make him military-style wear from material he bought locally. He was discharged a stripeless Private, but over the years he had promoted himself through the ranks and now wore the fake badge of a Chief Sergeant, which to him was the highest rank he could, even in his fantasy world, aspire to. Villagers called him the *samanja*, and woe betide whoever did not! Among Niba's post-war eccentricities was the dream of constructing a storey building out of bamboo. He did actually manage to build one, but when the last length of bamboo was nailed in, he realised he had not provided for a balcony and an internal staircase. He managed to contrive both internal and external stairs. When the project ended to his satisfaction, he realised that the building served no purpose at all. His wife suggested they use it for a barn. He was mad at her for daring to think such a thing. For a year the structure stood empty and doomed. Then a scattering of chickens she kept took a liking to it, and started carousing up and down its stairs. She stole up and pulled the front door open, and the chickens moved in. Thus was started the first local poultry in the village that won an award at an agric show. The samanja now earned a living rearing varied domestic stock. Every Friday evening his wife and seven children each carried a large cane basket full of chickens and set forth for the Saturday market, while he trailed with pigs and goats. He never bothered to hold on to the rope on his animals. All the way to Abakwa he would say 'Mboh! Mboh! Mboh!' and the animals followed him dutifully.

Mbah had retrained in Burma as an orderly after his hearing was impaired on the battlefield. He had since his return worked at the local infirmary. Apart from doing written prescriptions, he performed every intervention that was in the nurse's domain, from administering injections to stitching cuts and sanitising wounds. He was even reputed for circumcising male babies. Of the four men, he was the most cool-headed. He led his wife and nine children to church four days a week, defying the dust and the mud on the six-kilometre trek they did to get there.

They were sitting on carved stools under a tree in the middle of the compound sharing a drink of palm wine from a large plastic jug which they had brought. The expansive foliage let through not one ray of the scorching sun. Their voices were a tenor higher than usual and it was not clear if their faculties were still intact.

'Ah, Number One!' said Mbah. 'Since you are here and look very much your old self, I suppose you left the people back home in good health and did your journey on a good footing.'

'They are all fine,' Ayonchugu replied. 'As for the journey,

I have had worse. Compared to some of my journeys in the past, this was like flying in a Dakota C47.'

'Were they that uncomfortable?' asked Saji.

'Who's talking about comfort?' Ayonchugu asked. 'Your comfort came when you got to the end of your journey alive. It was war-time, remember? I was no Peter Thomas, the Lagos boy, but here I am.'

'I never had the opportunity to climb into one of those vehicles of the skies,' said Saji. 'In the desert it was marching, marching and marching on the sand all day in the scorching sun. At one time I felt my head spinning and thought I heard a sizzling sound, and for a moment was truly scared that my brains were getting fried!'

'They probably got fried anyway,' Niba dared to say. Saji glared at him and he pretended not to see his reaction. He hurried to add, 'No one returned with the same brains he took to the war. If you had come to Boma and had had to fight the Japs hundreds of miles into the dense jungle behind enemy lines as we Chindits did, without a single road leading there, you would have had your plane ride.'

'We were parachuted in to clear and dig in the jungle and create landing strips,' Ayonchugu said. 'I'd never worked harder in my life. In two days we levelled virgin forest the size of six football fields and turned the place into an impenetrable fortress.'

'That is why I keep saying, and no one seems to be listening, that young men today have all gone lazy,' Niba said. 'My farms suffered neglect because there were not enough hands to work them. I gave up farming for life-stock. To think I have four sons who are as old as I was when I went to war!' Niba shook his head in disappointment, and his medals jingled.

'Schooling has made them soft,' said Saji. 'What a drowse. Those men who fought in the German frontlines were real men. Ayonchugu's father was a man. And so was Niba's. Would we ever have real men in this territory again?'

'We can't tell unless there is a Third World War,' said Ayonchugu.

'It would be a war for weaklings,' said Niba. 'Today's

youths have all forgotten what it means to be brave. All they do is talk and talk and talk about which is the better party! Which region should get what number of representatives! We took arms to decide who had the better army! Wingate did! That was my janar!'

'You got it wrong there. Rommel had the better army!' said Saji. No one bothered to gainsay him, knowing how erratic he could become over people and things German.

'Sokomoto had it!' said Fuochu, intent on winding up someone.

'You must be mad!' exclaimed Saji. 'We are talking about armies that won the war. We are talking about good armies. Not evil armies.'

'What about bravery?' asked Fuochu. 'A Japanese soldier could stay back alone and ambush the enemy while his comrades retreated. That's what happened in Boma.'

'That was suicide,' said Ayonchugu. 'That was cowardice, not bravery.'

'It takes a brave person to practise that kind of cowardice,' said Niba.

'It takes any mad person to do it,' replied Saji.

'You boys are joking,' said Fuochu. 'None of you fought under Janar Shaw in Northeast Africa. He hardly ever lost a soja. He was my commander.'

'He lost no sojas because he fought no serious battles,' said Niba.

'What do you mean?' asked Fuochu, standing up and gesticulating as he spoke. 'War is not just about the battles. It is about information. We gathered intelligence about the Italian sojas and sent it back to our sojas. And you sit there and tell me we fought no battles? Did I earn my medals on a leisure trip?'

'Ho! Peace!' Mbah called out. 'The war was over some fifteen years ago. The Allies won. The Axis lost. We all fought for the Allies. So we all won.' Everyone shook their heads in agreement. 'Let's talk about today. Indeed, about now. We came here for two reasons – to see our comrade and to invite him to the meeting of the Kamerun Ex-Soldiers' National Union. As concerns the first reason – we all know what befell him when he was away at war. We do not wish to open old wounds. But we can't avoid noticing the scars. We would like our brother to tell us how he has been doing.'

Ayonchugu was cautious about what he said, for as yet he could not be sure if he could trust all the men. 'I have been doing quite fine,' he said.

'What?' asked Mbah, cupping his ears and leaning towards Ayonchugu.

'I carried on with my life in my new village!' Ayonchugu shouted. 'I guess if a stream kept going back to its source it would never be part of the sea!'

Mbah spoke again. 'I'm glad to hear that. At the same time, it takes a fool to point to his origins with his left hand. Your coming back here tells us you have not forgotten your roots. We know you have vested interest in this village. We are a team. What we want, we get. If ever you need our help, just ask and we will rally behind you. Is that not the case, sojas?'

'It is! It is!' they all agreed.

'I will remember your offer,' Ayonchugu said. 'I thank you all.'

'As we all know, there is a caterpillar in this village who makes believe he is a snake,' said Niba, loud enough for the whole neighbourhood to hear. 'He has attended meetings of the Kamerun Ex-Soldiers' National Union, whereas we all think he never fought. When he was taken to task about it some time ago, he claimed he was wounded while carrying out a secret mission for the army, and that Ayonchugu knew about it. Now is the time to know the truth. Even one day in battle would qualify him as one of us. Did Fingoba fight?'

Ayonchugu delayed answering, and Mbah spoke. 'This is not the best forum to put that question to Ayonchugu. I think we should stick to the purpose of our visit.' All heads nodded in agreement except Niba's. Mbah continued speaking. 'As you know, things are moving quite fast now, and it may be only a few months before Nigeria gains independence.'

'No later than 2nd April 1960, to be precise,' said Fuochu.

'That is a man who listens to the news,' Mbah said. 'We do not understand French, but we have all been listening to the news in English. We have learned that French Cameroun may also be released even sooner from the yoke of the French.'

'In a matter of weeks. January 1960,' said Fuochu.

'You are now showing off,' said Saji.

'Am I? For whose benefit? Yours?' Fuochu's retort smacked of sarcasm.

Mbah continued talking. 'We, the Cameroons, have an uncertain future, even if politicians are trying to tell us otherwise. London cannot keep control much longer. Now, we have for a while been debating these issues, and other issues of grave importance to us as veterans. As usual opinions are diverse. We would like you to attend our meeting, and contribute your voice to ours.'

'Just tell me the time and place, and I will join you,' said Ayonchugu.

'Good. G. H. Ashamba plans to discuss some of these things with veterans one of these days. Now, among the issues we have been discussing is that of a monument commemorating the battles we fought. Since the war ended, hardly has a month gone by without the radio telling us about a monument being inaugurated in France, England, India, Australia, America or even Boma. Now, the two questions have been these: Do we build a monument to honour those who died in the battlefield? Or do we build a monument for those who survived the war like us? Your contribution will be highly valued.'

Ayonchugu immediately thought of a third option, but said nothing.

The men left when Ndi's cellars were empty. Ayonchugu sat back and pondered what they had discussed. He sensed a certain naivety in the men. A monument was not something a group of impoverished ex-soldiers could just get up and build. Monuments, like the centuries-old statues of the Buddha and other gods he had seen in the Far East, or the pyramids in North Africa, or even the French steel tower whose name he could not remember, were all built to last. Ayonchugu saw some futility in the enterprise of the veterans. Were they planning on setting up a scarecrow that would ridicule the very essence of their effort?

CHAPTER TWENTY

Ex-soja goes fortune-telling

The day following the visit of the veterans, Ayonchugu went to sue Fon Fuotum and Ajong at the Customary Court of Abakwa Area Council. The clerk, popularly known as Pa Tafah, was a retired time-keeper for the PWD, volunteering for the court. After the paperwork was done Pa Tafah sat back and looked at Ayonchugu for a few moments in silence. In spite of his wrinkles and padded greying hair, the clerk was smartly dressed. Ayonchugu admired his well-ironed white shirt, striped black tie, black trousers and sparkling, pointed black shoes.

'Can I have my case number, please?' he asked.

'My son,' said Pa Tafah, 'I'm astonished at the calibre of people involved in this case. Do you think you stand a chance?'

'I'm counting on the laws of the land to work in my favour.'

'I've seen a lot in my days. There is the law, and there is power. The fon of Libah has never been made to appear in court. Do you realise you may have to leave the village irrespective of the outcome of the case?' Pa Tafah asked.

'I've not lived in Libah for close to fifteen years. I'm still alive.'

'This is going to be one case of the rat taking on the elephant in a wrestling bout,' Pa Tafah said.

'Don't forget that the fly got into the elephant's ear and caused its death,' Ayonchugu replied.

'And went to the grave with the elephant because it couldn't find a way out.'

'There was no grave; no one was ready to dig a grave that big. As for the fly, it left behind maggots which fed on the elephant's carcass and turned into more flies.' Ayonchugu smiled at the clerk in celebration. Pa Tafah heaved his shoulders, steeped a pen in a bottle of ink, wrote the case number and handed it to Ayonchugu.

'The case will come up in about two weeks. You can read and write, so you do not need the services of a court messenger. Read the notice board next week for the exact date and time. Good luck.'

When he returned home at Ndi's, Ayonchugu was debriefed by Tongembe. 'I managed to meet Ngelem today.'

'Our plan worked then?' asked Ayonchugu.

'It did work, with modifications though. I happened on an Igbo trader transporting goods. I convinced him to sell me some items at wholesale price. I went to Ajong's house, pretending to be a mobile Haussa trader with the ability to tell fortunes. And perhaps I have just found a new profession. I sold Ngelem and her co-wives some head-ties and jewellery at give-away prices, although I still bagged a profit.' Tongembe jingled the coins in his bag.

'And what do you think about her?'

'She is quite an impressive woman. But I think she is scared of something. She would not listen to her fortune in the presence of the other women.'

'But you still managed to talk to her?' Ayonchugu inquired.

'Sure. Very briefly in a passageway, as I made my way out of the compound. I'll meet her secretly again on Saturday in the school compound. I asked her to bring an item belonging to her husband. That really seemed to have scared her.'

'Do you think she will come?'

'I believe she will,' said Tongembe confidently. 'My commerce carried me over to your house. I met Moyu, our brother's son. He seemed to be quite *raisonable*. And hard-working too. He has rebuilt the house. The land all around the house has been cultivated. He grows tomatoes and every vegetable you can think of. I could not help but tell him who I was. He was quite shocked.'

'Did you call that one reasonable? Does he understand he has to keep silent about you?' Ndi asked.

'Yes. He's coming here tonight,' replied Tongembe.

'Did you see my grave?' asked Ayonchugu, forcing a smile.

Neither of the brothers seemed to be listening to him. Ndi shouted out through the open door to one of his wives way across the yard to serve dinner.

'While they are about that food, I'll shake hands with a friend behind the house,' Tongembe said, and stepped outside.

In the night Moyu came. He sat with the three men and listened with interest to their stories, and in one night learned more about the nature of the political conflicts that had besieged the world in the first half of the century than he had done in all his years of schooling up to Standard Four, when he escaped the teacher's cane to become a gardener. His father still considered him a disappointment.

That weekend, Tongembe completed a delicate job with a syringe and a drop of glue on two eggs. He then walked to the Government Primary School Libah, picked the padlock on the door of the Standard Two classroom and went in. He sat down at the teacher's table and waited for Ngelem like a hen incubating her eggs. They did not agree on a specific time. She had time only to promise that she would come after mid-day.

Ngelem came in shortly after. She was a little breathless. 'I actually came by and saw that the door was locked. I walked to the far end, went around to the back of the building before making my way back. I think there's a teacher in one of the classrooms. It might not be a good idea to stay here.'

'Have you brought an item belonging to your husband?' Tongembe asked.

She took out a skull-cap from her handbag and handed it to him. 'And what if the man I saw finds us out?' she asked.

'I know he won't. Trust my powers. When did your husband last wear this cap?' Tongembe asked.

'Many years ago. I took something he won't miss.'

'I work better with items that have been used recently. I will give this cap a try, though.'

'I'm here to talk about me anyway. Why bother about him?'

'Woman, all about you is tied up in this man. Let me see your hands. Good. Hold these.' He handed her two eggs. 'One is for your husband. The other is for you. Before we leave from

177

here today, you will tell by these eggs what shall become of you both in the few months or even weeks ahead. Choose your egg.'

She chose one of the eggs. He took back the eggs, held them over Ngelem's head, said some incantations in an alien language and walked around her three times. He stood in front of her and dropped the eggs on the floor. They both cracked. Ngelem's let forth water. The other egg was rotten. She looked at the water on the floor and shivered.

'Sit on the bench,' Tongembe said. After she had settled down, he addressed her in a solemn tone. 'Woman, your egg has nothing but water, as you can see. It is clean water. Pure, but not an egg. Your husband's egg stinks. And so does his life. Show me your palm.'

Ngelem held out her right hand, which trembled as he took it. He studied her palm for a few seconds, shook his head and released it. He took out a kola nut from his bag and peeled off its skin. He divided the skin in five parts. He threw the pieces of kola nut peelings on the floor, sat back and studied their disposition.

'Now, answer my questions,' he said in a firm tone. 'You are the leader of women's *takumbeng*, aren't you?'

'Yes, I am,' Ngelem replied.

'You are the most senior of seven wives.'

'Yes.'

'You have been with your husband for about sixteen years.'

'Yes.'

'You have two children. Two boys.' Tongembe bent down and read the kola nut peelings closely. 'Err...no...a boy and a girl.'

'Yes.'

'Your marriage is unhappy. In fact, I see here a lot of tears.' She said nothing. 'Your husband rarely comes to your room. Look at this piece here; its back is turned to this one.'

'He never comes to my room,' Ngelem said.

'You do not want him to come.' Tongembe pointed out a piece of kola nut peeling that lay apart from the others.

'No, I don't.'

'You hate the things he does.'

'Yes,' Ngelem answered.

'He is cruel to you,' said Tongembe.

'Yes.'

'You love another man,' he said, pointing at two of the pieces of kola nut peelings which were closest to each other. She said nothing.

'Woman, we have started this session; we must complete it. Answer yes or no. You love another man.'

'Perhaps,' she said, and her mouth started trembling and tears welled up in her eyes.

'I will take that for a yes.' She did not protest. 'I see here a grave. The man you loved died,' Tongembe said.

She wept bitterly. 'I'm doomed to be forever unhappy! I wish he had died in that war. My sorrows would have been less. He is alive and I'm the dead one. Cheuih!'

'Woman, are you willing to see your first husband?'

'It does not matter, does it? I long lost the larva of the beetle and the raffia bamboo on which it fed,' Ngelem said.

'Your fortune tells otherwise,' said Tongembe reassuringly. 'You could see your husband if you wished.'

'Of what use would that be if he does not wish to see me? Is my misery not bound to increase?'

'Perhaps he could take you out of your misery? Your fortune tells me things could be better.'

'I'm married to another man. Things can never be better.'

'But would you be willing to see him if he were willing to see you?' Tongembe asked.

'Yes. No! What would we say to each other? It's been eighteen years. Cheuih! Miserable me! Yes, I wish to see him.'

'Très bien. You will see him,' Tongembe said confidently.

'Impossible! I think I have stayed long enough. What is your fee?' Ngelem asked.

'Give my money after seeing him. Give me a minute,' Tongembe said and stepped out of the room.

Ngelem sat on the chair, dazed by the emotions that had been stirred in her. She was busy recollecting herself and wiping her eyes with the end of her wrapper when she sensed the return of the fortune-teller. She held out the money to him. The man gently took hold of her wrist. She looked up. It was the same face, albeit, older and tougher. The good eye looked at her without blinking. She took in a deep breath and clutched at her mouth to stop it from screaming, but it was not much use. Shivering as if she had suddenly developed a strong fever, she wept and crumbled in a heap on the floor.

When she recovered later, Ngelem proved to be adamant. She declared that she was sticking by her husband; if Ayonchugu thought he could, after all these years, suddenly erupt into her life and have her follow him like a sheep, he was gravely mistaken. She listened to his explanations about why he did not seek her out after the war, and actually broke out laughing amidst her tears and sniffs, at the even more bizarre reason he gave for wanting her back now. On her part, she refused to say a word to justify her marrying Ajong.

'In any case,' Ngelem added, 'the reasons were quite obvious. Whoever this quack you have employed to attempt to dishonour my marriage is, I wish never to see him again.'

'He is not a quack,' Ayonchugu said. 'He is....'

'I don't care who he is,' Ngelem cut in. 'And please, do me a favour,' she added. 'I wish never to see you again either. My husband can make sure you remain a ghost if you persist in your present mission,' she warned with a calm wickedness in her voice that took Ayonchugu aback.

The brothers returned home feeling stupid. The original plan was for Tongembe to meet her and pass on information that Ayonchugu wished to see her discretely. He went ahead with Tongembe's scheme because the latter convinced him he was going to explain everything to her and let her choose to see him or not. When Ayonchugu came from the Standard Four class, he was sure that Ngelem was going to welcome or be civil to him. Instead, Tongembe's theatrics backfired, leaving Ayonchugu very worried.

CHAPTER TWENTY-ONE

The deserter's limp

The Customary Court sat in an antiquated stone building located way behind the Magistrate's Court, facing an expanse of green fields teeming with rodents and some daredevil monkeys who were known to venture down to the grounds of the court and seize food from the hands of children. Eucalyptus and cypress trees provided a shade around the courtyard, where tree trunks were laid to serve as seats for people waiting to be called in for their cases.

Ayonchugu, a cross-section of his relatives and his war veteran friends sat in a small group, chatting and waiting patiently. Ayobang, a friend of his late father, was present too, puffing interminably on an antique clay pipe as if his life depended on it and saying nothing to anyone. They had all either come at Ayonchugu's invitation or their own volition to serve as potential witnesses.

A court messenger came out and invited the two parties to come into the courtroom. They all went in, sat down and waited for the chairman to call the court to order. Ayonchugu studied the chairman for the day. He was called Mofor. He was the most prominent councillor at the Abakwa Area Council. He was well respected for his perfect knowledge of the customs, mores and values of the people in all the villages that were under his jurisdiction. He was dressed in a *togo* and the cap on his greying hair had two red feathers and one pine.

Ayonchugu turned his attention to the six members of the panel who were going to assist the main judge. They too were all men of respectable standing as far as he could tell from their aspects and the red feathers in their caps. He believed he could have to a fair hearing.

Ayonchugu noted that Ajong was not in court. He and his father were being represented by some notables, most prominent among whom was Fingoba. The select group kept to themselves and spoke in whispers all the while.

'Silence everybody!' the chairman ordered. 'We are

starting now. Two matters have been brought to us today by Ayonchugu of Libah village. The first is a land matter, and the second is about marriage. We will deal with the land matter first. Is Ayonchugu or his representatives in court?'

'I'm here,' said Ayonchugu, raising his hand.

'Ayonchugu has accused Fon Fuotum and Prince Ajong of appropriating his land. Is the accused party or his representative here?'

'We are,' chorused the members of the defence.

'We invite Ayonchugu to make his case,' the chairman said.

Ayonchugu stood up and spoke. 'My father owned a piece of land at Ntako in Libah, which my brother and I used to farm. I went to fight in the second big war. When I came back in '46, my father's land was being cultivated by Ajong and his father, Fon Fuotum. All efforts by my family to stop them failed. I want this court to return the land to us, the rightful owners.'

'What makes you believe it was your father's land?' Mofor asked.

'He inherited it from his mother,' Ayonchugu answered.

'Did you say "his mother"?' Mofor looked from Ayonchugu to his six assistants in bewilderment.

'She was the titular Queen Mother of the former fon,' Ayonchugu explained.

'I see. What crop was being grown on the land?' Mofor inquired.

'Arabica coffee.'

'Did you ask them to stop farming on the land?'

'My brother did and was persecuted. He was virtually made an outcast in the village.'

'And you returned from the war in 1946?' Mofor asked, and when Ayonchugu nodded he continued, 'Why are you asserting your ownership only today?'

'I was traumatised by the war. I returned home hoping to find comfort in my family, but the same Ajong had taken my woman. My house was set on fire. I could not afford the cost of my cleansing rites, so I moved to another village to find some peace. After these many years, I'm now in a better frame of mind. That is why I have come to this court to ask Ajong and his father to give back my father's land and my wife and children.'

'We will stick to the land matter for now,' said Mofor. 'Where is your father?'

'He died in the 1920s.'

'Who can testify that the said land belonged to him?'

Ayobang, who was puffing away on his pipe, raised his hand. The chairman gave him permission to speak. He stood up slowly, took out the pipe from his mouth and held it in his left hand, and as he talked, smoke curled out of it into the air, filling the room with a raw tobacco aroma.

'Ayonchugu's father was my strong friend. He owned the land, I assure you. As a young man, he tapped all the raffia-palm bushes there, cultivated parts of the land, and planted the eucalyptus trees that are being sewn today for timber by Ajong and the fon. He was the first person to plant eucalyptus in my village. Many times, he organised working parties and we all went to work on that land for him. At the time Fuotum was our friend and used to come with us at Ayonchugu's father's invitation. Before he died, he told me how the land was to be shared among his sons. He also gave another person he trusted at the time the same information.'

'Who was this other person?' Mofor asked.

Ayobang was already returning his pipe to his mouth, but stopped short by an inch of his lower lip as he replied to the chairman's question. 'Fuotum,' the old man said. 'That was before he sat on the throne.' Pipe in mouth, he resumed his seat.

The chairman and his assistants whispered amongst themselves for a while, nodded in agreement and sat back. The chairman then called on the accused party to respond to the charge.

Fingoba stood up. 'The land belongs to Fon Fuotum, not to Ajong or to Ajong and the fon,' he said. 'In other words, these people have shown that they don't have a case by naming Ajong co-owner.' He looked at his opponents as spitefully as a small boy looks at an ant crawling up his leg. 'That said, I have here the land title. It clearly names Fon Fuotum the owner of the land.'

Fingoba limped up to the table and handed the document to the chairman who perused it and handed it over to the six-man panel. Three of them did not look at it at all.

'We have all heard the complainant and his witness,' said Ntumfor, one of the judges. 'This document was done five years ago. Ayonchugu says the land was occupied when he was at war. That was fifteen years or more ago. What is the proof that the land belonged to the fon back then?'

Fingoba adjusted the arms of his *togo* before talking.

'The facts are simple,' he said. 'The fon and the kwifon know who owns every piece of land in my village. They both say this land belongs to Fon Fuotum. Among the men seated here is Kwifon's messenger who will testify to that. The Queen of England's official has signed this land certificate. Is there anything higher than this to show ownership of land? I call on the chairman to dismiss this case.'

'We have listened to both sides. Now, is there anything else anyone wants to say before we move on?' asked Mofor.

Ndi raised his hand and Mofor nodded.

'I am Ayonchugu's big brother,' he said, standing up. 'I was expelled from the land forcefully at the height of the war, when the price of coffee went up. Ajong and Fon Fuotum asked me to sell my coffee to them and I refused because they were paying half of what I could get from European traders. Fon Fuotum had his militia lock me up in his private jail for three weeks. Next, I was handed over to the district police. They tortured me until I undertook never to return to the land. I plead with this court to ignore the modern documents and revert to the traditional basis of land ownership.'

Ndi sat down. The court was silent. The chairman conferred with his colleagues for a few minutes before addressing the court.

'We have decided to withhold the court's ruling on the land case and to give it together with the decision on the second matter. In the second matter, Ayonchugu accuses Ajong of taking his wife and children. We call on him to put his case before this court.'

Ayonchugu stood up. His good eye quickly scanned the

courtroom and came to rest on the seven judges.

'My fathers,' he began, 'in 1940 I married a woman called Ngelem. Everything on her head was settled. She came to live in my house and became heavy. The baby was not yet born when early in 1941, I joined the army and went to fight in the North. There, we won the war against the Italians and the Germans. I then proceeded to the Middle East, where I served in Palestine and Iraq, before being reassigned to South East Asia. Again, we won against the Japanese and renegade Burmese. I returned to my home in 1946, and discovered to my horror that my wife and children had been stolen by Ajong. I want them back.'

'Did you ask Ajong to return your woman when you came back from war?' asked Mofor.

'No. I was in no position to do that. I was non-existent.'

'How come?'

'In my village, a plot had been cooked up, and I was considered dead and buried. My grave is still there, waiting to be levelled the day I pay for my exhumation rites, which I can ill-afford even today. My house was burnt down. I was too disturbed to think straight, so I left for another village.'

'And now?' said Mofor.

'I have found some peace. I'm more mature. I want my wife and children back,' Ayonchugu said firmly.

'Can anyone testify that she was your woman?'

'Yes. Bobe Chia. He is my father-in-law. He is here.'

'Bobe Chia!' Mofor called out. 'We will listen to you.'

Bobe Chia, a neatly dressed elderly man who had his chin propped on his walking stick, was sitting at the back of the court, avoiding either party like a polygamist avoiding two disagreeing wives. He braced himself on his walking stick with both hands, got up slowly and walked reluctantly to the middle of the room.

'Did this man marry your daughter?' asked Mofor.

'Yes, he did,' Bobe Chia replied.

'Is she still married to him?'

'He died at the war. She remarried.'

There was a murmur around the room.

'Well, he is right here,' said the chairman, pointing at

Ayonchugu. 'Or am I to suppose that you are seeing his ghost?'
The people laughed. 'Supposing it's a ghost you are seeing, did
you return the things paid on her head to its family?'

'They won't take anything,' said Bobe Chia.

'Why?'

'I don't know,' Bobe Chia answered, shaking his head.

'Of course you know,' said Mofor, studying Bobe Chia's
face. 'At your age you should know.' Bobe Chia was silent. 'Did
you receive bride-price from Ajong?' Mofor asked.

'No, I didn't,' said Bobe Chia.

'Did you ever receive anything from him at all?'

'He was married to my daughter, so we did share trifles
now and again,' the old man explained.

'Like what?'

'Kola nuts, a bottle of wine, tobacco, and the like.'

'And some money, I suppose?' Mofor inquired.

'I never asked him for money,' Bobe Chia stated.

'But did he ever give you any?'

'Yes, but it was not the bride-price,' Bobe Chia stated
emphatically.

'What was it for?'

'All I can tell you is that there was no mention of bride-
price in the private transactions I had with Ajong, and I wish to
keep those transactions private.'

'In your opinion, is the marriage between Ajong and your
daughter valid?' the chairman asked.

'I doubt that it is. As I said, I have not taken any money
for her head from him. And from what she told me some time
ago, they have not lived as husband and wife for a long time.'

'And what did she mean by that?' Mofor asked.

'At your age you should understand,' Bobe Chia retorted.

'I do respect your age,' said Mofor. 'But I won't have you
disrespect this court. Do you have anything else to say?'

Bobe Chia nodded and spoke. 'I wish to tender my
apologies to Ayonchugu. I could have been a better father-in-
law to him if he had not died so soon after he joined the army.'

'I'm sure his ghost here seated has heard your apology.
Thank you indeed for coming here today. You may sit down.'
Mofor turned his attention to the defence bench. 'And now, we

wish to hear from this party. Is there any reason you people this way think Ayonchugu should not have his request granted?'

'Yes,' said Fingoba, getting on his good foot and putting a hand on the bad one for support as he approached the judges.

'Introduce yourself to this court,' Mofor said.

'My name is Fingoba. My title is Finjongfinchugu. I represent Ajong in this matter.'

'How long have you known the couple?' asked Mofor.

'For as long as they have been married.'

'Good. What do you have to tell us?'

'Firstly, the woman that man wants is married to another man,' said Fingoba. He signaled to one of the notables on his side and he brought him a deer-skin bag. He slowly slipped his right hand into the bag and pulled out a sheet of paper and held it up. 'I have here the marriage certificate.' He stood still and silent for some moments before returning the document into the bag. As the man turned to leave, Fingoba resumed speaking. 'Secondly, we have heard her father say he received things from Ajong. That was effectively acknowledging that his daughter was Ajong's wife. Who else but a father is best placed to acknowledge the fact that a daughter is married? Who else knows in his heart that he has indeed taken the bride-price? It is the act of taking that acknowledges bride-price, not the discussion of it. He may today be sounding regretful, as we hear from his apology to a ghost as the chairman puts it. But for the past seventeen or more years he has acknowledged Ajong as his son-in-law. Finally, and very importantly, Ayonchugu's request to have the children is very ridiculous. He is not their father. They were born long after he left for the war and long before he came back.'

Fingoba's eyes scanned the faces of the members of the panel and came to rest on the chairman for a few moments. He threw a disdainful look at Ayonchugu's side of the room, adjusted the flowing arms of his *togo* like a priest who had just finished serving communion, spun around, flung his good leg ahead and pulled in the bad one from behind him like a hydra and resumed his seat with a silent flourish in his limp.

'Don't sit too quickly,' said the chairman. 'I'm sure

members of the panel have a few questions for you.'

Fingoba stood up as ceremoniously as he had sat down and indicated with a nod of the head that he was ready for cross-examination. Ntumfor, the youngest member of the panel, spoke.

'There are a few things I want you, or anyone else, to clarify for me. You said that the children were born long after Ayonchugu had gone to war and long before he returned. Am I by this to understand that he is not their biological father?'

'Yes,' replied Fingoba.

'But she was heavy when he left for war,' Ntumfor stated. 'You certainly don't mean a few months when you talk about long after.'

'No. The first child passed on. She got married to Ajong and had two other children.'

'How could she marry when she was already married? Was there a divorce?' Ntumfor asked.

'A divorce was not necessary. Ayonchugu was dead when Ajong married her,' Fingoba explained.

'We all know he did not die because he is right here.' Ntumfor's voice had a hint of annoyance. 'Why does everyone keep saying he died when we all know he did not die?'

'He was reported dead,' said Fingoba.

'Where did that report come from?' Ntumfor asked.

'From the British High Command,' Fingoba replied.

'Before I return to you, can Ayonchugu's people tell us why they would not accept a return of the money for her head when everyone knew so well he had died in the war?'

Kwende spoke for the first time. 'We were not convinced that our son was dead,' he said. 'We only heard it rumoured that he had died. We received no letter reporting his death. We wanted Ngelem to remain our wife until our brother was officially confirmed dead. And were we certain he had died, we would, with her consent, have chosen which of our brothers was going to take her for his wife.'

'So in effect, Ajong acted on a rumour,' said Ntumfor.

One of the notables on Fingoba's side sprang to his feet and spoke with conviction. 'No. Not a rumour. He acted on first-hand evidence from a nobleman who saw him killed in the sands of North Africa.'

'And who was that man?' Ntumfor asked.

'That man was Finjongfinchugu,' replied the notable.

'The same one who has been speaking on Ajong's behalf today?' Ntumfor asked.

'The very same,' the nobleman insisted.

'But he has just told us that the information came from the British High Command,' said Mofor, now looking more alert.

'Can Fingoba tell this court exactly how that information came about?' Ntumfor requested.

Fingoba stood like a tree that had suffered the tortures of a storm the previous night and was waiting for the rising sun to revive its drooping branches and coerce its leaves to face skywards again. The sun seemed to be setting on him instead.

'I can only say what the information available at the time was,' he said. 'He was known to be dead. I suppose this session is not an investigation into how information in the army was passed on to civilians. Those were military secrets.' Three members of the panel nodded; Fingoba's voice went a tenor louder. 'This is not a court-martial, and it would certainly not be in the interest of the members of the panel to turn it into one. My honoured elders, let's not be diverted from the facts of this case. Ajong has a valid marriage with his wife, and I'm calling on the court to dismiss this impostor's ridiculous claim.'

Four members of the panel were seen nodding in agreement with Fingoba, and would, perhaps, have gladly avoided staking their necks over such delicate and alien matters as *military secrets*, but Ntumfor was not intimidated.

'This court has the duty to deliver justice in accordance with our customs and traditions,' Ntumfor stated. 'Things happening in the military are beyond our competence. But here we have a woman who remarried on the grounds that her husband had died in war. It turns out the source of that information may not be credible. The very person who was supposed to have brought that information to his people, and who was supposed to have witnessed the death of Ayonchugu first-hand, is the person here today saying it is not our business to establish the legal grounds of the marriage in question. Fingoba either had information from the High Command about Ayonchugu's death or saw it happen. It has nothing to do with military secrets. Neither the DO, nor the government in Gbuea, nor the Resident British Administrator, not even the Queen's Government in England, can fault us for wanting to know the truth.'

All eyes were now turned expectantly, questioningly, towards Fingoba, who seemed to have all of a sudden run out of words and zest. Members of his team got up and whispered things in his ears. They seemed to be urging him on to say something, but he stood as tongue-tied as Afo-a-Kom.

Mofor broke the prolonged embarrassing silence. 'And the marriage certificate you are presenting, when was it drawn up?' he asked.

'In 1953,' Fingoba said in a less forceful voice.

'In other words, both children were born before their parents got married?' Mofor said.

'Err...no,' Fingoba stammered. 'They were married before the children were born.'

'Do you therefore acknowledge that the said marriage certificate is irrelevant to your defence?' Mofor asked.

'I don't understand you,' said Fingoba, looking confused.

Mofor leaned forward and directed his speech to Fingoba. 'Ayonchugu is right here with us. There was no tangible proof of his death except your word. Ayonchugu's people refused to accept a refund of the money for her head. The woman's father did not formally receive bride-price from Ajong. The grounds for marriage were baseless, and I must say, traditionally, the marriage is null and void. As for the children, they were conceived even before the parents' so-called marriage in 1953 as indicated by the marriage certificate you have presented. By our customs and tradition, children belong to the person who is married – traditionally – to the woman who gives birth to them, unless that person gives up his claim and right to being their father. At the time the children were born, the recognised, legal husband to the woman was Ayonchugu, and he insists the children are his. Who can deny him that?'

The most elderly notable on Fingoba's side said a few loud words originally meant to be a whisper to him. He was then seen to pick up his cane and deer-skin bag, and to walk out steadily from the courtroom as if he had no reason being there in the first place. In the meantime the panel of six and the chairman conferred for a few minutes and seemed to come to an agreement. They sat back and waited for the chairman to speak.

'Ayonchugu, we have a few questions for you. Did you enlist in the army at the same time as Fingoba alias Finjongfinchugu?'

'Yes,' Ayonchugu answered.

'And you both fought battles?' Mofor continued.

'That's what soldiers did.'

'So you are both war veterans?'

'If you say so.'

Mofor looked annoyed. 'I would appreciate it if you give this court more exact answers, otherwise we would be obliged to hold you in contempt of court. Veteran or no veteran, you must respect this court,' said Mofor in his firmest tone yet. He opened a file in front of him and pulled out a sheet of paper and continued. 'This court must proceed in accordance with official directives. I have here a note from the DO stating as follows: "In his Honour's opinion, nothing should be done which might encourage ex-soldiers to believe that they can ignore the Customary Court. His Honour considers that no steps should be taken which might give them the impression that they are in a class by themselves and are therefore entitled in the matter of access to the Courts to different treatment from any other member of the community." Now that we are clear about that, give me straightforward answers. Which battles did Fingoba fight with you?'

'He is here,' said Ayonchugu, gesturing towards Fingoba. 'I think he is best placed to answer that question exactly.'

The chairman glared at Ayonchugu for a few seconds, then turned to look at Fingoba, who remained as taciturn as a cow awaiting slaughter.

'How many veterans of the First World War are here?' asked the chairman. Two hands went up. 'How many veterans of the Second World War are here?'

Nine hands shot up, including one from among the panel.

Fingoba's was the last to come up, and kept weighing down as if it was too heavy for him to keep straight up. He pulled back the ample arm of his *togo* right to his shoulder and propped his elbow on his walking stick, with his hand pointing upwards in front of him, just above his navel.

'Now we will begin with Fingoba alias Finjongfinchugu,' Mofor said. 'What was your Soldier's Service and Pay Book number?'

'Err...I have...err...forgotten,' Fingoba stuttered.

Mofor looked at the right corner of the room. 'The old man there by the wall. What was your Soldier's Service number?'

'Zweiundtwanzig-P-C-neunhunderedeins,' he rattled off without hesitation.

'Danke,' said Mofor. 'And you there, Second World War boys, from the left to the right, let's have your Soldier's Service and Pay Book numbers. Go!'

The first ex-soldier recited: 'Andreas Afunchwi Asongwe. Known to the Army as Corporal Fumchwi Esungwe. 13199A. Unit at engagement: 2410 Company, Army Pioneer Corps. Unit at discharge: 23rd Chindits Brigade, Boma.'

'Chinye Kangno Ncha. 13176. 3rd Heavy Anti Aircraft Regiment Workshop, Boma,' the second man said smoothly.

The rest of the veterans all effortlessly recited their numbers and other unsolicited information from memory. The chairman beamed at them, and turned again to Fingoba and said, 'I guess that has refreshed your memory. Your Soldier's Service and Pay Book or discharge number please.'

'That information is irrelevant to the matter being deliberated by this court,' said Fingoba. 'Eighteen years are not eighteen days.'

Mofor looked very unimpressed. 'Tell that to the German soldier over there. If I were in your boots, I would pray that my fate be better than Eddie Slovik's. Of course, you've never heard the name before. As you said, this case is not a court-martial. But your credentials as a WW2 soldier are dubious as far as this court is concerned. I will advise the fon of Libah that you be stripped of that red feather in your cap and of your agnomen until further investigations show whether you deserve to keep them or to be hanged.'

A murmur of approbation echoed in the courtroom, and Fingoba hung his head, which suddenly had grown heavier than his neck could carry. Two more notables on his side walked out.

'From the facts brought in front of us,' Mofor continued, 'and going strictly by our traditions and customs, of which this court is the enforcer in accordance with the law, the marriage between Ajong and the woman in question was never supposed to have taken place, and is therefore declared null and void by this court. Ayonchugu can have his wife and children back. Ajong can appeal this ruling or go to the DO for a review if he so wishes.

'On the matter of the land, I must stress here that land belongs to whoever occupies it effectively. We think that the fon of Libah has effectively cultivated the land under contention for a very long time. Members of Ayonchugu's family have had enough time before now to make a case in this court or any other court, and have not done so. The fon's authority does not extend to the courts, and therefore the court would be able to return land to Ayonchugu or his family if we found that the land had been illegally occupied by any third party. The fon has a land certificate to back his occupancy of the land. This court therefore dismisses Ayonchugu's claim of ownership of the said parcel of land. He may appeal this ruling or go to the DO for a review if he so desires. I thank my colleagues here for the work they have done today. I thank you all for coming here and wish you all peace in your hearts and a safe journey as you return to your homes. This session is over.'

None of the notables cared to join Fingoba as he limped out of the courtroom. Everyone looked away when his walking stick got stuck in a crevice on the steps outside and he tripped and fell over, and his cap came off and went rolling in the dusty earth path separating the green lawn from the verandah of the courthouse.

Ayonchugu's little crowd left the court feeling happier and more emancipated than when they came in, although no one felt the need to celebrate. The ruling had favoured them in the more important case. They comforted themselves by saying that land was just earth, something abundantly available, which no one came to the world with, and which in the end was only best seen as an ephemeral drudge. The fon was in the twilight of his life, they said, and they would see how much space he was going to occupy in the ground once he went missing.

One thing in particular bogged Ayonchugu and his people. Yes, they won a case. But how were they going to enforce the court's decision? Kwende led a discussion on the subject that afternoon, shortly after leaving the court. 'We all know Ajong. He won't respect the court's ruling. He won't give up Ngelem without another big fight. What do we do?'

'What if we went and asked the DO to send policemen to enforce the ruling?' suggested Niba.

'You speak like a stranger,' said Fuochu. 'Ayonchugu is not the first ex-soldier to go through this same thing. The last time it happened the DO's officials said the police did not have time to waste on such trivialities.'

'That was a long time ago,' said Mbah. 'The DO's people at the time said they were overwhelmed by too many complaints from ex-soldiers. Things have changed now. I too think we should talk to the DO.'

'And what if, in spite of everything, the woman refuses to come with me?' Ayonchugu reasoned. 'It might be wiser to talk her into leaving Ajong. Then, she would feel more at home in my house.'

'Why waste precious time?' asked Saji. 'Waylay her on her way to the market. Capture her and take her home. Simple!'

Pa Ayobang shook his head in agreement with Saji and addressed Ayonchugu. 'The difficulty I see in your case is of your making – you wish to have the woman's consent before taking her back. These are indeed strange times if a woman's consent has to be sought to get her to return to her rightful husband. Is it not said that a woman's flute makes no music? I need a couple of men with real balls. We will go over to Ajong's place and return with her!' The old man looked around, but nobody seemed ready to go with his idea. 'Where is Tongembe?' he asked nobody in particular.

CHAPTER TWENTY-TWO

The jewel and the brick wall

Ngelem was in the throes of her daily torments. They were torments she had endured for many years. They were years she had gone around being the accursed first wife who performed all the important functions of the household without enjoying any of its comforts. In public, she appeared to be effective and strong in her role as the wife of the second most powerful person in the village. He was the *ndifon* – the dauphin, a man with immense influence and wealth. She carried Ajong's bag whenever he was out on public functions; she served his wine, bowed down or on one knee, from the trusted calabash that was the second burden she had to tug along. She ran his harem of wives, ensuring that she understood their fertility patterns, sending them into the marital chamber at the appropriate time. Each wife cooked and served food on a different day, and it behoved her to put a schedule in place and taste his food before he ate it.

Hers was a position the younger wives envied. She ostensibly had unlimited access to the prince who never seemed to have enough of her. Their husband was a person for whom they performed wifely duties. They prostrated their bodies, minds and hearts before him, seeking that rare word or nod of approval that was so fulfilling to a spouse's very purpose. But everything seemed to end with Ngelem. A wife knew her husband had approved of her cooking when Ngelem asked her to prepare the same meal a second time in the same week. She knew she had pleased her lord when, in spite of not being in her period of fecundity, she was called to go to the matrimonial bedroom. Getting Ngelem's approval was as good as getting their husband's.

Ngelem was one of those rare gems of a woman whose husband had never had to take a calabash of palm wine to his father-in-law to humbly negotiate her return to the matrimonial home.

Had they known the deprivations, the desperation, the angst, the sadism that pervaded the relationship between Ajong and Ngelem, the younger wives would have been exceedingly thankful for their lot. Once in a while, they had an inkling that all was not well between her and their lord, and whispered things to one another. They could, however, not put a finger at anything in particular. Over the years, Ngelem and Ajong had become such master players at their game that no one could tell that their life together was bereft of harmony.

While the case was proceeding at the Customary Court, Ngelem and Ajong were in the master chamber. Everyone thought they were teaming together to battle Ayonchugu's claims or sharing a tender moment.

'So you were tricked into going there?' Ajong said in a most sarcastic tone. 'Did Ayonchugu trick you into revealing to him what a frigid old hag you are?'

'He did not lay a hand on me,' she answered indifferently.

'And so he only wanted you back. And now he wants my children too.'

'I hope he wins the case,' she said in a voice which indicated she had had enough of what present life had to offer.

'Win or no win, the ruling of the court is irrelevant to me and you know it,' he said in an off-handed manner.

'But not to me. I will go to him if he wins,' she stated.

'We are married. No court, talk less of the Customary Court, has the power of repeal over this marriage.'

'That won't stop me from going. I have passed the age to let someone else decide where I want to be.'

'You go alone. Await news of what I will do to the children.' His voice did not betray a single emotion, and this, to Ngelem, was more chilling than an outburst of threats.

'You dare not touch my children,' she warned.

'Did you say *your* children?' he retorted with a sneer.

'Yes, my children. You have used Chefor and Ebanga all these years to get your way with me. Now they are big. You can keep them, but I'm going.'

'Did I say I was going to keep them?'

'What do you mean?' she asked, her rising voice betraying

her fright.

'I said await news of what I will do to them.'

'You don't mean...you surely don't mean...!'

'Yes, woman. I mean that I will do to them what I did to those men. Nobody crosses my path and lives to celebrate.'

'You won't harm your own children!' she wept.

'Ha, *my* children you say at last! It's you I'm after. Do you know where your children are now?'

'Playing in the palace arena.'

'Wrong.'

'Where are they? Hey! My mother! I'm dead!'

'Not yet. You will have blood upon your head if you leave. First son or not, I'm going to be the fon of this village. I have the support of the DO. You shall be the queen. I don't care if you have been out of my bed for years. If I want you back there I will have you, frigid or not, disgusting old hag! I shall not be dishonoured. Now, get whoever cooked me the *ambaa* yesterday to prepare the same soup for my lunch.'

She looked at him steadily, trying to will some humanness into his unyielding soul. Feeling powerless, she wiped her eyes with her wrapper and left the room. She went through four rooms and came out by a side-door onto the courtyard of the women's quarters. Her heart missed a beat when she saw three wives buying wares from the Haussa fortune-teller.

After leaving instructions regarding Ajong's lunch with Wife Number Four, her legs carried her of their own accord to the salesman. When he had finished with the younger women, they respectfully stood back.

'Ayonchugu has won the case,' he whispered earnestly. 'Will you meet me in his house this evening? Promise me you will come.'

'I will be there.'

'Now buy something.'

She nodded discretely and bought the wick of a lamp.

CHAPTER TWENTY-THREE

A politician woos ex-sojas

On the evening of the day following the court case, Fuochu came and reminded Ayonchugu about the invitation the KENU had received from G. H. Ashamba. It was a good thing he came, otherwise Ayonchugu would have forgotten about the meeting. For a few days running, he had known that the political patriarch was around, but he had been too preoccupied by his own mission to Libah to care about G. H. Ashamba's.

It turned out to be a grand reunion of ex-soldiers who had been mobilised from the five surrounding villages. G. H. Ashamba was on hand to welcome 'the boys' in all smiles, and was playing the your-humble-servant game as they jumped off the sand-tipper he had hired to bring them in. The North African boys were there, as were the Burma boys. The proudest of them all was a handful of men who had seen action in WW1 and WW2. Some of the boys came in uniforms of sorts complete with rubber 'cane jar' sandals on their feet, while others had on military boots which had been jealously preserved under coats of black polish. They all had assorted medals jingling from their breast pockets.

It was a noisy and nostalgic affair, with lots of singing, foot-stamping salutes and rank calling. They managed to settle down following orders from Samanja Man-Pass-Man, a rock-solid sixty-two-year-old ex-chief sergeant who had fought every war since the turn of the century and emerged without a scratch. G. H. Ashamba welcomed them and promised to make the meeting one about the veterans, and less about himself, their humble host. He introduced some personalities who were with him. Ayonchugu was excited, although surprised that Moka was present.

'You boys did a formidable job for the world,' said G. H. Ashamba. 'Now is the time to do a job for your nation. I have been around for many years. I knew the Germans and I know the English. I know the French and I know French Cameroun. We have been moving in the dark, feeling our way and fumbling along. My experience with these people is like a firebrand and I will wave it for those of you who have the sense to follow the light. I have a question for you. In war, what is the number one rule?'

'Listen to the orders of your commander,' said someone.

'Good', said G. H. Ashamba. 'Some of your comrades are not with you today because they did not obey orders; they perished.' Ayonchugu moved uneasily in his seat. 'You are here today because you listened to the wise instructions of your commanders and executed them. Yet I do not purport to give you orders. By virtue of years and experience, I will give you advice. Our ancestors knew the importance of good advice; that is why they handed down proverbs and riddles to us.'

Some of the veterans had a good idea about what he was driving at and were not surprised at his next words. 'In a matter of months I will go to Lagos to attend the biggest ceremony of its kind ever in West Africa – the independence of Nigeria. We are talking about the once Independent Colony of Lagos and vast regions made up of ancient kingdoms, sultanates and emirates so diverse and divergent at one time that the prospect of making a single nation of them was rather distant. The French have also set a date for the independence of French Cameroun. That leaves you and me to decide what sort of destiny we want. In the months ahead, you will be called upon to make a choice about what you want. At that time, I entreat you to listen to the wisdom of our party. A wise man will not afford to lose both the larva of the beetle and the raffia bamboo. A wise man with no farms does not return to his impoverished home to meet hungry wives and children. He takes up his hoe and machete and goes over to work on his brother's farm. When the crops are ready, his brother will invite him to the harvest. Now, what if he is lucky to have two brothers – one estranged brother who grew up away from home and acquired different mannerisms and beliefs and even a different language, and one who is a bed-mate, even if he has daily disagreements with him as it is so often the case among family members? You think and decide for yourselves which of the brothers he would work with. As for me, my choice would be obvious....'

Ayonchugu was at first alert to every word spoken by the honorable man, but soon his mind wandered back and forth between the war years and the fleeting present.

'I have a special guest from Gbuea, who accepted to come all the way here to be part of this meeting. He is a son of the Coast. He is our son as well. He knows our traditions like a native. By accepting to be with us today, he is reaffirming our stance as one people. Welcome a great teacher. Welcome Moka!'

Ayonchugu looked up and saw Moka stand up and come forward. Samanja Man-Pass-Man shouted a command and all the boys sprang in a single go. He gave another order and they all greeted. Moka responded with a bow, and the men sat down. Moka started speaking.

'I thank the Honourable Ashamba for inviting me here today. He has given me the opportunity to see you, greet you, and honour you for the great heroes that you were, and still deserve to be. I have never before seen this many members of the KENU except during your parade on Empire Day. I was in the Gold Coast and saw the place occupied by veterans in the society. Some years back, they dared to stand up and ask for their due from the Colonial Government, and some of them paid with their lives. They not die in vain; Ghana is today an independent nation.

'Always remember that, as with the war of 1914, this was not our war. You were mostly recruited as volunteers. Volunteering leaves you with a choice. How many of you made that choice freely?'

Ayonchugu could see G. H. Ashamba cross and uncross his legs several times; he could see his face losing its merriness and his smile fading into a smirk, behind which his teeth glittered like a wild basenji's.

'Remember that we were pulled into war by the happenstance of being a United Nations Trust Territory. Had Germany won the first war, we would have been – God forbid! – on the side of the Axis in the second! No wonder then that the German media protested when they learned that Native troops were about to be recruited to fight on the European front. I did not know that it was a greater privilege to die on the European front. European front or not, you fought bravely against formidable warriors. The European front was only one of many fronts it took to fight and win the war.

'I knew very personally a soldier, a brave young man, who fought and returned to his home....' Ayonchugu heard his own story being told. Towards the end of the narration someone figured out who the story was about and shouted, 'Ayonchugu! Number One! Oyee!'

'Oyeeee!' shouted the others, stamping their feet on the ground. A finger pointed him out and before he knew what was happening, strong hands lifted him off the ground and threw him up. As he shuttled towards the ground he was caught and thrown up again. Ayonchugu was rattled by the suddenness of the whole episode, and when he finally was set on his feet he was indeed relieved.

Moka moved over to him and gave him a manly handshake and patted him on the back, while exchanging greetings. He then returned to his former position and continued his speech. G. H. Ashamba, meanwhile, sat scowling, unable to hide his rage as Moka digressed further from the tone he had set for the meeting.

'Veterans that you are, are all proud people. You achieved marvellous feats, and deserve the medals you all so proudly exhibit. You wallow in your own sense of achievement and this is quite comforting for you; you have earned the right to be proud. However, be it from the Colonial Government or from the traditional institutions, veterans have not had the support they needed to make their lot better. While you know best what your needs are, one does not have to visit a fortune-teller to know that you needed, and still need, special medical attention; that you deserved opportunities to acquire an education; that you should have been given priority in training and recruitment for jobs; that your children deserve good and free education; that you deserve a pension to cater to your infirmities, especially when you become old. And the list continues. In Europe, all sorts of projects have been implemented ever since the end of the war: Housing for Heroes projects, Education for Heroes projects, Health for Heroes projects, Monuments for Heroes projects. You name them. All soldiers who won the war are treated as heroes. So why do you deserve any less?

'These are the issues that you should be putting to those who are in power. Any formula for independence brought to you by any politician should address foremost the plight of your lot, for if the British leave without sorting out these issues, I tell you, our future politicians will never show you the concern that the nation for which you fought should show.

'And as far as the great political question of the day is concerned I have this to say: You do have fertile land and the energy to farm it. You do not have to work on another person's farm for a living. If you do not understand me, ask your neighbour and he will explain to you.'

G. H. Ashamba promptly got up and stormed into his house through the main door. Moka continued talking to the men.

'Ten years ago I sat in my office in Ngonibi pondering what my son may say about you men fifty, sixty or seventy years from then. I scribbled something which I titled "The Palm Tree Greens" on paper. I do not have that piece of paper here with me, but it sounded something like this:

> For a king the greens battled
>
> Came home quite rattled.
>
> Fodder for fire they often were,
>
> Sent forth the battle front to test,
>
> Elite troops may no onslaught bare
>
> Quartered safely in iron-clad nest.
>
> Hundreds'f thousands never returned
>
> In tombs worldwide they were interred;
>
> The no less brave were forgotten
>
> Rustic lives by misery to shorten.

We must here their plight unfold

Lest history us to ransom hold

That we saw but never were bold

To decry the pittance untold

On which the greens grew old...

And died.

We will remember them.

Moka paused, head bowed, while the men looked at him in silence, some nodding gravely as they gradually made sense of his words. Eventually, he lifted his head and spoke. 'My wish, my fervent wish for you men, is that any prophetic element in the lines I just recited be proven wrong one day. As for history, nothing can change it.'

He turned around to return to his seat and only then did the men start speaking, in low tones.

The sun set and it grew dark; oxygen was pumped into three Tilley lamps which were then lit and hung up from poles. The atmosphere was festive. There was food and a lot to drink. The voices of the men grew louder. Their bravado soared. They re-enacted scenes of bravery and cowardice from the war. They imitated the speeches of Wingate, Tottenham, Auchinlek, Wavell, Clavert and Churchill. They sang military songs and yodelled folk tunes creatively.

Ayonchugu wanted to meet Moka, who, sometime after his speech, left his seat and went into the house. Ayonchugu, holding a half-empty bottle of beer, went to the main door. It was manned by a huge unyielding man with a scowl on his face who started snarling in Haussa when Ayonchugu insisted on going inside.

'Why don't you bark? Carrier! *Linwan!*' Ayonchugu flung back at him. As he turned to leave, the door suddenly swung open and Moka emerged, looking baffled and hasty as if he had just seen spirits. When he saw Ayonchugu his countenance regained some candour and he said, 'Come with me,' and launched himself towards the car parking area. Ayonchugu swallowed his beer in three gulps, flung the bottle on the ground and trudged after Moka. They both got into his Austin A40 and shut the doors with loud bangs. Moka manoeuvred the car in a wild sway out of the yard and sped off down the dirt road.

'I will kill them both!' Moka said in a near-scream.

'Whom?'

'That bigot called Honourable Ashamba and that haggard quack in your village! I will begin with the wizard! I'm talking about your father-in-law. You shall be my witness! Then I will dedicate the rest of my life to hunting down that treacherous Ashamba until I get him!'

Ayonchugu knew better than to argue with him or to ask any questions. Still, he was a bit worried about Moka's driving. They emerged onto the Trunk A Highway. 'Driving fast on these gravelled roads in the night can be very dangerous. Our ancestors said an angry man....'

'Drop the ancestor crap!' Moka cut in in a loud voice. 'I'm not sure who mine are!'

Ayonchugu remained silent as they sped along for about two miles. Then he spoke. 'I do not intend to return to the village right now.'

'No? I thought the meeting was over.'

'I did not come to Libah for the meeting. I came on a mission to retrieve from Ajong and his father what was rightfully mine. We were in court yesterday.'

'Indeed?' asked Moka slowing down a little.

'The Customary Court said I could have Ngelem and the children back.'

'Indeed?' he said again and slowed down the car to the legal speed limit.

'Yes. I hope to return with them to Ngonibi. They are in Ajong's compound and I'm at a loss about how to take them out of the place. Ajong is powerful enough to defy the court.'

'Is she willing to come with you?'

'She confessed her dislike for him and implied that she still liked me. She promised to meet my brother yesterday and failed to show up. She sent information that she couldn't leave without her children. He is to see her again today. I guess the biggest problem now – as always – is Ajong.'

'So you need coercion of some kind then?' Moka asked.

'I'll need to convince her to come with me, or use force.'

'I'm sorry I did not ask your opinion before taking off. Are you willing to use force – now?

'Yes,' responded Ayonchugu.

Moka brought the car to a gritting halt. 'Your ex-soldier friends,' he said.

It took Ayonchugu a few seconds to realise what Moka was driving at. He nodded in agreement.

'From there we are off to Ngonibi for the next lap of tonight's mission,' Moka said.

Again Ayonchugu nodded, although he knew he could make that journey only when he knew exactly what had suddenly come upon his friend of old, and agreed with his plans. Moka did a u-turn and sped back into the village.

When they got to the road that branched off to the mansion, Moka stopped the car and said, 'I can't stand the sight of that man again. I will wait by the road. I'm sure you know what to do.'

Ayonchugu left the car and went to talk discretely to his friends. It took only a few minutes of groundwork by Fuochu to get enough volunteers for the job. While Ayonchugu and Moka went in search of Tongembe, Samanja Man-Pass-Man was leading a covert operation in quest of Ngelem and the children.

That night a handful of men stormed into Fingoba's compound. They met him sitting alone in his parlour, mournful, besieged by the troubles visited upon him by the return of Ayonchugu to the village.

Samanja Man-Pass-Man did not give room for ceremony. 'We are looking for Ngelem and her children,' he said. 'You know where they are. Take us there now!'

'I have not the least idea what you are talking about,' Fingoba said.

'Of course, you do. Either you tell us where they are, or we tell the Colonial Government that you deserted the army during the war. But even that would be doing you a favour. These boys are really angry now, and you may end up with no legs at all, instead of your leg-and-a-half,' the samanja threatened.

'I truly do not know, samanja. Since the court case I have not been able to see Ajong. He has threatened to kill me for losing the marriage case.'

'Not just for losing the case but also for lying to the whole village. Your disability was self-inflicted wasn't it? At least you should be able to tell the truth about what really happened to your leg tonight.'

Samanja Man-Pass-Man gave a disabling kick to the scar on Fingoba's withered leg. He howled in pain, and as the samanja got ready to deliver a second missile, Fingoba stammered, 'The children are in Kwifon's den. No one knows where the woman is.'

The samanja looked at him in disgust. 'It's a good thing you deserted,' he said. 'Just one kick and you sing like a weaver bird. If King George had had only men like you, he would certainly have lost the war. You are taking us to Kwifon's den right now.'

Fingoba's eyes widened in alarm. 'No please, I can't. That would be a sacrilege.'

'Don't worry. No one out of this group will know about it. If you don't take us there, we will go to Ajong and tell him how much you've told us tonight; you would be dead by morning. Your choice.' Samanja Man-Pass-Man turned to his companions and said, 'Let's get out of here.'

The men turned around and marched out of the room. They were gone only a short distance into the night when they heard Fingoba say, 'Wait for me! I will take you there.' They waited for him to join them. He came on crutches, pulling his bad leg painfully after him. They all set off in purposeful silence in the direction of the palace, taking the back roads.

Once they arrived at Kwifon's gateway, the men fell back and Fingoba went in through the members' entrance. After a long wait, he emerged, closely followed by two frightened teenagers. The samanja instructed some of the men to take them out of sight. He then turned to Fingoba and said, 'You indeed invite it upon yourself like the screeching cricket in the riddle. Kwifon's eyes are the very grasses you see around you.

A thorn does not discriminate whose foot it pierces. Be wise enough to return to the den, perform the necessary ablutions and take the members' exit when you leave. Farewell.'

The men were hardly gone when they heard the voice of Kwifon rolling out a litany of mournful notes. 'This is a strange hour for Kwifon to sound his voice,' Samanja Man-Pass-Man said. 'That fellow is certainly done with. I nearly feel sorry for him.'

The men walked on till they reached the *mitiee* that was at the centre of the village. Waiting for them there were Tongembe, Ndi and Moyu. The veterans handed the children over.

'Our job is done,' said Samanja Man-Pass-Man. 'Greet our comrade. Tell him we wish him good luck.' Without more fuss, he and his men went off into the darkness.

Sometime past mid-night, the party of five emerged at a milestone on the Trunk A Highway and found a car waiting. The back door opened and Ayonchugu stepped out. The children were ushered into the car, where their mother sat weeping inconsolably. The girl started crying too. Ayonchugu had a few words with his brothers and nephew, and then got into the front passenger seat. Moka started the car.

'We should be in Ngonibi before daylight,' muttered Ayonchugu.

'That depends on the state of the roads,' Moka responded. 'You know, this car is quite low. The last time I travelled that way only Land Rovers and mammy wagons could go all the way.'

CHAPTER TWENTY-FOUR

The story of Moka

Ayonchugu and Moka drove for a long time in silence while their backseat passengers tried to comfort one another. Ayonchugu could glean most of their conversation over the din of the car engine.

'Why would Tata keep us in Kwifon's den?' asked Chefor. 'Women don't go there. I'm not yet initiated.'

'I was very frightened. I kept imagining that spirits would come out and swallow us up!' said Ebanga.

'It did not happen, and here you are,' said Ngelem soothingly. 'Just calm down.'

Ayonchugu kept shaking his head. There still lurked in his subconscious the absolute terror of those moments in his childhood whenever children were told in whispers by an adult that Kwifon was going out. They would stay close to home, and when they heard the strikingly rhythmic notes warning of Kwifon's appearance, they would dive under their beds and lie there, trembling, barely breathing. Kwifon's music would sound as though it was from everywhere and yet from nowhere. It would grow oppressively louder and louder as the spirit approached, crushing their little bodies with the force of its all-paralysing notes until they felt like burying themselves in the ground for safety. Then, as the spirit went by and travelled further away, there would descend upon the atmosphere a prolonged heart-thumping silence, until birds returned with their chirping, and then the voice of an adult would call out to the children.

'Really, it was not as scary as I thought it would be,' Chefor said. 'Only Suh and Nformi were there. They told us many stories about the village.'

'They gave us achu with a lot of meat,' said Ebanga.

'Who were all those men who came for us?' asked Chefor.

'Don't ask questions now. These two men and their

208

friends have saved your life.'

'We imagined that we were about to be used for a sacrifice!' exclaimed Chefor.

'The gods won't allow that,' said Ngelem. 'It's been a long night. Have a rest.'

Ebanga laid her head on Ngelem's shoulder and soon fell asleep. Chefor leaned towards the window and looked vacantly into the approaching dawn.

Ayonchugu's mind was clear by now. He sat brooding over the developments of the night. Planning had been fortuitous. His mission had succeeded. Surely, Mengen would be happy. What about this woman, Ngelem? Was she indeed his wife? She looked withdrawn. His thoughts were interrupted by Moka, who started speaking without warning.

'You know, my father was a terribly embittered man.'

'Why?' Ayonchugu asked.

'My mother walked out on him with her lover. No one knew where they went. Duala, Enugu, Onitsha or even the Colony of Lagos. They both simply disappeared, and no one heard anything from them again. My father was left with three of us – all boys. He never remarried.'

'How did he manage to bring you up by himself?'

'Determination. He had a lot of that. I was encouraged to go to school by Catholic priests from Bojongo.'

'Is that not the place where the early missionaries built a beautiful church up in the mountains in the heart of the forest?'

'Yes. Papa had little money to send me to school. My brothers did not care about school. They hated going to church, being altar boys and being bullied by the priest. They went with Papa to the farm and teased me all the time. They would ask if I had managed to pinch Holy Communion from the Reverend Father. Later, they became very proud of me, and were excited each time I came back home from school. They would put together their meagre resources and give them to me.'

'So you were their *mukala*?' Ayonchugu said.

'Oh, yes. They actually called me that. When I was mid-way through primary school, the priest told me that an important government official was impressed with my results and had decided to sponsor me to the highest level.'

'Who was it?' Ayonchugu asked.

'I didn't ask that question until I went to the Teachers Training College in Calabar. I wrote to the priest in Bojongo through whom money was being channelled to me, asking to know who my benefactor was. He replied that he would seek the permission of my sponsor before telling me. Later, he informed me that his request was not granted. I threatened to withdraw from school if I didn't get the information.'

'I guess you were not serious about withdrawing?'

'I actually came back home to my father. By that time he had become a photographer. I started thinking about joining him in the profession. The one thing I came out with from my short experience in photography was my wife. One day I sat in for my father and went to photograph a family. She was there in all her natural beauty, waiting for me to claim her. I did. The priest sent me a letter saying that I needed not withdraw from school because the Catholic Mission had taken over full responsibility for my education. So I returned to Calabar and completed teacher training.

'I started teaching in Mamfe. Then I was offered the position of Headmaster of Catholic School Ngonibi, a struggling new school.'

'That was a long way from Mamfe,' Ayonchugu observed.

'Not just that. I had just got married. The mission convinced me to go. I owed them my success. You know how the Ngohnibi school performed so well that the missionaries decided to fund my studies in the Gold Coast. On my return last year, I was recruited by the Department of Education.

'Politicians have ever since been on my neck, trying to convince me to join one party or another. I've made it clear that I'm a civil servant and will do just my job, irrespective of which party is in power. My stance has not endeared me to any of the party leaders.'

'Obviously not. They call it "sitting on the fence".'

'Whatever. Now back to G. H. Ashamba. As you know, that is a name that has been in the power circles forever. He called the shots when the Germans were there, and still managed to crawl under the skin of the British. I'm sure you've heard how he managed to create a semblance of political neutrality and became an arbitrator between the Colonial Government and the Ziks, when in reality he was one of the propelling forces in Dr Zik's movement in the Eastern Territory.

'When I was still in Standard Six, he sent me a personal letter of congratulations for my excellent academic record. You can imagine how proud I was.'

'I once received such a letter myself. I know the feeling.'

'Again, after I resumed teacher training, he wrote to me saying it was a wise decision I had taken to complete my course. I wrote to my priestly sponsor demanding to know if G. H. Ashamba had anything to do with my education. The priest said yes, he had something to do with the education of all children the mission was sponsoring because he was a contributor to the fund established by them to assist achieving pupils. I dropped the matter. When I was working in Ngonibi G. H. Ashamba came to see me. He said he had only been passing through the village and having learned I was headmaster there, had stopped by for a chat. We discussed politics, naturally, and disagreed on so many things that when he left he looked like a father whose favourite son had let him down.

'While I was in the Gold Coast I wrote a letter congratulating him on the contribution he was making to the advancement of education in this territory. We kept a stream of polite communication going between us until I returned. I'd made him understand that I was more interested in intellectual debates, in underlying truths than in political affiliations. We had tended to find a lot of common ground in the former than in the latter. When he invited me to the meeting of the veterans, he seemed to have forgotten that fact. After my address yesterday, he told me that I was a most ungrateful young man. I said I had nothing to be grateful to him for. He said I had everything to be grateful to him for. He said I'd just blown my chances of becoming *somebody*. He then launched into the story of my education...of my life....'

It was dawn when the car drove into Ayonchugu's compound. Its exhausted and sleep-deprived passengers crawled out, stretching and yawning liberally, mouths wide open. The only person who remained in the car was Ngelem. Mengen, with Nkahfi hard at her heels, came rushing towards the car, in utter amazement at the sudden early morning invasion. She greeted Moka with all the fuss. His attention kept straying towards Nkahfi. Mengen noticed him studying the boy and said, 'You do recognise my little husband, don't you? This is Nkahfi who was born about the same time as your son.' She turned to the boy and said, 'Stop rubbing your eyes and say good morning to the HM.'

'Of course I do recognise him,' said Moka. 'He's grown a lot. It never ceases to amaze me how quickly children grow.'

'I still remember the day you paid a fine for not being able to immediately tell him from your son,' Mengen said.

'I was also thinking about that day,' Moka said, nodding.

Mengen turned to the teenagers, greeted them warmly and invited everyone into the house. The children went in with Nkahfi. Mengen approached the car and peered in through the glass of the passenger door. The door opened from within and she greeted in Binibi. Ngelem responded in Libah.

'Please come into the house and warm yourself,' she said.

Ngelem came out of the car ever so collectedly and went with Mengen to join the children.

Ayonchugu and Moka went to the men's section of the house, where a fire burnt on logs.

'You look terribly upset,' Ayonchugu remarked.

Moka nodded and said, 'When I look at Mengen I feel a great heaviness in my heart. I feel a strong sense of loss. I should be happy, yet I'm not. I feel like weeping.'

'I understand. All these wasted years.'

'Right now, I'm exhausted. But I'm going to see this through to the end this very day.'

'I think you should wait a day or two before confronting Nyarong,' Ayonchugu suggested. 'Also, let's go together.'

Moka shook his head. 'I can't wait,' he replied. 'This is not the kind of visit for which to take along a son-in-law. Don't worry. I won't strangle him – just yet. What I want very urgently from him now is information.'

'Do let me go with you,' Ayonchugu offered. 'I'll stay outside.'

'Agreed,' Moka replied. 'Just don't do anything unless there is a real fight.'

After breakfast Ayonchugu took Mengen to one side and told her who the lady and the two children were. Mengen just kept gaping at him.

'Why are you not saying anything?' he asked her.

'My lord, what's there to say?' Mengen replied.

'Are you happy now that I have brought them?'

'It is a good thing. I should be happy.'

'Good. The teacher is going somewhere soon. When he is done, we are all going to sit down and have a real family talk before he returns to Gbuea. I'll get him some smoked antelope – if he would accept it. Don't forget to put together something for Matalina. Some *egusi* or *koki*.'

'I know what to do,' Mengen said.

'I leave it to you then.'

'Where are they going to sleep?' Mengen asked. 'Well, not the children. I mean...the woman.'

'The day is still young. I can bother about that later.'

The next half-hour saw Ayonchugu and Moka going at a fast and purposeful pace along the jagged forest tracks which took them to Nyarong's. But for the men's footfalls, the place was silent and the huts looked vacated. Ayonchugu stayed within earshot while Moka approached the door of the building that was decorated with fetishes. He was about to knock when Nyarong spoke.

'Come in teacher. You hardly slept at all and you woke up with the chickens.'

Moka stepped into a room with a low bamboo ceiling, and, slightly stooping, peered at the man he had come to confront. He was sitting, Buddha-like, at the far corner.

'Sit down, teacher. I was expecting you. I'm receiving nobody today until I'm done with you.'

'No Nyarong. It is the other way round. You are receiving no one until *I* am done with you.'

'I expected you to say even that. Be cautioned. The day

has not come when the one-eyed see more than the two-eyed, and in this case the seven-eyed. The youngster at the top of the mountain thinks he has conquered the village below because it is lying at his feet. The hawk thought mother hen....'

'Nyarong, I have come to ask you some important questions and would need straight answers. Where is the woman called Atemnji?'

'Take a seat. How the impatient scares away the grasshoppers in the heat of the sun! The patient waits until nightfall and then lights a lamp. The grasshoppers come to him. You are....'

'Where is Atemnji? I ask again.'

'The seven spirits see everything that was, that is, and that will be. But they stay dumb until the chink of the coin gives them speech. Drop a coin on the platter.'

'Nyarong, you know in your ingenuity that I have not come here for divination. Once upon a time, you and your assistant ran away from Kanke with a pregnant woman. Next thing anyone alive remembers, you arrive in this village with a little girl. What happened to her mother?'

'I owe you nothing, young man. That includes the answer to your question. Sunrise is most conducive for harvesting my medicine plants. That's the back of my head you are seeing. If you would excuse me....'

Nyarong sprang to his feet as he was talking and unhooked a bag from a wall post, picked up his sheathed knife and strung it around his waist and in one sweeping move seemingly unlikely for his age, he was out of the door, pulling it shut behind him. Moka sat in the sudden darkness of the room, head bowed for a few seconds, then got up and felt his way to the door, pushed it open and stepped out. Nyarong had vanished. Moka stood in the empty yard, stupefied, wondering what next to do.

'Ayo!' he called.

'Are you ok, HM?' asked Ayonchugu coming from the side of the building.

'Nyarong has just escaped. Did you see him?'

'No. I heard you talking with him. Then I thought I heard him leaving, and hurried over.'

'The old crook! I will get him yet!' Moka said, his voice full of anger.

'Let's go and talk to Nwenmufu,' Moka suggested. 'He probably knows as much as Nyarong.'

'Good idea. Where does he live?'

'You see that path over there,' said Ayonchugu, pointing in the direction of a track that went through the bushes behind the dwelling. 'It leads to his hut.'

CHAPTER TWENTY-FIVE

On the tracks of a mysterious woman
Nwenmufu not only talked willingly but also offered to take the men to the village where he had carried out Nyarong's most hideous orders many years before. They drove for a whole day, left Moka's car at the end of the road, and continued on foot until they came to a village which was lost in the heart of the forest.

The men walked the length of a street that traversed the village. There were huts on either side of the street. Every hut had a branch of nkeng stuck above the door. The men shouted out greetings left and right to the villagers who came to their doors to look at them. No one talked to them, but they noticed that some of the villagers waved branches of nkeng in response to their greetings. At a short distance after the last house on the street the men came to a grotto.

'It happened around here,' said Nwenmufu.

'Are you sure?' Moka asked.

'Yes,' he answered. 'My life has depended on tracks. I can't miss one when I have been there before. This shrine was not here. But it did happen at this end of the village.'

'Let's talk to the villagers,' Moka suggested.

'Do you understand their language?' asked Ayonchugu.

'I can't say until I hear them talk,' Nwenmufu responded.

The villagers turned out to be unhelpful; they simply stared back, taciturn, blank faced, or walked away at the approach of the three men. They were becoming exasperated when they saw some children going about. Nwenmufu called out to them and they came running. Using signs and whatever words he could find, he managed to make himself understood. The children responded, each saying something or adding to what another had said, and the old man kept shaking his head.

'They say we must carry nkeng. They say that Nkeng was here just this morning with a man. Nkeng is a woman. They say food will rain on the village this year; that she and the man are this morning just up the road that is crying. That's as much as I could put together.'

'What do they mean by "the road that is crying"?' asked Moka.

'It might be that the woman was crying,' Nwenmufu said.

'Ask them if that's what they mean. Can they describe the woman?

The old man talked to the children, listened to them for a while and turned and spoke to the men. 'She was crying, they say. I think the description is hers. She could not have remained perpetually young.'

'Why do they call her Nkeng?' asked Moka.

The response came in a question. Did they not know *the Nkeng*?

'They could not be gone too far,' said Ayonchugu. 'We may catch up with them yet.' As he spoke he started to move. Moka was hard at his heels, and Nwenmufu shuffled after them.

They were hurrying towards the exit of the village when one of the children ran after them shouting something in earnest.

'He is saying we must carry nkeng,' Nwenmufu explained. 'I'll ask him why.' Nwenmufu spoke to the boy, and reported that he was not sure he understood what the child was saying.

'The voice of a child is the voice of the gods,' Ayonchugu said. 'I suggest we carry the plant. It seems they thrive on it here.' He stepped into the bushes and in a few moments returned with a long plant. He used a folding knife to cut it into three, and gave each of them a length of it.

Thus began the chase across the land for the woman the men now simply referred to as Nkeng. It was a long chase for a target that was determinedly elusive. Their spirits were kept up by the fact that Nkeng was actually moving in-land, in the very direction from which the three men had set out.

A new day broke with Ngelem and Mengen receiving Tongembe in Ngonibi. As yet, Ngelem did not know exactly who he was, although she had long suspected that he was as much a fortune-teller as a monkey was a gorilla. She was so engrossed in her own musings that she did not at first bother asking him to explain himself, or his sudden pervading presence in her life. She knew time was the solution to many mysteries, and if he was one of the mysteries her life was so replete with, so be it.

Information came to her in a round-about manner. Mengen was no polyglot like Nyarong, and even though Ayonchugu spoke the Libah language with Nkahfi, who had acquired it with ease, she could barely understand a few greetings. Ngelem could speak some Binibi which she had picked up mostly from Ngonibi traders. She set to interpreting Tongembe's words for Mengen. She noticed that he was very selective about the information he divulged. She learned that he was Ayonchugu's big brother who had lived most of his life out of the village. He did not say where.

As Tongembe relaxed in the hospitality accorded him, he began speaking more freely. In a subsequent discussion with Ngelem, he informed her about the happenings in Libah since her departure.

'Libah is boiling over. The fon has disappeared.'

'At last. But alas! I have no more tears to shed.'

'Libah is in turmoil over the arrest of very important personalities and witnesses will be called to testify against them in their trial.'

'Is Ajong making it to the throne?' Ngelem asked.

'He has been arrested for at least one assassination. Will you testify against him?'

'A woman's flute makes no sound. I can't.'

'Yes, you can. It is being handled by the police. They will listen to you.'

'Would that not be as good as trying to get a foothold in excrements with my walking stick?'

'No,' Tongembe replied. 'You will neither be rubbing yourself in mire nor will you be wasting your time. His crimes are not only against you. Lots of wrongs have to be righted.'

'I won't want to be in the same room with him again.'

'You could speak to the police.'

'I may do that.'

'Fingoba is dead. Ajong again is thought to be involved.'

Ngelem performed a short spontaneous dirge. 'How did it happen?' she asked.

'Do you consult a necromancer on the death of a dog?'

'Definitely not,' Ngelem replied. 'But you still may want to satisfy your curiosity.'

'He was found dead by the roadside the morning you left,' Tongembe revealed. 'His skin was all burnt, but not his clothes. They were all said to be intact.'

'Kwifon's retribution,' Ngelem said, tapping her shoulders lightly with the tips of her fingers in horror.

'Mm. The thorn not discriminating whose foot it pierces.'

As the day wore on she found herself feeling at home with Tongembe who never ran out of speech or ideas. Their interaction inevitably brought them to a discussion about the fortune-telling session. He was apologetic about misleading her about his identity.

'It was important for us to know if you still cared for Ayonchugu,' he explained. 'It was the only way I could think of getting you to talk with my brother.'

'And what if I said I did not care for him?' Ngelem asked.

'We could have changed our strategy but not called off the venture.'

'What else are you still concealing from me?'

'Nothing,' Tongembe replied.

'Absolutely?' Ngelem did not look convinced.

'*Absolument.*'

'Where have you been all these years? You know, when I was getting married to Ayonchugu I was told he had a brother in French Cameroun and another in the tin mines of Jos. Which of them are you?'

Tongembe thought for a moment and decided that she was safe to confide in. He told her about himself.

'You have not told me about your wife and children.'

'The war in *Indo-Chine* finished me. That which could have made me a husband and a father was blown off, and the stump that is left is only good enough for my regular handshake with my friend down there.'

'I'm so sorry,' Ngelem said, her voice full of compassion.

'You don't have to be,' Tongembe said. 'Those who ought

to be have outlawed and are bent on hunting me down.'

'All of that will change with the coming of independence.'

'I'm sure it will.'

Ayonchugu's friend, Kelechi, was on his way on an unannounced visit to Ngonibi. He was accompanied by a woman whom he kept referring to as "Mother".

For two days, Kelechi and the woman had travelled non-stop from a town in Eastern Nigeria to the frontier village of Ekom. They had canoed across a hippopotamus- and crocodile-infested river, and continued on foot until they had reached Mamfe. From there they had hitched-hiked on a *gongoro* lorry, trekked for some miles, and reached the first of their destinations in a land which was still as virgin as it had been for centuries.

She plucked two nkeng stems and handed one to him saying, 'Son, hold this. We are in the Land of Nkeng. The world, open as it is, holds a thousand mysteries. Sometimes we are privileged to be let into some. Today, you will see another side of me. I will answer your questions, but the story of a lifetime cannot be told standing up.'

She then led him through a linear settlement of wooden huts, whose rustic inhabitants recognised her and waved excitedly with nkeng plants. She acknowledged them by holding up her plant. She brought him to a well-tended grotto at the far end of the village. In the middle of the grotto was a stone slab.

'This altar is the footstool of Nkeng,' she said. 'It is a receptacle for my tears. I sat on the ground in the first few years of my pilgrimage here. The villagers planted this rock when Nkeng became a cult. I planted every single one of these plants. They are made up of thirty clumps. Each clump represents a year from the day my misery began. What misery!'

She crumbled onto the ground and wept for a long time, supplicating and invoking in a language known only to her. When her lamentation ended, she planted her nkeng stem and tried to explain her actions to Kelechi.

'This village once suffered a long-running drought, causing some people to flee. And then one day, a woman came along and gave birth to a kid which did not survive. You won't believe a human being gave birth to a goat, but they did. Since then, the skies have been opening just at the right moment to water this land. In this village I'm treated as a priestess or even a goddess of abundance.'

'What became of the woman?' Kelechi asked.

'As I said, it is a world of mysteries,' replied the woman. 'Each shall be unraveled at the right time. As for me, these people do not know where I came from. What I know is that they decorate their doors with nkeng and pray for my return. When I delay in coming, they panic.'

With her face still awash with tears, Kelechi and his mother walked through the village. From one side of the street they heard people shout out, 'With whom do you dwell?' and from the other side came the answer, 'I dwell with Nkeng!' The couple left the village as unobtrusively as they had come in, without speaking a word to anyone.

Now, the closer Kelechi and his mother got to Ngonibi, the clearer it became to him that she was reluctant to continue the journey. At one point she suggested they call it off. Her increasing disinclination to complete the trip had the opposite effect on him. He was particularly worried about one thing and sought to clarify it with his mother.

'Mother, why are we going to Ngohnibi?' Kelechi asked.

'You keep asking the same question over and over. I never tire of answering you. We are going to see my daughter. So look forward to seeing your sister.'

'Daughter? Sister?' Kelechi said, looking perplexed. 'I thought....'

'Don't think too much, Kele. This has been a long journey and your mind needs a rest.'

As on many occasions in his life, he kept silent, preferring to let things unfold.

Now, as they entered the village of Ngonibi, she began to tremble all over. She shielded her face with her wrapper and shrouded herself up like the pudic wife of a Bororo man.

'Son, I want you to promise me something.'

'What is it, Mother?' Kelechi asked.

'Promise that you will always treat me as your mother.'

221

'Of course, I promise.'

'Even if you find out that I have not been completely truthful with you. Please, promise,' she pleaded.

'I'm not sure about that,' Kelechi replied. 'It all depends on the nature of what you have been hiding from me.'

'I've not hurt anybody,' his mother said. 'I've only hidden certain things from you.'

'I'll try to understand why you did that.'

'One can't be afraid of falling when one is already lying on the ground. Please, son, I only wish for you not to let me be grounded forever. Give me a hand and I'll be on my feet again.' These were her last words before they stepped over the threshold, and bore their bedraggled selves towards Ayonchugu's smoking room.

'Anybody dey dey?' Kelechi called out.

Tongembe came to the door, closely followed by Ngelem.

'Na dis be Ayonchugu him house? Tell'am say him mother don come,' the stranger announced.

'Indeed! Where is she?' asked Tongembe.

'Right here,' said Kelechi, gesturing towards his mother. 'Tell him Kelechi of Chindits Brigade, son of Igkoegba is here too!'

'Are you his friend?'Tongembe asked.

'More than his friend. We fought in the war. He saved my life and I saved his. We are brothers. We are survivors.'

'Come in my, brother. I'm his brother. Sit down.'

Ngelem greeted the visitors and went over to Mengen's kitchen.

'Are you sure you are brothers?' Kelechi asked.

'Same father, same mother,' Tongembe replied.

Now Kelechi was confused indeed. Did Tongembe not recognise his mother? Did they come to the wrong place? He turned to his female companion. She was withdrawn and wrapped up in spite of the warmth in the room. Most likely, something had failed to register in his mind correctly, and he thought it might be safer not to pursue the matter further then. He was no longer certain why he and his mother came into that house.

'Where did you see action together?' Tongembe asked.

'In Boma. We first met in Mombassa and got to be friends. And from then our fortunes were tied together. We lived through bad and worse times together. We saw horror together on Crucifixion Day. He was our Number One.'

'Number One?' Tongembe said.

'Yes.'

'And you were Number what?'

'Err...I did not have a number.' Kelechi paused in thought for a while. 'There was only a Number One, I believe.'

Ngelem returned with water for the visitors and announced that food would be ready in a moment. Mengen followed after a while with a basket full of *achu* and set it on the table. She greeted the visitors and turned to leave. The woman, meanwhile, upon setting her eyes on Mengen started trembling all over again. As Mengen walked out, the woman started sobbing uncontrollably. Kelechi tried to comfort her, but his actions only caused her to belch out a heart-rending lamentation. In only a couple of minutes the atmosphere changed, and already, a neighbour's voice could be heard asking from across the fence what the matter was.

'She is mine. Wooeih! Wooeih! She is my very own. The skies and the earth, the gods and the spirits from whom nothing hides, the evil man and his companion, they all bear witness that she is mine. Wooeih!'

'Mother, can you tell me what this crying is all about?' Kelechi said. 'You can tell us everything. After all, we are in your son's house.'

'Not my son's house, Kele. My daughter's house. Who will ever believe me?' she mourned.

'Mother, you are embarrassing me,' Kelechi said to her in his language. 'We are here to see your son. You know I do not have the best memory. What I'm sure about is that all along, this trip has been about your son, and never about your daughter. I count on your sanity, so that we do not both embarrass ourselves in front of these people.'

'Am I mad?' she asked. 'Let people think what they will. Daughter it is. The truth is etched out with a searing knife in my mind and heart. It is palpable, moving about and breathing. Let me weep. The truth is in the blood that no amount of my tears can dilute. So let me weep.' Her lamentation went up a tenor.

Kelechi turned to the people who had been showering them with their hospitality, but who had suddenly become speechless. He gestured apologetically, hauled the woman onto her wobbly feet and propelled her towards the door. He led her at a fast pace across the yard to the exit of the compound. Her piteous cries could be heard for a while as they travelled further and further away.

'The Nkeng is after the *ngonitong*,' Nwenmufu hypothesised.

'Are you suggesting that she may actually be heading for Ngohnibi?' Moka asked, as he drove the car along the earth road.

'That is my belief,' replied Nwenmufu.

'Assuming she is after the *ngonitong*, who is the man with her?' Ayonchugu asked. 'She is supposed to be a loner.'

'I don't know,' Nwenmufu replied.

It turned out that the old man could be right after all. Intelligence garnered indicated that the couple was seen heading for Ngohnibi, and that the woman was shrouded, as in a burkha. The men concurred that this was not the consequence of some exaggerated sense of religious piety, but most likely an attempt to stay undiscovered.

'Only two people in this part of the world know her real identity,' Moka said. 'Why would she conceal herself?'

'Fear,' Nwenmufu replied. 'Raw and traumatising fear of Nyarong.'

When the men pulled up at the entrance to Ayonchugu's residence, an exhausted Nwenmufu was aided out of the car. He painstakingly shuffled after the men into the house. Ayonchugu expressed surprise when he saw Tongembe. Little time was spent on pleasantries, though. The three men were soon being told the story of the woman and her son.

'Raving mad, both of them were,' said Tongembe.

'Even the man?' asked Ayonchugu.

'Yes, even he. I learned their language from Nigerians in Kumba. He told her to remember that he was mad and counted on her to do the thinking.'

'They initially appeared really normal, but for her dressing. By the way, how many languages do you speak?' Ngelem asked Tongembe.

'Whom were they looking for specifically?' asked Moka.

'I think the man was saner than the woman,' said Tongembe. 'He said they were looking for you.'

'Are you sure?' asked Ayonchugu.

'Of course. The woman said she was looking for her daughter. She was adamant about it and broke down when food was brought to them. He hauled her away and they disappeared as suddenly as they had appeared. Pathetic when two mad people disagree.'

'Who served the food?' asked Ayonchugu looking at Tongembe.

'*Quelle question!* The women served the food, of course. You don't think it was I, do you?'

'Obviously not you. Which of the women served her?'

'I brought in water and she washed her hands,' Ngelem said. 'Mengen brought in food, and then the tears started raining. Mengen, did you notice how that woman wept when you came in?'

'Yes, I did. She said the truth was palpable, breathing and moving about. Strange way of speaking.'

'Strange indeed,' Tongembe agreed. 'She said that her raining tears could not dilute the truth. I believe sometimes even a mad person can sound quite lucid until betrayed by action.'

'It was the man who declared her mad and whisked her off, as famished as they had come,' Ngelem said. 'Did you notice how gaunt she looked? Poor creatures. At least they should have had a bite before continuing their wandering.'

'Which way did they go?' asked Moka.

'That way,' said Ngelem, pointing eastwards.

'Shall we go then?' Moka asked, looking at the men. 'Do come with us if you wish,' he said to Tongembe.

'What are you people after?' Tongembe asked.

'The couple,' said Moka. 'They are the key to secrets we wish to be let into.'

CHAPTER TWENTY-SIX

The loudest scream ever

Nyarong had been wandering up in the hills for some days in search of Salifu and his cattle. He had beaten the plains of Ndop, the lowlands of Mbui, and scrambled up the hills of Aghem, Kom, Metah, Bui, and Misaje, all in vain. He was greatly distraught. Salifu and five hundred cows had vanished without a trace!

He pronounced curse after curse on Salifu and his nomadic lot in every language he knew, but only got echoes of his own impotent voice mocking at him from the wilds. Was it true he had been double-crossed? Oh that he had Bag-of-Evil! What he could have done to the wandering animal! Wipe out the miserable filcher with a bolt! Or send a swarm of wild bees to plant their stings on every part of his mangled body and on those of his wretched woman and his tiny daughter who ran away each time she saw him coming up the hill! Was he so finished that even a *ganakoh* had no awe of him now? And all because of that devil of a woman called Atemnji! May her spirit know no peace! Oh that he had that bag again!

And what was this happening to him? Twice he had felt the earth spin and seen the ground come up and slap his face so badly that he had lain unconscious for hours. Every joint in his body was lit up in a rage against him, and his head was pulsating and clanging with the force of a blacksmith's hammer. Sores had erupted on the soles of his flat thick-layered feet. He had developed a fever and was overcome by dizziness. Wherever he looked, life around him was vibrating in a dance of masquerades; he could not focus enough to find a leaf that could assuage his deliriums and aches. All he wanted now was Nwenmufu, who would nurse him back to health. Then he would be up on his feet again and go after that *nyamfikah* called Salifu.

Mm! The teacher! A good lad he used to be. He was all a

man could wish his son to be. He studied abroad. He wore neat foreign clothes like G. H. Ashamba. He spoke like a book. He was Headmaster. All of that because he was provided the means to go to school. And had not the big man promised to ensure he goes far in the government? All these years he had kept his word. Out of fear, of course. Who could break a blood oath taken on the *tigi ngang*, the very same fetish-pot upon which he depended to suppress his enemies and grow his riches?

Everything had been going as planned. And then out of nowhere came the teacher asking questions about that devil of a woman Atemnji. His world was once again shattered, and he was on the move – not before the teacher had left with Ayonchugu, but shortly after. The disappearing trick had worked out perfectly. By stepping into a dark corner just in the inside left corner of the door and pushing the sliding door shut from within with his walking stick, he had made it look as though he had stepped outside. A log he had pushed through the eaves from inside had landed outside just by the door, creating the impression that he was moving outside. Nwenmufu would have confirmed that he had disappeared. Of course, Nwenmufu would never tell the truth about Atemnji.

If only he had found Salifu! He would have been on his way to Northern Nigeria, from where he would have sent information to his lackeys about his new location. His present situation was pushing him to fall back on the most feasible alternative, one full of risks, but the one way he was sure of staying alive, unsuspectingly close to home.

He was thirsty and hungry and very sick. He was suffering from everything. Sheer will power kept him going, and even that was waning. He came to perch at the top of a cliff, knowing full well down below in the valley was water. He could either drink the water or drown in it. Either way, he was sure to feel some relief from the intense malaise that consumed him. He stumbled down a rough track, holding on to grasses and shrubs, rolled over a few times and finally found himself in the valley and a few paces away from the banks of a swashing stream. There he lay sprawled, bruised and exhausted, unable to make another move, his aged body failing to respond to his tortured will.

From the opposite bank a man and a woman watched the struggling man finally come to rest in the valley, as inert as dead. He pulled off his shoes, dashed across the stream, stepping on stones and splashing in water, and in a moment, scrambled up the embankment. He grasped the man and expertly hauled him over his left shoulder, slid down the embankment, waded through the water and returned to the other side of the stream. He carefully placed the old man on the grass, face up.

The woman bent down to attend to the invalid and instead recoiled in shock. She stood upright and looked up to the skies as if for help. Her entire frame stiffened momentarily. She opened her mouth, breathed in a generous amount of air, and then let it out in a raw, ear-shattering wail. Then she spun around and started running towards the road, waving her hands about as if that would ward off the encounter she had just had with the devil himself.

Her cries reached the ears of the men coming up the road, and they all turned and rushed in the direction of the voice, with Ayonchugu and Tongembe in the lead. She saw the men and ran towards them.

'Let her through!' shouted Ayonchugu as Tongembe attempted to grab her. 'Get ready to face whatever she is running away from instead!'

They both stepped aside and she ran past. She did not go far, before running out of breath. She tripped and fell down. Moka ran up to her and helped her onto her feet.

CHAPTER TWENTY-SEVEN

The bag-of-evil is found

If you were a stranger with a patient ear and were kind enough to offer a bottle of stout to any of the inhabitants of Kanke, you would soon be entertained with Ligibi's extraordinary story, which came in as many versions as there were raconteurs. When two young idle men had the opportunity one late afternoon to be asked to talk about Ligibi and Bag-of-Evil, they gladly obliged.

The listener on this occasion was a big Haussa man with a permanent scowl who introduced himself as Ali. He clearly had come from far away; his motorcycle was cooling down in front of the bar, while he conversed with his barefooted companions – Tantoh and Agbor. They were in their twenties and wore shabby shorts and tee-shirts with holes in them. They were drinking and smoking Gold Filters, blowing foul-smelling air between stained teeth.

'The man you are looking for is called Ligibi,' said Tantoh.

'So are you sure he has the item?' Ali.

'He not only has it,' said Agbor. 'He is stuck with it. Who here does not know that bag? He threw it in the river, and when he returned home, believe you me, it was hanging on the wall!'

'He even forgot it in the market, and it was returned to him by Faï, the market sweeper,' said Tantoh. 'There's no way he can rid himself of that bag.'

'Can you boys tell me what is inside the bag?'

'Of course we can,' said Tantoh. 'Everybody knows. It has thunder and bees.'

'There's also a piece of wood, a seven-pine bundle of brooms and an ox-tail wand,' his companion added.

'It has a script which describes a hundred uses of the bag,' Tantoh said. 'It is written in Aka-uku-aka.'

'It would take a trip to the land of the Mouns to get that

229

translated,' said Ali. 'Give me an example of a feat the bag has performed,' he requested.

'Ok,' said Tantoh. 'One day Ligibi's mother returned home and said she had no food for him because the bunch of plantains she had hoped to prepare that evening had been stolen from her farm. Ravaged by hunger that night, Ligibi opened the bag and sent malaria to the thief. Then he thought that making the thief ill was not going to stop him from feeling hungry. He told the bag that he wanted the plantains returned – to his mother's house! That same evening her mother's farming companion knocked on the door. She was wet and shivering, and was carrying a big bunch of plantains on her head.'

'She had been unable to set it down in her own house!' Agbor said.

'You know, Ligibi was a weakling,' Tantoh explained. 'He used to be scoffed at for not being man enough.'

'But when he had that bag people stopped mocking at him,' Agbor said.

'Those who didn't, learned a lesson.' Tantoh stuck his cigarette in his mouth, leaned backwards and sucked hard on it. He held his breath for a few moments, then let smoke stream out of his nostrils like the exhaust of an old car running on diesel. Tantoh continued speaking. 'When his father died, he got drunk at the funeral. Was it not Tabifor who said that Ligibi had at last become a man by inheriting his father's property which included his mother? Where is Tabufor today?' Tantoh coughed and spat on the floor.

Agbor took over. 'Ligibi pointed a finger at him and told him he would rot on his deathbed and neither his wife nor his mother would be able to help him. Tabifor laughed and called it a curse from a chicken. Believe you me, a year to the day of the incident, Tabifor lay dying. His condition was so bad that he was totally isolated.'

'His food was served to him tied to a bamboo pole and pushed through a hole in his confinement,' Tantoh said. 'Did we not dig his grave even before he died? Fear that bag!' he exclaimed.

The two fellows went on and on about the mysterious bag

and its owner, while their companion leant back and half closed his eyes as if he did not take their stories seriously. His apparent indifference fired the men up, and one man competed to outdo the other over his knowledge of Ligibi and the bag. Ali ordered a second round of beer and some cigarettes.

Agbor and Tantoh said that Ligibi came to be known as the-man-with-the-evil-mouth, and people avoided faulting him. He relished the new-found awe in which people held him. He made demands on people and got whatever he wanted. Over time, he so believed in his own personal grandeur that he started abandoning the bag and still getting results. Who knows, he may have desisted entirely from using the bag, if strange things had not started happening to him.

At one point, the men claimed, Ligibi stayed for a year without sending the bag on a mission. One morning he was woken up by the very teasing buzz of a bee. He tried all day to see, catch or send away the annoying bee to no avail. He was becoming despondent when in the evening, it occurred to him that the bee might be related to the bag. He opened it, wondering what exactly he was going to find inside. Then things started falling in place. There was the distinct buzz of a bee coming from the bundle in the bag. He thought for a long while and decided to take action. Two weeks previously, his neighbour's goats had broken their tethers and come into his compound and eaten vegetables in his mother's garden. She had gone over to the neighbour's compound and had an argument with the man, who had refused to take responsibility for his children's careless handling of the goats.

"Time to experiment," he mumbled. He placed the buzzing bundle in front of him and said: "Mete out immediate punishment on Mabu's goats for destroying my mother's garden and depriving us of much-needed vegetables." Immediately, a bee flew out of the bundle. Shortly after, he heard the buzz not of one, but of a whole swarm of bees passing over his roof. Shortly after, there was a stampede. Goats could be heard bleating in Mabu's compound.

In the morning, he heard Mabu's wife weeping as if she was at a funeral and went over to see how much disaster the bees had caused. He found Mabu and his sons digging a grave to bury seven bloated carcasses. He mumbled some words of sympathy. When he was leaving, Mabu drew attention to the side of his face which was swollen. He admitted having been stung early that morning as well.

'He had learned yet another lesson about sending the bag's inhabitants on a mission,' said Tantoh.

'He must be ready to welcome them back when they returned,' Agbor concluded for his companion.

'I like your stories,' said Ali, whose scowled face briefly relaxed into a smile before assuming its usual severity. He placed some coins on the table and said, 'Get yourselves some more beer.'

When the drinks were opened and placed before them, the young men resumed their stories. 'All what we've told you happened long ago,' said Tantoh.

'Yes, a very long time ago,' Agbor emphasised.

'Ligibi finally mastered the craft of using the bag and no longer suffered the sort of mishaps he suffered before,' Tantoh said.

'Those mishaps actually left him limping,' said Abgor.

'And that was not the only thing that happened,' Tantoh said.

'Not at all,' Agbor replied. 'He married a very beautiful girl, but she left him after three years for an older man. It was rumoured that he could not get *it* up.'

'One evening recently,' Tantoh said, 'Ligibi was sitting in his house in deep thought. For some time, owing to the caution with which people had come to treat him, no one had done anything to incur his wrath. Nobody had reported anyone to him in the silent hope that he would use his bad mouth to put them in their place. He was worried that the elements in the bag could soon start agitating and he would know no peace until he sent them on a blood-letting mission. He thought down the years, looking for actions that called for retribution. He thought about Nyarong. "Why not?" he asked himself.'

'Why not?' Abgor repeated, and took over from his mate. 'Ligibi brought out the bag from the depths of his soot-stained bamboo cupboard and peered inside it. The prominent eyes of a chameleon stared back at him. "Lightning will it be then," he mumbled to himself. He spoke into the bag. "Many years ago a man came into Kanke; he was welcomed because people believed he was bringing them good. He did show his good side. But he could change hue like the chameleon. For every good he did in the day, there was thrice as much evil fomented in the night. I present you Sona's case. Nyarong had three children by his wife. Nyarong got her pregnant with a fourth and then abducted her. Wherever Nyarong is, lightning and thunder must destroy him now!'" Agbor paused and took a sip from his bottle, held it up and gauged its contents.

Tantoh took over. 'Nyarong closed the bag for a few seconds and then opened it again. The chameleon was gone. He took out the piece of wood and went outside and stuck it into a banana stem. It was time for the uneasy wait. Anything could go wrong, you know. Lightning and thunder are no bee sting. He waited for only as long as it takes to cook a pot of beans, but it was like waiting for two market days.'

Tantoh and Agbor finished their third bottles of beer. They each lit a cigarette and bid their time. The stranger waited patiently. When it was clear that he was not ready to buy them another drink, Tantoh decided to round off the story.

'Ligibi heard a roar in the skies and heavy drops of rain pelted down on his roof. Lightening flared down on his house, followed by an enormous bang that was heard fifty miles away. Ligibi was air-lifted and smashed in a heap outside, where he lay, unconscious. When he finally woke up, only one side of his body could move or feel anything. He managed to peer with one good eye at the banana plant into which he had stuck the wood to receive the elements. It was still standing upright and fresh. Where had he gone wrong? He opened his mouth to cry out, but he only croaked and fell back.'

'I guess you know that lightning and thunder work only when the facts are accurate,' said Agbor.

'Take me to Ligibi's,' said the stranger. 'I want the bag.'

'Stranger,' Agbor said, 'you must be as unyielding as a white cow to want it in spite of all what we've told you.'

'I don't want the bag for myself. My master wants it. Have you ever heard of G. H. Ashamba? He's a very powerful man.'

CHAPTER TWENTY-EIGHT

The story of Atemnji

Atemnji was sobbing uncontrollably. The men gave her time to recover, but her cries only grew louder and her eyes let flow tears like a generous palm tree lets flow wine – in an unceasing trickle. Nwenmufu, who had started recounting his own part of the story, stopped talking and went with Ayonchugu to Nyarong's hut. Warm vapour had filled the room. Nyarong was prostrate in bed exactly as the men had placed him when he regained consciousness after being attended to by Nwenmufu. His breathing was still laboured and his gross sweaty body shivered spasmodically now and again.

'Do you think he will get out of this?' Ayonchugu asked.

'Yes,' replied Nwenmufu. 'These are the very best herbs.' As he spoke, he shoved some dry twigs into the fire and poured more water into the cauldron. Muttering and shaking their heads all the way, they went back to join the others.

Atemnji had calmed down, but the flow of tears was not yet capped. Nwenmufu settled down and continued his story.

'Nyarong was greatly feared. I too was afraid of him. As we progressed in our escape from Kanke, I realised that he was not carrying Bag-of-Evil. I knew that without that bag, Nyarong was totally powerless; he had only his reputation to scare anyone. From then on, I knew I was free from bondage to him.

'The woman gave birth. That night Nyarong went away and in the morning, and returned with a nanny goat and its kid. Shortly after, he ordered me to kill her and walked away. I raised my knife and the woman screamed. I stuck it into the kid, which crumbled on its feeble legs without uttering even a little bleat. I whispered to the woman to flee as far as she could and let our paths never cross.

'I caught up with Nyarong. He gave me the baby. From then on, I was her mother and father. She fed on the goat's milk. Our journeys took us through most of French Equatorial

Africa and back. We never stayed in the same village for more than a few months. We used our knowledge of herbs to cure ailments along the way, and were welcomed wherever we went.

'As the child grew up, she tended to be more attached to me than to her father. Sometimes, I thought he actually hated her. He had hoped the baby would be a boy. One day he confessed to me he was convinced she was not his. When we came to Ngonibi she was already as tall as this.' He indicated the height by holding out his hand in front of him.

The woman began sobbing uncontrollably again. Nwenmufu interrupted his story for the second time, and again, stepped out with Ayonchugu to check on Nyarong.

It was just past midday and the sun was at its zenith against a clear sky. As they walked across the yard, they could see Tongembe who was stationed at the entrance to the compound, sending back people who were trickling in for consultation. They went into the sick-man's hut. Nyarong lay exactly as they had left him. Nwenmufu lifted the medicine pot from the fire and placed it close to Nyarong's bed and opened it. Hot vapour came out and spread under the bed, infusing into the cushion of plantain leaves that served as a mattress. Nyarong stirred. The men left him and returned to the waiting room. The woman had collected herself and was recounting her story at last.

'When I told Sona that I had good news for him I really meant it. I was pregnant and truly by my husband. I had been to see Nyarong, but any woman who knows herself knows who the father of her child is. Yet I could not make a special ceremony of this pregnancy. Instead of bringing happiness, the pregnancy caused my husband to hate me completely. He wouldn't eat my food. He wouldn't talk to me. He wouldn't even look at me or acknowledge my presence. Whenever I looked at his door across from my kitchen, I felt hatred coming my way like evil spirits. I was getting set to run away to my parents when I accidentally overheard him telling my son how he was sharpening his knife to kill a pregnant nanny goat and bury it in a coffin and have people dance on its grave. I fled to Nyarong's. He was the one person I believed at the time could protect me. How I regret that journey! I have wished a thousand times I had gone to my parents! Nwenmufu has told you about the rest of my ordeal.'

'It was a terrible ordeal indeed,' Ayonchugu said. 'How did you survive it?'

'When morning came I was still lying as he had left me, on the same spot, with the stiff carcass of the kid by me, its tongue sticking out. Poor thing. I wished I were dead too. My whole body felt dead already. So why was my mind still alive? The first person I saw in the morning must have been a wayfarer. He peered at me and must have concluded I was dead. He plucked a branch of nkeng and dropped it on my inert body and went his way. I managed to grasp the plant with benumbed hands and later understood that my grip on the plant had been so firm that my rescuers had let me hold on to it. I did not understand the language of the people of the nearby village who rescued me, and must have nodded when they asked me if I gave birth to the kid. A medicine-woman – she must have been the village mid-wife, confirmed that I had indeed given birth – to the kid.'

'You are lucky they let you live,' said Nwenmufu. 'Where I came from, that would be interpreted as a sign of malediction and you would be killed to pacify the gods.'

'Not those people,' Atemnji said. 'Instead, I was held in awe as one who was going to reverse the fortunes of the people of that village, which had for many years suffered from famine. They must have consulted their oracle or a sorcerer who said I was a harbinger of good luck. It was foretold that a woman would have an exceptional kind of birth before the famine could end. My star was indeed shining as that year the harvest was good and the animals started returning to the forest.

'When I felt strong, I left the village. In memory of my lost daughter, I returned there once a year to plant nkeng on the site where she was torn off my breast.'

'I now understand how the cult around you developed,' Kelechi said.

'When I mourn for my daughter, they think I'm supplicating the gods to send them a good harvest. So much for my cult status.' Atemnji paused for breath and used the end of her wrapper to dry her eyes.

Ayonchugu sat head bowed; Moka was looking at her face and missing not a word of what she was saying, taking in every gesture she made.

'I could not go back to my husband,' Atemnji continued. 'I could not go after Nyarong. I travelled to the Colony of Lagos where I traded in anything that could be bought and sold. I sold fish, guru-guru, groundnuts, akara, mai-mai in tin cups, and lots more. When I had enough capital I went to the tin mines of Jos and sold food to the workers there. They ate on credit and paid at the end of the month. But they were treated like slaves and they started striking. I lost my capital when they were not paid. I relocated and started again from scratch.'

'How did you manage to know many soldiers?' Moka asked Atemnji.

'The war came; suddenly, my town was teeming with young recruits. I sold things to them. One day I volunteered. I wanted to be a soldier so that when I returned, I would fight Nyarong with sophisticated weapons. But I was rejected. I could not be a nurse. I was unfit to be anything else, except a laundry girl at the local barracks. I refused to sign up. I stayed around long enough to get to know some of the young men well. It was rumoured that in the army they ate only lousy European food that never filled the stomach. I started making sweet potato biscuits for departing soldiers. Even after the war, I continued to make and sell akara at Arakan Barracks.'

'What did you think happened to your daughter? Did you try to find her?' Moka asked.

'I did. When I had enough money I came to the Cameroons. I investigated every medicine-man who matched Nyarong's description and finally traced him to Ngonibi. My horror of him returned. I still managed to visit the village and tried to discover my girl to no avail. The following year, after Nkeng, I returned to Ngonibi more determined and in full disguise. I finally saw her. She looked healthy and strong. During a later visit, I found out that she was married to an ex-soldier. I found out about him.'

'So you knew me!' Ayonchugu exclaimed, his eye widening in disbelief.

'Yes, I did,' Atemnji replied. 'A long time back. Your name.

Your original village. I spied on my daughter many times going about as a bride. She looked happy and settled. I saw her pregnant with my grandson. I was happy too, but heart-broken at the same time. Do you know what it feels like to walk past your own daughter and for her not to know you? Or to try talking to your grandson and he runs away in fright screaming "Juju! Juju!?" You feel worthless and suicidal.'

'Why didn't you talk to me?' Ayonchugu asked in a voice tinged with regret.

'I was afraid of Nyarong,' Atemnji replied. 'Whenever I thought about him, I felt paralised. I thought you'd be on his side. I went to the ex-soldiers' association where I talked about you, claiming you were my son. I hoped to get their sympathy. Kelechi came to me and said he wanted to find out more about the soldier behind that name. You know Kelechi's memory is poor. But he was absolutely sure the man meant a lot to him. He took me to his house and showed me pictures of himself and others taken in India and Burma. I saw my daughter's husband in some.'

'I was very happy at the opportunity to learn more about myself from someone who knew me closely in the war,' Kelechi said.

'Now I was in a greater dilemma,' Atemnji continued. 'I had said Ayonchugu was my son. I was afraid of being seen as a liar if I said he was my son-in-law. I tried to justify myself by reasoning that in my culture, your first daughter's husband is treated like the first son of the family. Kelechi was bent on keeping the link he had just found to his days at war. He offered to lodge me, with the intention of travelling to the Cameroons to meet Ayonchugu. I stayed with him. Before long, he was treating me like his real mother. Indeed, he became a son to me as well. I also became his guide. Whenever I came to perform nkeng, I told him I was going to see my son. He wanted to come along. Either his job kept him back or I looked for an excuse to dissuade him. One day he received a letter from Ayonchugu and was truly jubilant and read it out to me.'

'I remember that letter,' Kelechi said. 'I replied, didn't I?'

'Yes, you did. You started asking more and more questions. Why was I always going on and on about my daughter-in-law and hardly ever about my son? Why did he never write to me? How come Ayonchugu had not replied to the letters you had sent him through me? The questions had become too many and it was quite clear to me you had become more discerning. I realised I had told enough half-truths. This year I was determined to reveal everything. So together, we travelled to Land of Nkeng, where I performed my annual ritual.'

'It was surreal,' Kelechi said. 'I saw a very new side of her. She asked me to leave all my questions until we came to our final destination.'

'He was accommodating most of the way,' Atemnji said. 'As we got closer to Ngonibi, I was overcome by fear. I wanted to go back to Nigeria. He wouldn't hear about it. By the time we reached Ayonchugu's house I was calm, though still afraid. I had to face my fate.'

'How often has many a man been seen to be totally serene, coherent, and putting on a show of temerity on the eve of their own suicide?' Kelechi asked, and everyone looked at him, as if surprised he could be that discerning and expressive.

'We arrived at Ayonchugu's house and my daughter came to serve us food. My own very daughter!' Atemnji said, her face beaming in amazement. 'I was so emotionally embroiled that I could stand it no longer. The truth tumbled out of me in spite of all the planning I'd done to reveal it gradually. You can imagine what it must have been like for Kelechi. There I was, clearly a stranger in that house, breaking down in front of all those people and making ridiculous claims. Do you blame him for thinking I'm mad? Perhaps I am. You couldn't live through what I've lived through and be normal. All my life has been a lie from the day I slept with the devil next door!'

While she was talking, they were aware of weak groans coming from Nyarong. Now, they clearly heard him calling out for Nwenmufu.

'The medicine is working,' Nwenmufu said. 'Now that he is talking, let's go and see him.'

'I can't face him!' cried the woman. 'You people go.'

'I assure you he is harmless,' he insisted.

'I will come with her later,' said Tongembe, who had given

up his post and joined them.

'It might be better that way,' Nwenmufu said, and led the way to Nyarong's hut, followed by Ayonchugu and Moka.

Vapour from the clay medicine pot had filled up the room. Nyarong lay in a sweaty heap, face up, a whizzing sound erupting from his massive chest, the fever gone.

'Who's with you?' the sick man asked in a deep unsteady voice.

'Moka and Ayonchugu,' replied Nwenmufu.

'It was long laid down that I would die in the presence of my son,' Nyarong said. 'Where is he?'

'Right here, behind me,' said Nwenmufu.

'Can you come closer, son? I know you look at me and hate me. Beware! Water evaporates and blood clots. Can you come closer?' Moka moved to the side of the bed and peered down at Nyarong. 'Is that the teacher?'

'Yes. It's I,' Moka answered.

'I won't ask you to give me your hand because I know you won't. I tell you, I have done my duty by you.' Nyarong gasped, clutched the sides of the bed with trembling hands, and tried to turn his head towards Moka. 'You ask the big government man. He has all the details. Up in the hills, the rest is there, five hundred in number. You can have them all. They are all yours now.'

'What is he talking about?' asked Moka, looking at Nwenmufu.

'His cows. They now belong to you.'

'I don't need anything from you, Nyarong,' Moka said.

'No, you don't,' Nyarong said. He breathed noisily like a horse that had been running uphill for a long time, and managed to say something during each egression. 'You have everything. I'm proud...I did my duty by you. The government man...he kept his word. Your education. Your work. He did it all. I sent him to do it.'

'He is referring to G. H. Ashamba,' Nwenmufu explained.

'No, Nyarong,' Moka said. 'You did not do me any good. You took away that which was most precious to me. You ruined my family.'

'I'm your family. I planned things...to be good for you.'

'And what about my mother? What did you do to her?'

'I...did what I had to do,' Nyarong said.

'Did you? Did you have to kill her, Nyarong?' Moka asked in a loud voice.

'She was...no good...to anybody,' Nyarong managed to say.

'And so you killed her!' Moka retorted.

Nyarong shook his head slowly. 'She...was going to die anyway...I was surprised she made it that far.'

'You aren't my family,' said Moka. 'I won't have your cows. For your information, I talked with your government friend before coming in quest of you. He has stolen everything and taken it through Northern Cameroons to Nigeria.'

Nyarong's breath suddenly became more laboured and he tried to grasp the sides of the bamboo bed with unsteady perspiring hands.

'Nyarong, the ghosts of a hundred souls which perished at your hands won't let you rest. I will conjure them myself to haunt you.' Moka turned around and whispered, 'Get me my mother.' Turning back to Nyarong he said, 'Nyarong, you did a lot of evil all your life. You have your chance now to make peace with the world here and that of your ancestors. What do you have to say about all the evil things you did?'

Nyarong's answer came out in a whisper. 'Do you judge your father? Beware, son.'

'You are not my father until you assume responsibility for the lives you ruined,' Moka said.

'I did what I had to do. I'm saying no more.'

Moka turned to Atemnji and said, 'Come forward.'

The woman came and stood by Nyarong's bed. She bent down and peered into the sick man's eyes, which had lost their glare. Nyarong's eyes closed and opened again. The apparition was still there, peering ominously into his soul. His whole body started agitating and his breath came out in gaggles.

Outside, the sun disappeared behind thick black clouds that came rushing in from the south and the distant roar of thunder could be heard. Pellets of rain thumped the dusty grounds and were instantly swallowed up by the dry, thirsty earth.

'The dead are not dead Nyarong,' whispered the woman.

You and I forever.'

Nyarong whimpered like an animal caught in a trap. His eyes widened and bulged, and he struggled to breathe. His mouth opened as if to scream, but nothing came out. He managed to lift his trembling hands as if attempting to shield himself. A huge spasm overrode his effort and his hands fell back listlessly by his sides.

Outside, the surrounding forests swished and grunted under the lashing of a brewing storm. Gusts of ever intensifying winds blew leaves all over, and several branches ripped off from trees could be heard crashing onto the ground. There was a flash and a bang from the skies. Nyarong's hut shook from its brittle roof right down to its fragile foundation. The roof of the building was whipped off and an outburst of heavy rain sent everyone running for cover in the nearest standing hut. The seven poles holding up Nyarong's house toppled over.

CHAPTER TWENTY-NINE

The last meeting

Ayonchugu left Ngonibi for the first time in three months to meet with his comrades in Libah. He rode some of the way, and boarded a squealing rickety Volkswagen bus for the rest of the journey. He had enough time while he made the journey to reflect on the past months, which had been eventful for him and his relatives.

He had seen a lot of tears flow as family trees had been redrawn. Mengen's had kept his shoulders wet for several nights. Her devotion to Nyarong had been total. She had been the most emotionally tested, feeling revulsion and at the same time a deep-seated sympathy for him. She had been the only one to mourn him, and for her sake, he had been given an ordinary burial.

'Do you think I'm normal?' she asked Ayonchugu about three weeks after meeting Atemnji.

'Of course, you are,' Ayonchugu replied. 'That is why you are able to ask such a question.'

'My mother's story makes me sad. But to me it is like listening to a fireside tale. What's wrong with me?' she cried.

'Again, I say nothing is wrong with you,' Ayonchugu reassured her. 'You need time to take in all what has happened.'

'Does a child need time to have feelings towards her mother?' Mengen asked in a pained voice.

'No,' Ayonchugu replied.

'Then why is my own mother such a stranger to me? Do you think I'm treating her the way a daughter should?'

'Megemuo, I think you are trying. Our bodies cannot put on a light hue in old age.'

'Maybe if I spoke the same language as her, things would be different.'

'Maybe.'

'The HM my brother! I feel it. I always liked him.'

'So did I.'

Ayonchugu had seen how Ngelem was struggling with her loyalties and emotions in the face of the sudden invasion of people in her erstwhile secluded life, and had decided to leave her alone in the understanding that she would go towards the people she wished to be close to. She was already doing delightfully well with Ngelem's teenagers, who were now the undisputed centre of Nkahfi's life. She was deferring to Ngelem, but the language barrier limited their interaction.

Moka tried to be light-hearted about many things, but left no one fooled about how he felt about the reunion with Atemnji. He called Ayonchugu 'son-in-law'; he joked that Ayonchugu would have to pay him the bride-price all over on Mengen's head. He promised to take Nkahfi in future to the city of Gbuea to see his carbon print. 'What is a carbon print?' the child asked. 'Bring me your English reader.' The child brought him the book. Moka chose a picture at random, gave him a white sheet of paper and asked him to place it on the picture and trace it with a pencil. When he was about to leave the boy rushed to him brandishing the drawing and saying he still hadn't told him what a carbon print was. Moka smiled at him, looked at the drawing and said indeed the drawing was not a real carbon print; he would know what it was exactly when he came to Gbuea. He drove off with Atemnji and Kelechi.

Ayonchugu quickly found out that Ngelem's post-war frigidity had become second-nature, and this was rather a relief for him. These days, she often brought Tongembe his meals and chatted away with him while he roofed Ayonchugu's new stone house with corrugated metal sheets. She and Tongembe had confided in each other and were carrying on just very well in a lien that was driven by mutual empathy.

Ayonchugu caught up with his friends and the following day they left for an important meeting of the KENU in Mankan village. He and Fuochu were both pushing along their black high-framed Raleigh bicycles, and from the look of things, would push them all the way to the meeting and back. Saji's severe form was being pushed along by Teneslaw and Niba in a wheel chair. Mbah was lagging behind, calmer than ever, his lips moving in silent recital of the rosary. Afungchwi was in Abakwa on temporary employment with the PWD and had sent word that he would attend the meeting if he was given time off.

Kangno was with them today. He was a lanky fellow who sounded like all his energy found an outlet through his mouth, until one got to know that he worked all day building and mending things. He was presently in the middle of a story about a man who used to be in his company.

'This man, as I said, was a sergeant in the 3rd Reg'men Heavy Anti-Aircraft Workshop in Boma. He was from the Go'cos. He was a very very good worker. He could build anything. He repaired everything the white men repaired and some they could not. He built a new jeep one day from three jeeps that the Japs had destroyed.'

'In one day?' Niba asked.

'Don't be stupid. He completed it one day.'

'I see. But must you call me stupid?'

'Did I call you stupid? I said you should not be stupid.'

'What's the difference?'

'Hold it boys,' Ayonchugu said. 'You were telling us about this man from the Go'cos.'

'Yes. He hated the way the white boys were treating him. They sent a boy who did not respect him to work with him. He did things and the boy took the credit. And the medals. It was always like that. We had our kitchen far away from theirs because they said they did not want our smelly bush food to infect theirs. Twenty of them ate the quantity of meat that forty of us ate. They seemed to be throwing food to the dogs when they gave us something. We were working together because that was the only way to win the war. They treated us like children. They called us bush men.'

'We all know those things. You were talking about the sergeant from the Go'cos,' Niba dared to remind him.

'Am I talking about someone else now?' Kangno asked. 'I was saying that he hated the way he was treated. He answered rudely to our commander. They reduced his rank to corporal. He built a new jeep from old abandoned wrecks. They said he should not drive it. He was very very angry and shouted at the commander. They took off all his stripes and gave him one more chance. He asked us to mutiny. We did. He was dismissed and told to prepare to return home. He became mad. He went to his cabin and got a gun. He lay on the ground and crawled ever so carefully to the commander's office. Then he pointed the gun at his heart and shot him.'

'Shot his own commander!' exclaimed Niba.

'Yes, he did. And that's not all. He dashed up to the Officers' Mess and shot into officers and wounded four. Then he escaped to the main road. A passenger car was driving by. He shot at it and wounded the driver.'

'And nobody could stop him?' Niba asked.

'He was a damn good soja. But they shot him in the end. Then they said he shot himself. There was an investigation. The case went on for weeks. The doctor said he was shot in the back. That was the problem. Why should a soja be shot in the back? We started talking loudly. Then they sent a doctor to see what we were eating. They checked where we were sleeping and the things were using. After that they gave us more meat, and even sugar and milk. They sent us mattresses, mosquito nets and blankets. We did not need the blankets. You remember we normally served for three years without leave. This time around we were driven off to another camp like from here to Ndu and we stayed there just having fun for two weeks.'

'So the Go'cos man did not die in vain,' Fuochu said.

'Not at all,' Kangno said. 'He did not deserve to die, though.'

'But he shot people,' Niba said.

'People treated him like nothing,' Kangno said.

'And still are doing no better,' Saji said. 'When will the payment come?' he asked.

'What payment?' Ayonchugu inquired.

'The payment KENU told us to apply for,' replied Saji.

'I do not have time to waste,' said Kangno. 'Nothing will come of it.'

'Applying won't hurt,' said Fuochu. 'If it comes, fair enough. If it doesn't, that won't be the end of my life. I still have my hands.'

'What about those who have no hands?' asked Saji.

'They have tax exemption,' said Niba.

'All veterans have tax exemption,' said Kangno.

'Do they? I have paid tax all these years!' cried Ayonchugu.

'That is because you live in that lost village of yours,' Kangno said. 'You must get your exemption card signed soon.'

Suddenly, Fuochu put up his hands and gave the silence signal. 'Listen boys. I hear vibrations like military trucks.'

'They are in your head,' said Kangno and they all burst out in laughter.

'I hear them sometimes myself, with Bren machine gunfire and zooming Hurricane bombers,' said Teneslaw. 'That happens especially after a very hard day's work.'

'This is serious boys. I definitely hear them approaching,' Fuochu insisted.

'I think this is serious indeed,' Saji said. 'I think I can hear them too.'

Three minutes later the first of the trucks came by. It was a conventional personnel carrier, with two back-to-back benches running along its back. Armed soldiers occupied every space available, looking taciturn and menacing. The men stepped onto the turf by the roadside and saluted the men in the truck. The commander saluted them back. For about fifteen minutes, a truck went by every thirty seconds, just as the dust behind the preceding truck settled.

'This is fun, fellows! Who were those bad boys?' asked Niba excitedly when the trucks had all gone past.

'The 5QONR,' Ayonchugu replied.

'The 5QONR?' Niba asked, looking blank.

'Fifth Queen's Own Nigeria Regiment,' Ayonchugu said. 'I'm sure you still can read,' he added.

'The one in Enugu?'

'Sure.'

'Why are they here?'

'Does this man ever know current affairs?' Fuochu asked. 'They have been training along the border with French Cameroun.'

'Training for what?' Niba asked.

'Stupid question again,' Kangno said, looking at Niba disdainfully. 'What do soldiers train for?'

'It is called territorial integrity,' Ayonchugu explained. 'UPC insurgents have been coming into our region and causing trouble. The 5QONR has been containing them.'

'I see,' Niba said.

'You do not see anything,' Kangno said. 'I'm sure you have more questions to ask, but would rather not show your ignorance. Are you aware that French Cameroun became independent a few weeks back?'

'Who is not?' Niba asked. 'Are they not called La République of Cameroun now? I have had enough of your treating me like your lackey. After all, we both had the same rank in the army.'

'That is if we had a rank at all, sergeant. By the way it is La Republic de Cameroun.'

'Peace you two. Must you always disagree like two jealous wives?' asked Ayonchugu.

'Is he not the one who is always trashing my ideas about?' Niba complained, a deep frown now darkening even further his face.

'You always have questions,' Kangno said. 'Never any ideas. That's tiresome.'

'There he goes again,' Niba sighed.

'At your command, samanja!' Kangno saluted.

By this time, they had arrived in Mankan and were making their way to the village community hall.

'A little change of topic may usher in some peace, gentlemen,' Fuochu said. 'Who would ever have thought that Cameroun would gain its independence before Nigeria?'

'They are less divided than the regions over this way,' Saji said.

'Maybe,' said Mbah, who had all along kept silent. 'What with the hassles involved in uniting the Independent Colony of

Lagos, the Northern, Eastern and Western Regions, the situation in Nigeria is more complex. The English want to make sure they leave behind a real nation, not warring brothers.'

'What will become of us when Nigeria becomes independent?' asked Niba.

'I think our independence will come at the same time as Nigeria's,' said Saji.

'That is not possible,' Mbah said. 'It was long made clear that we are not part of Nigeria. It's only for convenience that we still share some services. Nigeria is to become independent in a few months from now, they say. We are going to remain a Trust Territory for a while longer.'

'Not forever I hope,' Teneslaw said.

'Surely not forever,' Mbah said. 'Listen to the news. You boys must trust our leaders. They are mostly men of faith. They are working out the best deal for our future.'

'Is there anything like men of faith in politics?' Saji asked.

The men kept their sometimes lively, sometimes quarrelsome discussion until they arrived at the meeting grounds. The nearly three hundred ex-servicemen present were a disorder of physical presentations. There were those with missing limbs, those with missing eyes, missing ears, detached or gnarled noses, misshaped hips, trimmed fingers, displaced vertebrae, and scarred heads. There were those who had all their members intact, but had disturbed faculties. There were those who looked really fine, until they boasted to you, with an X-ray to prove their point that bullets were until this day still safely lodged in their skulls or spines and hips. There were also those who, by some unexplained, unjustified law of chance, had not a single mental or physical scar, although they had fought at no less challenging fronts.

Old friends shouted out to one another in military slang, and acted out for the twentieth time memorable scenes from their companies. It was always a great reunion, and the men more than felt compensated for the long distances they trekked to get to these meetings.

The meeting began as usual, with the bowing of heads in

silent remembrance of those who had died since the previous meeting. Announcements. Reports. Contributions for membership update. Collection for the bereaved. Collection for the seriously disabled. Collection for the monument project. Collection to sponsor a delegation to see the administration about unpaid stipends. Collection for a delegation to see government officials about the status of veterans in a future independent nation.

None of the collections was above five shillings. Half of the members paid up; the other half could ill-afford a contribution of any kind, and undertook for the umpteenth time to pay their share sometime in the future.

When it came to the monument project, an old debate about whether to build for the dead or for the living resurfaced. Someone was not satisfied with the resolutions at the previous meeting in this regard. Someone did not trust that the artist, a mere village smith, could produce the quality of work the veterans wanted. Someone thought that the cost was too high; another person thought the cost was too low. The meeting was in a long-running stalemate. Ayonchugu indicated that he wished to talk, and was given the floor.

'My dear comrades,' he began, 'I have listened to sojas speak. Why are we so divided over trivialities? Does it really matter whether the picture we see on the moon is that of a human, or an animal, or a rock or even smoke? What matters is that the moon shines and gives us light. Our monument should celebrate both the living and the dead. We all fought an honourable war. We were Allied soldiers and each of us, dead or alive, is a monument.'

He could see heads nodding.

'We did not get up one morning and choose to go and start a war so that at the end of it we would build ourselves a monument. We were called up, the willing and the unwilling, and some of us knew not why we were out there, but only knew we had to do our part for the King of England. If someone had to build a monument for us it should have been that king, or as it is the case today, his beautiful daughter. The Commonwealth is known to have been erecting structures the world over, celebrating the heroism of the living and the dead in the wars. We are still to see one of such structures close to home.'

His eye scanned the audience and came to rest on his nearest neighbour to the left. Both sides of his rubber sandals had gone under the fired knife many times. His glance fleeted upwards to the man's waist, past his sac-cloth belt, right up to the bronze and silver medals lined up on the pockets of his ragged shirt.

'We all know that nothing can make up for our sacrifices,' he continued. 'Did we trade our services, our lives, our loved ones, our limbs, our education, our everything, for a trifle? We, barefooted boys of the African Pioneer Corps, of the Royal West African Frontier Force, of the King's African Rifles, are still to be acknowledged for what our sacrifices were worth. The financial part may forever remain a dream. We can't celebrate ourselves in a monument, although some would say, like the proverbial lizard, we should. No. We did what we did. I tell you, there will come a generation of men and women; it may be in our lifetime or when we are dead of misery and gone. That generation will look upon our works and build us a monument as large as the conical rock in the heart of Ngonibi.'

Ayonchugu sat down to a deafening round of applause and shouts of "Number One! Number One!"

Glossary of non-English terms

achu	(Generic Cameroonianism) a meal of pounded cocoyam and green banana eaten with a yellow sauce (*njaniki*)
alakata pepper	a wild peppery seed believed to have spiritual and therapeutic properties
ambaa	A greenish-black sauce made with crushed cocoyam leaves
ananah	(Mbili) an auberginous fruit from a tree found at sacred places (*mitie*)
atege	(Mbili) storage room (esp. for wine)
badi	(Mbili/Ngemba) a calabash fitted with a strap and a circular base for stability
egusi	(Generic West African) pumpkin seed
finjongfinchugu	(Mbili) star-of-war (a knight, commander, etc.)
fon	(Generic Cameroonianism) traditional ruler of a village in the Grassfields
ganakoh	(Generic Ngemba (German orig.)) cattle drover
gongoro (lorry)	(West African Pidgin English) an old truck
koki	(Generic Cameroonianisn) a cooked meal of a mixture of crushed beans or corn and palm oil
kwifon	(Ngemba) a secret society with legislative and judiciary powers. Kwifon tends to be treated as 'a person'.
kwiemuluh	(Mbili) a rite of recognition of maturity by palace
mangisa	(Mbili) one of a multitude of dance groups. Plays music on a stringed instrument with both hands.
mankare	(Ngemba) farm beds made by burning organic matter under a heap of soil
manyanga	(Generic Cameroonianism) oil obtained from heating kennel
Manyi	(Generic Cameroonianism) a mother of twins (*masc.* Tanyi)
megemuo	(Mbili) mother-of-child
minjang	(Ngemba) a game played by children with pebbles
mishugu	(Mbili) tiny edible frogs fished in some lakes in the Grassfields

mitiee	(Mbili) a sacred place, an altar, a shrine
mukala	(Generic Cameroonianism) whiteman or albino
musanga	(Ngemba) cowries, necklace
(mi) ngemba(le)	(Ngemba) "(I) say"; used to call for attention
ndamu	(Ngemba) celebration/rites/activities (especially by women) on the birth of a baby
ndong	(Ngemba) a small calabash with a long neck and hole at its tip. (In another context - a flute)
ngonitong	(Mbili/Bafut folktale) a beautiful girl, a maiden
ngunibom	(Mbili) a painful stomach condition
njaniki	(Ngemba) a yellow soup that accompanies achu
njogmassi	(Gen. Cam. of German origin) forced labour
njoh	(Mbili) kola nut peelings (used in divination)
nkang	(Grassfields of Cameroon) corn beer
ntum	(Ngemba) loincloth worn in Grassfields style
pfeng	(Mbili) a sixty-centimetre to one-metre long bamboo cylinder used as a wind instrument
samanja	(RWAFF slang) sergeant-major
tamboo	(Mbili) male neighbour (fem. megemboo)
tamukum	(Ngemba) founder or manager of a traditional dance group
tiemuo	(Mbili) father-of-child
tigi ngang	(Mbili) medicine-pot
togo	(Ngemba) hand-made formal Grassfields wear
waniboh	(Mbili) one of many masked dance groups which have xylophones as main musical instrument

ACKNOWLEDGMENTS

I owe a great deal to Dr Funwi F. Ayuninjam of the Central State University of Ohio, USA, for his patient reading and insightful editorial suggestions on my drafts.

I thank Drs. Paul Mbufong, Victor N. Cheo, Nobert K. Mbulai, Charly Ndi Chia, P. A. Abety, Andrew Ngeh, as well as Mr Stacey Hirons who reviewed my manuscript. I am grateful to Messrs. Mathew Takwi, Oliver Bayliss, Roland Kwemain and Thiery Kuwan for their input in more ways than I can elaborate upon here.

I am indebted to the memory of many ex-servicemen whom I knew in my childhood. In 2006, Pa Andreas Afungchwi Asongwe, a distant relative of mine and a veteran of the North African Campaign, shared his WW2 experiences with me; I was devastated by his death two years later and started writing this novel. I was particularly lucky in 2010 to meet Pa Kangno Ncha and Pa Lucas Mbah, both WW2 veterans of the Burma Campaign. I spent two evenings chatting away with Pa Kangno Ncha, who at about ninety, surprisingly spoke with the lucidity of a nineteen-year-old. Veteran Mbah was deaf; his silent but profound gaze told a story more touching than any number of words could tell. I have used the names of all three veteran soldiers in *Traded for a Trifle* as a tribute to them. However, their characters, like all others in the novel, are absolutely fictional.

I am grateful to the staff of the National Archives in Buea who helped trace a number of useful documents.

I thank my compatriots of the UK-based Bongabi, ANEESCam and Mbeligi for their encouragement.

I received the greatest support from Gwen and our kids. They endured my long absences from home quite bravely and gave me the drive to carry on. Mine, this novel is for you too.

Abety Gwandi, 14th July 2013
www.abetygwandi.com

www.ingramcontent.com/pod-product-compliance
Lightning Source LLC
Chambersburg PA
CBHW050406260626
47156CB00003B/889